Erotic Fantasies
For Romantic Couples

Bella Beaudoin

PublishAmerica

Baltimore

First printing

ISBN: 1-59286-765-0
PUBLISHED BY PUBLISHAMERICA BOOK PUBLISHERS
www.publishamerica.com
Baltimore

Printed in the United States of America

I dedicate the writing of this journal to all the people in my life that fill me with love and hope and happiness:

To Chris who gave me wings and helped me to soar in my heart with the angels; who helped me to open my eyes and see myself as other people see me, knowing that they see a good person - a person full of love and compassion - a person full of hope and life ...

To Rusty who showed me that people who really care never leave your side regardless of the consequences to their own lives;

To Kevin who taught me to open my heart and to trust it wherever it may lead me in this life .... To never settle for less than .... To always go after the best .... To love someone enough to set them free even when it hurts you more than words can express ...

To Dawn who taught me that there are people who have enough love and goodness in their hearts to forgive what the world may see as unforgivable. I love you sis!

And most importantly to my darling Michael, my partner, my soul mate, my encourager, the love of my life, my motivator, my inspiration, and often my kick in the butt - who had faith in me and my abilities when I myself had no faith left...

To these special people who complete my life and surround me with unconditional love and acceptance I say humbly...Thank you; I am honored to have you in my life...

TABLE OF CONTENTS:

Hi …My name is Bella and I hope that you enjoy reading my short stories of erotica. I am a college-educated mother of two who currently home schools my children. I have written children's stories and romance in the past but this is my first (though hopefully not my last) collection of short erotic stories for romantic couples.

I think I can best describe what I write by telling you what I DO NOT write. In my stories you will NEVER find bestiality, pedophilia, or incestuous relationships. There is plenty of that type of stuff already on the market so if that's what you are looking for, please put down my book and keep looking. I do not write anything with serious violence or rape either although in role playing scenes there may be mild, consensual bondage. Now you know what I do not write about so let's move on to what I do write about.

I am heavy into romance, sharing, caring, experimenting, sensuality, and yes sex! I believe that great sex comes from a culmination of emotions and sharing and my stories reflect this. There are many physical ways for caring couples to pleasure each other and you will probably find most of them in my writings at some time or another if you continue to read my stories. I think that two adults in love, making love to each other and with each other is a beautiful experience and as such is nothing to be ashamed of so my sex scenes may tend to be very graphic. If this type of explicit description offends you, please read no further.

There may also be times when I touch on different fetishes. I have many friends who have various fetishes in their sexual lives and they have been made to feel embarrassment over the years because of them. I truly feel that there is nothing wrong with indulging in a sexual fetish as long as it is a harmless one that hurts no one physically, mentally, or emotionally. Fetishes are merely preferences that the "normal" people in society do not understand and so they do as people always have - they label them and they condemn them as being "abnormal." Who decides what is normal anyhow? Sometimes society has a tendency to label anything that is different as abnormal but is being different really a bad thing? Just think how boring the world would be if no one was different. Could you really live with millions of people exactly like you in every way? Would you really want to?

My writings usually lean toward reality and so they may include adultery or pre-marital relationships on occasion. In no way do I condone such activities but as an adult I know they are very much a part of everyday life in the real world and as such they do enter into my stories at times. Enough said for now as I carefully step down off my soapbox to avoid injury. If you still are interested in reading some sensual, sexual, and often romantic stories as a couple or just for your own pleasure, read on and I truly hope that you enjoy!

CHAPTER 1
BEACH BLANKET BEAUTY

BEACH BLANKET BEAUTY

Alexia snuggled deeper into the comforter, pulling it tight around her shoulders, pretending it was Paul's strong arms holding her tight. She wished it was Paul and her tears fell as she realized she would never again feel those loving arms around her. She missed his strong, tall body. She longed to look again into his sexy brown eyes. Her fingers itched to run through his curly, dark hair. Alexia gazed out over the water watching the painted beauty of the sky as the sun set, leaving behind only the pink streaks of color as proof that it had ever been there. She thought how the last two years could have so easily been nothing more than a dream. She could almost pretend it was a dream if only the proof that Paul was real wasn't growing inside of her day by day.

The wind was starting to pick up and the evening air was getting cool but Alexia was not ready to go home yet, not ready to face the dark house, not ready to spend another night alone. She closed her eyes and lifted her face to the breeze feeling comforted by the way it brushed her fiery red hair back from her brow. For a few moments she let herself relax. She enjoyed the sound of the waves crashing against the shoreline and the salty smell in the air. The steady rhythm of the ebb and flow soothed her weary mind.

Her life had been so different when all of this had started. She had been married. She had been content in her small home with her little garden in the back. Her days had been spent on volunteer work and spoiling her precious pups. Back then everything seemed to be firmly in place for Alexia. Now she tried to recall what had changed. When had her life become so confusing?

She shifted slightly on the sand, trying to calm the restless child poking her ribs, wondering if he sensed her mood. Her hand slid down to her belly, now slightly swollen at six months along. She felt the skin ripple under her fingers and wondered if it was a hand or a foot moving. Alexia smiled at the thought that very soon she would be bringing this little miracle into the world. Then sadness overtook her as she remembered that Paul would never see what their love had brought to be.

She leaned back against the tree behind her and closed her tired eyes again, letting her mind start to replay the events that had led her to be here today. She wanted to stop the mini movie that kept going over and over in her head but she couldn't make it go away. It invaded every thought, every dream, and every daydream. Alexia needed to be able to not think, needed to be able to stop remembering before she drove herself crazy with all the should haves in her head. It was too easy to see what she should have done now that it was too late. Alexia knew what she had to do.

She had to pull herself together and make a home for her and her child. She had to be both mother and father to him because it was her fault that he had no father. She only hoped that her mistakes would not follow them both as they started their new life together.

Alexia curled into a ball on her side and tucked her arm up under her head as she stared out at the reflection of the moon dancing on the water. Slowly her weary eyes started to close and soon she drifted off into a deep sleep. The dream was not a peaceful one. Alexia always had the same dream lately, a dream where Paul was walking away from her never to return. The last look in his eyes was one of pain, betrayal, and overwhelming sadness. Why had she told him she didn't love him when her heart ached for him more with every beat?

Many times over the years Alexia had suffered because of her stubborn red headed pride and this was no exception. Paul had come along at a time when she most needed him in her life but he had told her from the beginning that he wanted no strings attached to their relationship. They had started out as buddies, friends who had similar interests and enjoyed each other's company. Quickly things had escalated to the point where Paul had become her best friend and she desired his company more than anything in the world. Still, Alexia refused to admit she had fallen in love with him.

Then came that fateful night, the night Bradley had come home drunk and confessed to Alexia that he had been seeing another woman for the last several months. She wasn't really shocked. A part of her had already known what was going on. All the business trips and nights at the office that kept getting later and later had clued her in quite awhile ago. She had said nothing because after growing up being shuffled from foster home to foster home, her marriage to Bradley had offered her a sense of stability and security that she craved in her life. Oh, he hadn't wanted children and Alexia did but she was willing to give up that dream to feel safe. Now the safety had been ripped from her and her mind went numb as she listened to her husband of five years telling her how he was moving out tomorrow and would be filing for divorce as soon as possible. She stared at his face, barely registering his cruel words as she remembered how he looked without the proof of drinking on his face. He was a handsome man, well-built and muscular with dirty blonde hair and piercing blue eyes.

Alexia couldn't even cry. She was so stunned, so shocked, so afraid of being alone. Bradley went into the guestroom and locked the door. Alexia sat staring at that dark brown door for what seemed like an eternity before the ringing of the phone jogged her into motion. Quickly she yanked up the receiver and uttered a throaty hello.

"Alexia?" The voice on the other end was Paul. "I was wondering if you would like to go to the beach tonight? Some friends are having a midnight barbecue and when I asked what I should bring they told me to bring a beach blanket beauty and just have fun so of course I thought of you my dear friend."

His voice was so sweet, so soft and tender that Alexia had a hard time not letting him hear the tears that were stuck in her throat. After several minutes she agreed to go in the cheeriest tone she could muster up and told Paul to give her fifteen minutes to change. As soon as she heard the phone click, Alexia ran to her room and quickly pulled on her bikini and wrap as the tears slid silently down her face. She heard Paul's car pull into the driveway and dashed to the bathroom to splash cold water on her puffy eyes, hoping beyond hope that he wouldn't notice she had been crying.

Paul rang the doorbell several times before Alexia answered. *Why do women always take so long?* he wondered, but as soon as she opened the door he knew something was wrong. The smile she put on for him and the cheery, almost animated way she greeted him let him know she was not ready to talk about whatever was bothering her tonight. But when she hugged him, it was all he could do not to pull her trembling body close to his own. He made himself let her go, knowing she was married and that this friendship was all he could ever have of her. He told her from the start that he would never ask for anything more but it was killing him, loving her and wanting her so badly, and yet unable to say anything to her. Paul knew he loved Alexia enough to live this torture of being so close to her but unable to have her in his life the way he wanted her ... as his wife and life partner.

It had started to drizzle just as they reached the party and so it came as no surprise when Paul's friends decided to call it quits and go home earlier than planned. The sky had grown dark very quickly and the air became damp and cool. Streaks of heat lightening lit up the darkness every few seconds, giving the feeling of impending danger but still Paul and Alexia decided to stay a little while. Both of them had always loved walking in the warm summer rain, feeling the soft spray caressing their upturned faces. It was just one of the many things they had in common. As they strolled the beach together, Paul's arm fell around Alexia's shoulders in a light, friendly embrace, offering her more warmth and comfort than mere words ever could. Her shaking had calmed but it was clear that she was deep in thought. He felt her weight shift and she leaned against his side causing his arm to slip down around her waist, his hand resting lightly just above her hip. Alexia's head leaned against his shoulder and Paul found himself intoxicated by the way the scent of her shampoo flooded his senses.

When Paul turned to look at Alexia he only intended to tell her what a great friend she was and how much that friendship meant to him. He wanted her to know that he would be there for her no matter what the problem was that she was facing. She would not have to deal with it alone. His eyes met hers and he found himself totally engrossed in her beauty, unable to utter his well-rehearsed speech.

Neither of them was quite sure how it had happened but suddenly Alexia was in his arms, her swollen breasts pressed firmly to his chest, her slender hips pushing against the noticeable bulge in his cut off jeans, her lips locked tight on his, and her tongue exploring wildly.

Paul knew Alexia was upset tonight, knew he should pull away from her, but he couldn't let go of her willing body now that he finally had her in his full embrace. Alexia felt Paul's arms tighten around her pulling her closer to his hard body. At first his lips were gentle against hers but as Alexia slightly parted her mouth and let her tongue sneak out to tease Paul his kiss became more passionate. She pulled back from him and stared into his eyes for just a few minutes before she leaned forward and began to trace the outline of his lips with the tip of her warm wet tongue. Paul's tongue darted out to meet hers and began a seductive duel with it that had her blood boiling in just a short time. As Alexia's tongue retreated into her own mouth, Paul's followed lovingly, giving her the chance to suck on it, driving him wild with desire.

For just a split second Alexia considered stopping but she needed the comfort of being with someone she loved. Slowly she undid the wrap at her waist and the strings that held her bikini bottom in place on her slender hips. She moved her arm around behind her back and untied her bikini top, letting it fall to the sand and pressing her now bare body against Paul's strong chest. She wiggled from side to side enjoying the feeling of the springy hairs on his body stroking her breasts. A gasp caught in her throat as she felt Paul's hand slide between their bodies and cup her aching breast, his thumb and forefinger gently teasing her nipple into erectness until she moaned with uncontrollable desire for more of his touch. Alexia knew there was no stopping now. She wanted Paul more than she had ever wanted anyone before. She needed him to satisfy her longings.

Paul dropped to his knees pulling Alexia down with him. He spread out her wrap and gently leaned her back onto it, bending down to place butterfly kisses over her smiling face. As Paul slid off his shorts Alexia saw the enormous erection he had and knew for certain that she affected him the same way he affected her. Her hand reached out tentatively and grasped his hot cock feeling the thick wet pre-cum sliding down his shaft. As Alexia ran her thumb gingerly over the swollen head of Paul's cock she heard him moan lightly and looking up she saw his eyes close as he leaned his head back. Quickly she turned onto one side and leaned her head toward him, her tongue testing the tip of his cock, loving the salty taste of the thick fluid there. Paul's hand reached out and his fingers entangled in Alexia's hair, pulling her head closer to him as she opened her willing throat and took his cock deep into it. She began to make small swallowing motions, the action causing her soft throat to milk Paul's shaft, squeezing it over and over in soft caresses. Her tongue slid up and down the underside of his shaft sending electric waves to every part of his hot body.

Unable to take any more sweet torture, Paul pulled away and lay Alexia back down on her wrap taking his place beside her. His head dipped and his lips surrounded her nipple sucking gently but urgently. Alexia arched her back and pushed herself up against Paul's mouth as her hands pulled at his head, pressing his mouth more firmly against her. When her grip eased Paul pulled his lips from her now erect nipple, carefully sliding his teeth against it as he did so, making Alexia beg for him not to stop. He moved his mouth to cover hers and began to kiss her so passionately that she could barely breathe. As he slid his mouth down to her neck, Paul's hand moved between Alexia's thighs.

Feeling his fingers as they played in her dripping bush, Alexia instinctively opened her legs wider, allowing Paul to explore. As his forefinger slowly circled and teased her throbbing clit, his second finger slid inside her wet slit, deep into the warm hole that was waiting there. Paul never let his lips leave Alexia's moist skin, nibbling and kissing over her neck, her ears, her face, her breasts as he felt the growing wetness in his hand that proved she was getting more excited with every touch. As Alexia started to thrust up against his hand, Paul slid another finger deep inside her wet pussy and began to slowly fuck her with them, loving the feeling of her juices as they ran down the back of his hand. With his first finger he began to massage her clit more vigorously, stopping now and then to press directly on it and delighting in her squeals of pleasure when he did. Paul noticed Alexia's breathing become heavier and felt the thrusting of her hips against him become faster and harder. He knew she would cum soon and he whispered into her ear asking her to tell him when it was time. His own body was showing signs of wanting to cum too. His cock was a hard, quivering monster begging for release but Paul wanted to know Alexia was satisfied first, wanted to know he had brought her joy like she had never felt before.

Suddenly Alexia's body became rigid and her pussy muscles gripped Paul's fingers very tightly. He knew even before she moaned out, "Oh, God, I'm cumming Paul!" Her whole body was consumed by the orgasm, his fingers being gripped in wave after wave of pure pleasure by her wet pussy. It was all Paul could do not to shoot his cum all over her side as he lay there watching her climax but through her moans he heard her cry out, "Fuck me Paul! Fuck me now, pleeeeease?"

Once was all Alexia had to ask him. Before she had even reached the end of her climax Paul was on top of her. He shoved his hungry cock into her in one swift stroke, filling her pussy so full that she could feel him stretching her inner walls. Alexia's legs wrapped around Paul's waist and pulled him into her deeper than even he knew he could go. Their hot, sweaty bodies began to move together in a rhythm all their own. It was as if they were one person, so perfectly did their bodies respond to each other. Paul could still feel Alexia's pussy grasping his cock in the aftermath of her first orgasm He loved the way he slid in and out of her so easily, so smoothly. He loved the way she kept moaning his name over and over again, telling him how good he felt inside of her, telling him how much pleasure he was giving her with his touch.

Alexia dug her nails into Paul's back, totally consumed by her passion but still careful not to draw blood. She felt him thrust harder and she met him with an equal intensity. She had never felt like this before, even with Bradley. Bradley had never taken the time to show Alexia what an orgasm was like. He just expected to get his and once he was satisfied he would go to sleep and leave Alexia feeling like there must be something more but not able to figure out what. Paul had already given her more physical pleasure than Bradley had throughout their marriage and he had done it because he wanted to and not because she had asked for it.

Paul rolled onto his back, pulling Alexia over with him so that she was straddling him with his cock still buried deep inside of her. Alexia began to move up and down, allowing him to see his cock sliding in and out of her, glistening with her cum. She slipped one hand around between Paul's thighs and began to play with his balls as she rode him, feeling them tighten and draw up in her hand. With her other hand she reached for Paul's hands and led them to her breasts. Alexia threw back her head and her long red hair blew in the wind, tickling Paul's thighs. As she felt Paul's hands squeezing her sensitive nipples and his thrusting became more uncontrolled, Alexia knew he would cum very soon. She also knew that the feeling of his hot cum hitting her pussy would send her over the edge once more into that wonderful new place he had opened up for her.

All of a sudden Paul's hands grasped Alexia's waist and slammed her down on him hard, holding her there. Alexia felt the hot wet volcano that exploded inside of her and her own body reacted by exploding too. This climax was far stronger than the first because with every new spurt of hot fluid that filled her, her pussy began to contract again. Her quiet moans turned into screams of passion and then whimpers of contentment as she drooped forward onto Paul, totally spent from the last two hours of lovemaking.

Alexia stirred in her sleep. This was the part of the dream memory she wished she could change. This was where things took a turn for the worst and she wanted to wake up but she knew that when she did she would still be in her dream, only she would be further along. Paul and Alexia had fallen asleep together on the beach that night, cuddled in each other's arms. The next morning as day began to dawn they had awakened, still entwined with each other. In the light of day Paul had thought he was seeing things more clearly. He couldn't come between Alexia and her husband. He couldn't break up her marriage. He lay for along time before she stirred just watching her sleep, memorizing every feature, counting every breath she took, and deciding how to handle the situation. Paul knew he had lost control and now he must make things better.

As Alexia's eyes opened she looked up at Paul with all the love and lust she felt in her heart for him. She was rather surprised when all she got in return was a small smile and an offhanded comment about the silly things moonlight and beaches can cause people to do. Silly? Is that how Paul thought of making love with her, as just a silly thing?

After being thrown away by her husband and giving herself so fully to Paul, Alexia had expected love in return. Now she was remembering the many times he had told her he wanted a no strings attached relationship. Apparently her feelings were the only ones that had changed the night before. Hurt quickly turned into anger as Alexia realized that she had been stupid to fall for him after he had been so clear in what he wanted from her.

As the anger built and Paul sat there talking about the many things they could do together as friends, Alexia's head began to spin. Suddenly she found herself yelling at Paul, telling him that he was not her friend or he would never have taken advantage of her the night before. The look of pain in his eyes should have stopped her cold but her own pain was so strong it pushed her forward. She told him they could not be friends anymore because she knew now she could not trust him. She screamed about not being able to love him even as a friend after he had used her, but the whole time her heart was crying out that it was too late because she already loved him. Tears of hurt began to roll down Alexia's cheeks in a steady stream as she watched Paul stand up, pull on his clothes, and slowly walk away from her forever. When she could breath normally again, Alexia had walked home to her quiet house. She found a note on the table saying good bye along with Bradley's house keys. Slowly she walked into the bedroom and fell onto the bed, crying herself to sleep as she realized that she was all alone in the world again.

Two months went by quickly when you slept them away and sleep was all that Alexia did. Bradley had been sending her a check for her expenses so there was no need for her to work. Paul should have been on his way to becoming a memory but Alexia still thought about him every day. Alexia had not been feeling well lately and she was going on the assumption that it was a mild case of depression until the vomiting started. It was only then that she realized she had not had a period since that night on the beach but still she didn't panic. After all it was only that once without protection so chances were slim that she was pregnant. Still, just to be safe, Alexia went to the doctor. When the doctor gave Alexia the "happy news" she cried. She knew she could never tell Paul. She did not want him to come back to her because he felt an obligation and a child was better off with one parent if the alternative was two that did not love each other. Alexia thought how much different things would have been if Paul had just loved her the way she had loved him. They could have been a great family but now she had to figure out what to do. Bradley would not support a baby that was not his and she could not expect him to.

The night air had turned cold and Alexia was moaning in her sleep. She kept begging Paul to love her, to want her, to hold her forever and never let her go. In her semi-awakened state she imagined she could hear him answering her, telling her he did love her and that he would cherish her for the rest of their lives if she would only let him. It wasn't until she rolled over and her blanket slipped away that the loud exclamation from Paul brought her fully awake and she realized he was really there with her.

"Alexia, why didn't you tell me?" Paul asked in a whisper as he stared at her growing belly. Alexia couldn't answer she was so astonished to see him standing there. "It doesn't matter now, Darling," he continued, "I love you and I am never going to let you push me away again!"

As her eyes filled with tears all Alexia could do was hold out her open arms to him. Paul wasted no time moving into her embrace and claiming her sweet lips with his own. He felt the baby kick against his stomach and with a wicked grin he crooned, "I think maybe we should let junior know daddy is back by rocking him to sleep." Alexia nodded silently.

Paul gently removed her clothes and then his own. They made slow, sweet love all night long as they planned their future together. He spent hours just kissing every inch of her exposed flesh, especially the stretched tummy that held the proof of their love.

CHAPTER 2
COLLEGE DAZE

COLLEGE DAZE

This was a really tough week for me and what can be called tough for me would be a vacation for other people. You see, I like to stay very busy at college. I like to have too much work to do. Not so much that I need help but enough to fight off boredom anyhow. Today I didn't have enough work to keep me busy through the morning faculty meeting so I was not looking forward to the rest of the day with so much free time on my hands.

To give my mind something to do I sat around and fantasized about a couple of the people on the faculty that have really caught my eye this year. Micah is a medium height dark haired, brown eyed brooder that simply exudes sexuality all over the place in a you-can't-touch-this sort of way. He is definitely a challenge if there ever was one. And one I would love to get the chance to take. And then there's Melanie. A tall blonde haired beauty with crystal blue eyes and a body to die for. Just thinking about her luscious lips and how soft they must be makes my pussy wet. To have a threesome with the two of them would be heavenly.

As the lunch bell sounded loudly Melanie came over and asked if I would like to go out to eat with her and Micah, and a couple of the new teachers. After the daydreaming I had been doing all morning I couldn't pass up the chance to get on friendlier terms with them so I accepted with a smile. We ended up going to a small diner just down the street from the college. I don't eat out much at all so I asked everyone what they would recommend. Melanie, Micah and I ordered the same meals after much thought. The knowledge that we all had the same taste in food made me pulse deep inside my pussy. I mean really, just think about it. If you have one thing common with someone, chances are you'll have other things in common too. And the more things people have in common, the more chance there is that they will also share more personal preferences, perhaps even erotic ones.

I don't normally order dessert after meals being a health conscious person but with my hormones raging out of control I needed something chocolate and I needed it fast! With no real work waiting for me to finish up I decided to take a long lunch. When our waiter came over and asked us if we would be having dessert today, I quickly replied that I'd be having a slice of double chocolate fudge cake with chocolate silk icing. As I finished giving my order I heard moaning from the other side of the table. Melanie and Micah both said that sounded scrumptious and that they would have the same. The other teachers decided against dessert and bid us farewell. Suddenly I found myself left alone with the two people I desired more than anything else in this world. The thought that the three of us were all alone made my pussy wet. I could feel the wetness as it seeped between my thighs, making them slide easily against each other as I crossed my legs. I don't wear panties often so when I cross my legs just right and swing the one on top at a steady pace I can make myself cum with almost no effort at all. And right then, staring at two people I had been wanting for almost a full school year now, I could think of nothing more exciting than cumming without them even knowing what I was doing.

While we were waiting for our cake we chatted about little things. I found out Melanie is single by choice, a career woman with very little worries about her future. Micah is a widower with a small daughter that he is raising alone. Of course finding out Micah was free to date excited me so much that I started to swing my leg even faster, feeling the wetness and heat growing as my clit responded to the rhythmic friction.

When our cake finally made it to our table in the hands of an extremely sexy waiter, we started to eat with obvious enjoyment. My hormones raging uncontrollably now, needing release from the pressure my secret masturbating technique had built up between my thighs, I ate every sweet bite with as much sexual innuendo as I possibly could. For good measure I threw in a lot of soft but satisfactory moaning. My moans grew louder as I felt the damn burst in an explosive climax and my cum flowed freely down the inside of my thighs. Watching Melanie and Micah from underneath my half-closed eyelashes, I knew I had them both totally mesmerized by my obvious sensuality. When our waiter returned again and asked if we needed anything else or if we were ready for the check, both Melanie and Micah had to clear their throats before they could speak.

We rode back to the college together in Micah's car. I sat in the front with him, which gave me a little time to test the waters by rubbing Micah's leg without being noticed by Melanie. I smiled to myself as I watched the bulge in his Dockers grow. When we reached the college parking lot Micah told us to go on in and he would be there in a moment. I figured he was going to jerk off before he joined us in the front office.

Melanie and I walked inside in complete silence. We walked quickly to the elevators. Once inside the elevator we were alone at last except, of course, there was the school's security camera staring down at us. I love to be watched so the idea that someone could see everything we were doing made me very horny again. I reached behind Melanie and slid my hand down her sexy, firm ass. Slowly I let one finger follow the crack in her ass going all the way down to her juncture. At first she was startled by my touch and she jumped but she didn't pull away from my hand. Then I watched as she seemed to relax and her eyes closed, enjoying the feeling of my hand on her.

Knowing the long ride up would take several minutes; I slid my hand further down her leg to the top of the slit in her black mini skirt. It was barely high enough to let me reach between her legs without doing too much bending and it looked like I was leaning back on the railing at the rear of the elevator car. When my exploring fingers reached her slit again, she instinctively spread her legs just a little. It gave me enough space to reach the front of her most sensitive of areas as my finger followed the silk string of her thongs forward. When I finally reached her clit, I pressed the hard little knob firmly and she let out a loud moan.

Smiling, I leaned over and whispered in her ear softly, "Do you like the way that feels, Melanie?"

"Oh, God, yes, Bobbi, yes, I like it a lot!" she gasped, trying to look calm for the camera but failing miserably.

"Do you want more?" I asked in a teasing tone of voice, knowing that her body was begging for the same release that mine had cried out for earlier at the diner. "Tell me what you want Melanie, tell me now!"

In response to my questions Melanie pushed herself down against my hand and groaned loudly, no longer trying to hide the lust that consumed her. She was breathing very hard now and her voice was barely audible as she spoke, "I want to cum, Bobbi!"

I looked up to see how many more floors we had to go and knowing we had only seconds before reaching our destination, I ran my finger on the inside of her wet pussy lips, touching her clit just as the elevator stopped. Quickly I pulled away my hand and stood up. As I moved to pass her I looked her straight in the eyes and raised my wet finger to my mouth so she could watch as I sucked her juices off. I heard her passionate groan just before I looked away.

I had nothing to do for the rest of the day, but I was smiling anyway. Every time I would catch Melanie's eye I would put my finger in my mouth. The look she gave me then was more than merely a look of lust. It was a look of absolute need, raw desire that had to be quenched as soon as possible.

I caught Micah watching Melanie and me off and on throughout the day. On his face was a look I can only describe as lust, awe and embarrassment all rolled into one. I wondered which emotion was the strongest and decided to find out for myself if the lust would win out. I caught Micah's eye across the room. I stood up and walked into one of the empty filing rooms, turned around, and looking him straight in his sexy brown eyes, I closed the door, never looking away. The room was fairly empty of everything except some furniture that had been discarded from various offices. I sat down in a black leather chair behind an old folding table and propped up my feet. I don't normally wear dresses to work but today was unusually hot for mid May and I had wanted to feel the breeze on my legs. I slid the hem of my skirt up my thighs just far enough that no one would be able to tell if I was wearing panties or not. I undid two buttons and was working on the third when Micah walked in.

He looked back to see if anyone had seen him come in. Thinking the coast was clear, he closed the door quietly and turned around to face me. One look and he froze in his steps.

"Awww, Micah, Don't be shy now," I said with a husky, lust-filled voice.

"Maybe we shouldn't be in here," he replied quietly, "someone could walk in on us at any time."

With an impish twinkle in my eyes I whispered softly, "Then lock the door, Sexy, and come over here. I want to see how that bulge in your pants is doing." He walked back and I heard the clink as the door lock clicked closed.

He walked over to where I sat behind the table muttering, "We really shouldn't. It's not a good idea, Bobbi."

"Well you can always leave, Micah," I said smoothly, "if you don't want to spend time with me."

I reached across the table and rubbed the bulge I saw on the outside of his pants. I could feel his cock throbbing, jumping at my soft touch. Ever so slowly I unbuckled his belt, undid his button, pulled down his zipper and let his pants drop to the floor. He was wearing silk boxers and I pulled his hard cock out from the opening of them, relishing how it appeared to be begging for my touch. Micah surprised me. He has a much bigger cock than I imagined. It must be a full 8 inches long at least and its thickness is incredible. The head was still a very dark purple, so I knew that he never did get rid of the hard-on I gave him earlier that day at lunch.

The pre-cum was thick and copious. I stuck out my tongue and licked it up. Micah let out a quiet moan as I stuck the tip of my tongue in his hole trying to get more of his pre-cum. Slowly I moved my tongue round and round the swollen head of his rock solid cock. I put my hand on his hips, holding him in place, not letting him push forward. I slipped my fingers inside his waistband and pulled down his boxers until his beautiful cock sprung free. I leaned forward and let my warm wet tongue circle his belly button as I took his throbbing head into my hand again and wrapped my fingers around his hot shaft. I kissed the tip of his dripping rod, sliding the head into my mouth and swirling my tongue around it. Reaching up I massaged his balls gently but firmly. His cock and balls jumped in my hands. Using my other hand as my tongue worked steadily, I stroked his shaft. I made sure to move very slowly at first, increasing my speed as his breathing got faster and became more ragged. Then all at once I stopped everything. Still holding his cock firmly I looked up into his surprised eyes. I grinned at him, and opened my mouth as if I was going to say something really important at that moment but then instead of speaking I slid his cock into my hungry throat. I took him in all the way to the base, deep throating him until only his balls were left outside my lips. I massaged him with my throat as I swallowed him over and over. I could feel his balls tightening as I kept swallowing. I ran my tongue along the underside of his over-aroused shaft and massaged his balls. I held the deep throat for as long as possible, until I felt the need to breathe again. Slowly I pulled his delicious cock out of my warm mouth. Massaging his balls with one hand, I had to use my free one to pull his hands from my hair and to keep him from thrusting back into my mouth. Once he stopped moving and became very still I started sucking him in and out of my mouth. I started slow and easy. I gradually increased my speed and the pressure I was exerting on his cock. Occasionally I would slow down or stop to deep throat him again. I could feel his balls getting tighter and more drawn every time I did this. I knew he was close because the whole time I could hear him grinding his teeth to keep quiet. I knew he was going to cum very soon and I was starved for the taste of his cum.

"Bobbi, stop! I'm going to cum!" he said between gritted teeth. Even while he was telling me to stop, his hands had found their way back into my hair and were pulling my head closer to him. I knew that if I deep throated him just once more I would be swallowing my coveted prize.

Wanting to taste him so much I was dripping now, I deep throated him again, reaching behind him to grab his ass and holding him deep in my throat. One swallow is all it took before he erupted in my throat. Not being able to stay quiet any longer he let out several loud groans as he continued to shoot hot spurts of cum deep in my throat. Every swallow was milking his cock, trying to get every last drop of his salty cream. Feeling suddenly weak in the knees he leaned back against the wall as his climax finished and he slipped from between my lips. Just then we heard a soft knock at the door. Micah jumped and pulled his pants up quickly, his face turning red as I walked from behind the table to answer the door. Before I opened it I looked over to see Micah leaning against the wall, his body half hidden in the shadows. I opened the door and came face to face with Melanie.

"Melanie, darling, do come in," I said saucily. As she entered I locked the door behind her, anticipating a second course for my sexual appetite, which was now raring and ready for more.

She had a confused look on her face as she began to speak. "I was just wanting to ....." I took her beautiful blonde head between my hands and cut off her sentence with a smoldering kiss, letting her taste Micah's cum on my tongue. Still holding her head I pulled away and looked into her questioning eyes. She hadn't seen Micah come in and still didn't realize he was standing there in the shadows. She wasn't quite sure what she had tasted in my mouth never having tasted a man's cum before. I led her over to the table, with her back to Micah. Propping her tight ass on the edge of it I knelt down in front of her. Glancing up into her lust filled eyes I slid my hands up her creamy thighs, lifting her skirt as I moved. When I got near the top of her thighs I watched her lick her lips. Without any conscious thought she spread her legs wider for me. It was then that realized Melanie no longer had her thong on.

"Oh naughty Melanie," I teased, "What ever could have happened to your panties? Did you lose them somewhere?"

She tried to stammer out a reply but ended up just groaning as I slipped my finger into her hot wet pussy. Pushing her further onto the table, I spread her legs apart. I leaned forward and sucked her juices from her inner thighs. Melanie closed her eyes and let her head fall back as her back arched, thrusting her breasts forward. I started licking her wet pussy slowly, covering her entire mound in short slow strokes. I spread her swollen lips apart and began to lick the opening to her wet pussy, circling her clit with my tongue. I slid one hand up her flat tummy to her breast and I massaged her erect nipples through the silk fabric of her bra, causing a deep moan to escape her throat. She looked at me with a deep animal lust clouding her blue eyes.

In a voice that was husky with passion I whispered to her, "Take your blouse and bra off and let me see you, Melanie. " She sat up and did as I instructed her. Her areolas were a dark, dusky rose color against the creamy ivory of her well-shaped globes. Her erect nipples were very big and adorned her breasts like cherries on a sundae. Gazing on her beauty I could feel my own juices starting to slide down my thighs. I rose up and took one luscious nipple into my wanton mouth, sucking gently. Melanie leaned her head back again. Suddenly she jerked and sucked in her breath.

"Bobbi, Wh…wh…what's going on here?" she stuttered, noticing Micah standing against the wall. With his hard, throbbing cock held firmly in his hand Micah stood up and moved to join us at the table.

He never spoke a word but simply smiled at Melanie before he leaned over her shoulder to suck on her other nipple. Melanie groaned and lay back flat onto the table. I moved and slid two fingers into her tight, wet pussy. Using my thumb I rubbed her clit hard and fast, pumping my fingers in and out of her pussy. I leaned down and sucked on her throbbing clit, pulling it into my mouth like a tiny cock. I slipped a third finger into her wetness and I could feel the beginnings of her orgasm. I sucked harder, pumped faster and I felt her start to cum. Quickly I moved my mouth to suck up all her juices, making her cum even harder. As her throbbing calmed I looked up at her, her cum shining all over my face. Micah was watching us while he continued stroking his hard glistening cock. Climbing onto the table I leaned down and kissed Melanie again, letting her taste her own cum mingled with Micah's in my mouth. As I was kissing her I felt her hand move along my leg up to my dripping pussy. She slid her fingers into my wet cunt. I reached down and moved her fingers in and out of me slowly. I took her hand and slid one finger up to my clit and made her rub it. I groaned against her mouth.

Suddenly I felt my skirt being lifted from behind me. I looked back and saw Micah slide his swollen and throbbing cock into my hot, wet pussy hole. I returned my gaze to Melanie who was now busy opening my blouse. I moaned loudly as she began sucking on my braless, erect nipples. Melanie rubbed my clit hard and fast while Micah held my hips and pumped his hot rod into my aching pussy.

I found myself so turned on I couldn't speak. I reached for Melanie's pussy again and started rubbing her clit in time with how she was rubbing mine. She groaned against my nipples and rubbed me even harder and faster. I felt Micah slip out of my pussy and looked back in wonder, watching as he slowly slid his cock into my ass. I felt his swollen head slip in and I throbbed in response. I felt Melanie slide under me and start eating at my wet pussy, slipping her tongue deep inside of me. Aroused now beyond all belief, I rocked back against Micah, forcing him to slide into my ass faster and deeper than he had been. I rocked back and forth on Micah's hot rod, causing Melanie's tongue to rub faster on my swollen clit. Feeling the deep stirrings of my orgasm starting, I move faster than ever before, in and out.

"Ohhhh, My God, yesssssss," I groaned as I orgasmed with a force that made my whole body tremble and quiver, "I'm cummingggggggggggg!!"

Micah slid out of my tight ass and came all over Melanie's face and breasts. To my surprise, she licked up everything her tongue could reach. Micah handed her his handkerchief but I quickly moved to use my tongue to lap up everything she had been unable to get to.

"You really are becoming nasty, aren't you, Melanie my dear?" I said with a sly grin. She replied with a grin of her own and a twinkle in her eye that promised we would see just how nasty she could get one day.

Slowly and carefully we all dressed, helping each other a little, stealing small gropes here and there. I pulled my skirt into place and buttoned my blouse. Melanie unlocked the door and slipped out first. A few minutes later Micah followed her. I stood there alone for a while, enjoying replaying our afternoon over and over in my mind, knowing it would not be a one time event, knowing that the best was yet to come. Smiling from ear to ear I went back into the office. I could see plenty of smirks on people's faces and I knew that all the questions I would get would be more than enough to keep me busy the rest of the day.

CHAPTER 3
THE GOOD HUMOR MAN

THE GOOD HUMOR MAN

Carmen smiled when she heard the bell of the ice cream truck ringing. Grabbing the change she kept in a small cup on the table by her door, she hurried out to wait by the curb. She knew that kids would come from every direction to buy their favorite ice cream cone or ice pop from the Good Humor man. Just barely the middle of June and already the heat wave was astounding. Temperatures had not dipped below eighty degrees this week even at night so the cold refreshment was a welcome treat for all.

Carmen stood at the back of the line with the other adults, letting the eager little ones have first choice. After all, they were the ones playing out in the heat all day while the grown ups stayed inside wondering how they had ever lived without air conditioning. Even in her halter top and short shorts, Carmen could feel the sweat running down her body in streams, soaking the space between her breasts and tickling the back of her neck.

It seemed like she waited forever but actually it was a matter of less than fifteen minutes for the kids to make their purchases and disappear back into their various yards. Carmen stepped back and let the other adults order first knowing that by going last she would be able to spend some extra time with Chris, the new driver for the good humor truck. Chris had caught her attention from the very first day he started this route, almost six months ago now. She had been in the middle of a pillow fight with the neighbor's kids when she heard the familiar bell ringing. Even though it was too cold for her to want ice cream, she had scurried out to meet the truck, planning on talking for a few minutes with old Mr. Wilson. Mr. Wilson had run the ice cream truck for years now, since Carmen herself had been a young girl, and she still enjoyed talking to the elderly man whenever she could.

As Carmen had reached the truck, her hair disheveled, her clothes askew, and her make-up all but gone, she yelled out a hardy, "Boy, am I ever glad to see you!" She knew that her enthusiastic welcome always brought a quick smile to Mr. Wilson's wrinkled face and she did so love to make him smile. This kind old man had been more than an ice cream vendor to Carmen. He had been a friend, always making time to listen to her when she was down or upset, always sneaking extra toppings on her favorite cone to cheer her sadness. Carmen waited to hear his bemused chuckle as she watched the doors on the side of the truck slide open.

"You must really love ice cream," said a deep voice. Startled, Carmen had jerked up her head and found herself staring into the eyes of one of the handsomest men she had ever seen. Her first thought was that he was laughing at her as she caught the impish gleam in his eyes. She instinctively knew that she should feel defensive and yet she didn't feel that way at all. As a matter of fact, Carmen wasn't exactly sure what it was she was feeling but somewhere deep inside of her she felt a stirring. Odd that a total stranger would affect her that way.

Her cheeks beginning to heat up Carmen stammered, "Ss...sss...sorry about that. I was expecting my old friend Mr. Wilson." Suddenly realizing that this stranger was in Mr. Wilson's truck she squared her shoulders and looked him directly in the eyes. With as much authority as she could force into her quivering voice, Carmen demanded, "And, by the way, who are you and what are you doing in that truck anyhow?" She saw the twinkle come into his eyes again and her cheeks burned a bright red but her stare never wavered from his face.

Chris managed to hold back the amusement in his voice as he stared at the young, clearly agitated lady standing before him. He had to make himself stare at her eyes so that his gaze would not wander down to her firm, ripe breasts and the outline of her erect nipples that was clearly visible through her thin shirt. The fire in her eyes excited him and he was glad that the truck hid the lower part of his body, sure she would be offended if she could see the bulge that had appeared in his pants.

"Hi, my name is Chris and I will be running this truck for Mr. Wilson from now on. His heart is getting weaker and the doctor has told him not to be out in the heat any more than necessary. Mr. Wilson said he has kept generations of kids on this street happy with his ice cream for as long as he can remember and he was not about to stop now. I was in the doctor's office that day, cleaning as it were, and half-heartedly told him to hire me. After all, anything is better than emptying trashcans and scrubbing toilets for a living. To my surprise he did so on the spot. He had me fitted for a uniform that very afternoon and by the following Friday I was the new Good Humor man."

Carmen listened attentively through his whole speech but her mind was racing to other thoughts. How could one man be so gorgeous that she found it hard to think clearly? She kept telling herself to get a grip. Never before had she been so attracted to someone she didn't even know. What if he was a con man out to steal profits from Mr. Wilson? Carmen knew instinctively that the man she was looking at would never hurt anyone on purpose. She wasn't sure how she knew but she was absolutely positive of the fact.

Carmen continued to meet the ice cream truck every afternoon and slowly she and Chris came to be friends. He kept her informed about Mr. Wilson's health and she kept him amused by her stories of the kids in her neighborhood. Every day she would saunter up to the truck window and order her favorite cone, a double dipped chocolate covered cherry delight. After the first few weeks Chris managed to always have it ready when her turn to order finally came. Carmen noticed that after Chris would turn off his bell, he didn't leave the street. Rather, he would drive down to the shaded parking lot outside of the public playground and park there. She finally worked up enough courage to ask him why and she was very surprised by his response.

Chris told her that her street was his last stop of the day and he hated to go home with so much daylight left. He would bring along a favorite book of poetry or sometimes his old 35mm camera and whittle away his early evening hours reading in the shade or snapping photos of the animals he saw in the park. Having the same interests herself, Carmen asked if she might join him sometime. The way his face lit up as he uttered a fast "Sure you can" in her direction made it clear that he enjoyed her company very much. Carmen thought how that was good because she definitely enjoyed being with him too.

As the two new friends had become closer, there came times when one might accidentally brush against the other while they were walking together.

Carmen was surprised at how this contact made electrical pulses spread throughout her body and then return to concentrate on her one small spot. She noticed that after spending time with Chris, even though it was always perfectly innocent, she would come home to find her pussy so wet with desire that she would have to change her panties. And one day as she leaned across him to retrieve a book from the other end of the picnic table, she slipped and found her hand firmly planted on his crotch. Chris gave a nervous laugh and pulled away quickly but in just the few minutes her hand had lingered, Carmen had felt his cock spring to life under her fingers. She wondered why Chris hadn't kissed her, why he hadn't asked her not to stop.

Over time the two had grown closer and often Chris would give Carmen a light kiss on the lips as he left her at her home. Carmen felt the desire for more but not once did Chris try to go further than that little peck. After several more weeks of wet panties, severe frustration, and many cold showers, Carmen got brave enough to make the first move. After all she reasoned with herself, maybe Chris was just very shy and needed a little prodding to get his libido going. Keeping this thought firmly in the front of her mind, Carmen waited for Saturday night when they would be going to a movie together. As always they had a great deal of fun, laughing and cutting up until an usher threatened to remove them from cinema. Afterwards they walked home hand in hand, enjoying the comfortable silence, the beautiful moonlight, and the soft breeze blowing at their faces. When the couple reached Carmen's front door at last, Chris leaned down to give her the customary brush on her lips. Without any more thought, Carmen wrapped her arms tightly around his neck and pulled his lips closer, stretching up and capturing them with her own.

She kissed him carefully and softly at first, slowly deepening the kiss, pulling his tongue into her hot mouth to suck it gently. She could feel Chris responding as his arms found their way around her slender waist and he pulled her close. His hands slid lightly up her sides and the skin beneath his fingers began to tingle in expectation. Carmen could feel his cock growing hard as he pressed it against her, could feel her pussy quivering with excitement at the thought that he wanted her. Her whole body burned like a raging inferno of passion and desire. She moaned loudly into his mouth as she felt Chris's hands find her breasts. Her nipples were already straining against the thin silk fabric of her blouse but they grew even harder at his touch. She closed her eyes and melted against him, waiting to feel him undo her buttons, waiting to feel his bare skin on hers.

Suddenly Carmen could not feel Chris anymore. She opened her eyes and looked at him in confusion as he backed away from her. "Not now, not yet," he whispered, "I have something special planned." Carmen knew the disappointment showed on her face but she managed to hold back her tears. He hadn't said no to her. He had simply said not now. Still, she wondered if now would ever come as she watched Chris turn and walk down the street toward his truck without saying another word.

The next day Carmen had run out to meet the truck just as always but when the crowd cleared and she got her turn at the window, Chris did not have her customary cone waiting. Instead he gave her a bright smile and asked if she would like to go to the park with him for a few hours. He promised her that once they were there he would definitely give her that chocolate covered cherry delight. Carmen wondered why she couldn't have her ice cream now. She would still go with him anyway but Chris insisted that she wait for her treat.

When Chris reached the park he didn't pull into his usual space but instead he drove around the maintenance building to the extra parking lot behind. Carmen found this rather odd since no one ever used that lot unless there was a special event taking place. It was completely cut off from everything by the dense trees surrounding it and the building in front of it. Without speaking a word Chris moved to the back of the truck and opened the freezer. He glanced back at Carmen over his broad shoulder and the sneaky gleam in his eyes told her that he was up to something. But what could it be?

Chris crooked his finger at Carmen, motioning for her to join him in the back of the truck. She immediately jumped to her feet and started toward him. As she got within arms reach, he reached out and grabbed her, pulling her to him in one swift motion and covering her surprised mouth with his own. The kiss heated her up immediately and Carmen responded with utter abandonment to her passions. She could feel her pussy growing hotter and wetter by the second and she hoped with all her heart that Chris wasn't going to stop this time. Just as her body reached a point where it cried out for fulfillment, Chris picked Carmen up in his arms and placed her ass firmly on the small counter against the back wall. Carmen could clearly see that his cock was swollen and throbbing and so she was amazed when, instead of pulling it out, he dropped to his knees in front of her.

Slowly and gently his hands caressed her right leg and then lifted it high. He removed her shoe and began to kiss the base of her foot, working his way over her toes, across her ankle, and up her calf, stopping to suck on the underside of her knee. His lips found the inside of her thigh and he nibbled softly on the muscle there. When Carmen felt his hot, wet tongue touching the crease where her crotch met her thigh, she moaned loudly and leaned back against the wall of the truck.

Chris dropped her leg carefully and moved to her left one, repeating the process slowly, building her anticipation. When his warm mouth again met her crotch, Chris stopped abruptly. He leaned back on his heels and looked up at her with a lusty smile. Carmen felt her skin burning with desire under his hands as he removed her panties and tossed them to the floor.

"Are you ready for your chocolate covered cherry delight, Carmen?" He asked with just the slightest hint of mischief in his voice. Carmen thought he must have surely been kidding. No way could he want her to stop now to eat ice cream. She decided he must be teasing her and that she was going to play along with it and see how fast he backtracked. She nodded her head quietly. "I think I will share with you today if you don't mind," his sexy voice continued. Every word he spoke made her wet pussy throb harder. Carmen closed her eyes and nodded again. She felt Chris move as he stood up and she wondered how far he would go with his teasing. When she heard the freezer door open she kept her eyes closed but decided that if he actually made the cone she would teach him a lesson by making him wait while she ate it.

When Carmen felt Chris move between her legs again she figured he had decided to give up his little game and finish what they had started. She gasped out loud when she felt something ice cold touch the inside of her thigh. Opening her eyes and looking down she saw Chris and as he looked up at her she could see the frozen chocolate covered cherry between his lips. The smile in his eyes was full of love as he pushed her back again and parted her legs wide. Carmen felt the coldness traveling up her leg toward her hot pussy and she wondered what Chris planned on doing with it. She didn't have to wait long to find out. Chris moved his mouth over her swollen lips and with one fast push, his tongue drove the cherry deep inside of Carmen's dripping cunt. The coldness excited her, made her hotter, made her pussy muscles flex, holding the cherry deep inside of her. The sensation was new to Carmen, feeling such coldness in the center of her hottest spot, and she wiggled a little, but Chris was not done yet. One by one he took the last three frozen cherries in his mouth and deposited them along with the first one inside her throbbing pussy. The cold pressure was exquisite, unlike anything Carmen had ever felt before. Chris left them there for several minutes until the heat of Carmen's body started to melt the chocolate and he could see it oozing from her pussy hole mixed with her own juices. His cock grew harder as he listened to her moans of pleasure and when he was unable to wait any longer, he moved his hot mouth to her well-trimmed bush. Chris let his tongue slowly lap over her entire mound before it traveled deeper, seeking out her swollen pussy lips. He drew first one and then the other into his mouth to suck on it. Slowly he covered her hot, wet, throbbing pussy and kissed it just like he kissed her sweet mouth. Carmen moaned and grabbed at his hair, trying to pull his lips up to hers, but Chris had something else in mind.

When she finally eased her hold on him, Chris took one hand and gently spread open the wet lips of Carmen's pussy. His tongue teased her clit, making tiny circles all around it before moving further down to her hole. He hungrily lapped up the melted chocolate and sex juices running freely from her heated cave. And then Chris pushed his mouth tight against Carmen's pussy and she felt his tongue dive deep inside of her. He felt so good that Carmen couldn't think straight and it took her several minutes to realize what he was doing. Chris was licking the remaining chocolate off the nearest cherry. Carmen could feel the cherry turning over and over under his exploring tongue. He took his time and before long Carmen was screaming out in ecstasy. Only when every last bit of chocolate had been licked off did Chris suck the cherry from her excited pussy. Carmen felt it pop out of her and the sensation brought on a sudden climax. Chris waited for her moaning to calm and then he moved his lips to hers, his tongue pushing the cherry between them, sharing his treat with her as he bit it in two and allowed her half to fall into her waiting mouth. When the cherry was gone, Chris again dropped between her soft, wet, creamy thighs and went after the next cherry in the same way. By the time all four cherries had been licked clean of their chocolate coating and shared freely with Carmen's soft mouth, Chris felt like his aching, rigid cock was going to burst. Listening to Carmen cum again every time he sucked another cherry from her hot cunt had made him hornier than he could ever remember being.

With Chris's lips still on hers and the last taste of cherry sliding down her throat Carmen moaned in complete satisfaction. Her pussy was not only hot and wet but it was throbbing hard. She was so aroused that she could hardly wait to feel Chris enter her. Her hands slid to his pants and she released the button they found, followed by undoing the zipper, and finished by practically yanking them down to his ankles. He wasn't wearing any underwear and as she raised back up his huge, dripping cock brushed her cheek. Feeling the wetness of his pre-cum she turned and let her tongue massage the tip of it. She could tell by the guttural sound that came from Chris that he liked what she was doing. But when she pulled the swollen head of his throbbing cock into her lips and started stroking it with the tip of her tongue he let out a loud moan and pulled away.

Turning his back to her he fumbled in the pockets of his pants. After watching for several minutes, Carmen realized that he was looking for a rubber. "Don't bother," she said in a husky, lust filled whisper, "I can't have kids and I get tested every six months for disease." Chris looked shocked but turned back to her and once again pulled her close to him. Carmen's legs found their way around his waist and looking down between them she watched Chris take his throbbing rod firmly in hand and place it at the opening of her pussy. He seemed hesitant to slide it in and unable to wait, Carmen used her legs to pull him toward her, letting him watch as her pussy swallowed his hard cock. The sound that came from his lips could only be described as animalistic. The groan vibrated the walls of the truck.

Carmen could feel his whole body trembling against her as they slowly began to fuck together. The sound of suction became louder as Chris slid in and out of her dripping pussy, moaning every time her muscles would tighten to hold him in. She could feel his heart beating against her own, his breath tickling the side of her face, his hands holding her tight. The sexual tension that had been throbbing deep inside of Carmen for the last several months was threatening to explode with a ferocious bang. Her hips began to rock faster and harder, her ass slapping against Chris's balls as she fucked him, forcing his cock to move in and out of her tight pussy hole. Suddenly Chris slid one hand down between them and covering the hair on her swollen mound, he slid his middle finger deep inside her hot pussy, letting it fuck her right along with his enormous cock. His thumb he pressed tight against her swollen clit which now stood erect and as hard as a marble.

Carmen slid her hand around behind Chris, her nails digging lightly into his ass as he continued to pump at her furiously. Feeling his body starting to quiver as his muscles tensed, she quickly slid her finger into his asshole, feeling the muscles grasp at it as he let out a loud yell, "I'm cumming, Baby, I'm cumminggggggggggg!"

The sound of his exclamation mingled with the hot spurts of cum that Carmen could feel hitting the inner walls of her dripping tunnel of love sent her into her own explosive climax. She called out his name as she came, declaring her undying love for him. They trembled in each other's arms until they both reached that state of comfortable afterglow and then they slowly dressed each other. As they sat there in the front of the truck, staring into each other's eyes, Carmen and Chris realized that they were soul mates, they were meant to be together forever, they were two parts of one whole.

Several weeks later Chris had given Carmen an ice cream cone with an engagement ring hidden in it. The gem was shaped like a small cherry and surrounded by crushed diamonds that sparkled like the mischievous gleam in his eyes the day she had first met him. Every Day when she heard the bell on his truck she would run out to meet him, waiting first for all the kids to leave, and then the adults, so that they could be alone.

Every trip to the good humor truck brought Carmen a new and unexpected treat, though she knew in her heart that her chocolate covered cherry delight would always be her favorite.

CABIN OF LOVE

CHAPTER 4

CABIN OF LOVE

I'm still not clear in my head exactly how it all happened. I guess that's why I'm jotting down what I can remember about that night. I am hoping that maybe it will help me to come to an understanding of what Michael and I did that night and why.

My hubby Michael and I had just moved back to the area where we had both grown up in beautiful western Maryland after four years away, and I was happy to be back home again. Michael and I had stayed with family members for the first month while we worked on finding a home. Eventually we found a small, cozy place at the base of the mountains. It was kind of hidden away from the crowds in a wooded area with only three other homes close by. The house that we bought was a four bedroom beautiful pine log cabin with a loft over half of the main floor, and one of those wrap-around porches that we could sit on and sip lemonade as the sun set. It wasn't really very big, but that porch sold me. I had always wanted a porch like that, where you could walk around the entire house without ever leaving it.

The mortgage payment was a little higher than we wanted but we figured that we could always rent one of the spare bedrooms and charge them a third of what we were paying. That would easily bring the monthly payment back into our range. The only snag in our plan was that Michael had had some problems in the past with roommates and was leery about trying to find a suitable renter. I don't usually like dealing with strangers but I really wanted that little cabin in the woods, so I told Michael that I would do the interviewing and find someone to share our home. Reluctantly, he agreed. After we signed the mounds of papers and moved into my dream home, I had to figure out what was the best way to advertise for a renter. I finally decided the best way was to list an ad in the local newspaper and to put Michael's cell phone number down as a contact number so that I wouldn't miss any potential "catches." Whenever an interview was required I could always meet them in public to make sure they weren't the proverbial "nut case" before bringing them home to show them our place.

I placed my ad the very next morning. It read: Looking for SWM/SWF to share small, private cabin in the woods with happily married couple. Applicant must be open-minded and agree to pay utilities in addition to rent of $450 per mo. Please call 410-555-5656 between 7 am and 8 pm and ask for Irene. Short, sweet, and to the point! I put in the open mindedness part because I didn't want some super opinionated prude telling us how we should be living. Looking back, maybe I should have left that part out. What's done is done, as my old grand pappy would say. No use crying over spilled milk.

Since I had planned on doing the interviewing, I kept Michael's phone with me at all times. Unfortunately, due to a mental lapse on my part, I forgot to take his phone with me when I went shopping that Friday morning. Michael stayed home and was relaxing on our new front porch. The phone ringing woke him from the peaceful sleep that he had drifted into.

Needless to say, when I got home we had acquired new boarder. Michael was pretty pleased by his choice until he looked into my smoldering eyes and realized that I was livid. I screamed in a voice that left no doubt as to my anger, "Dammit Michael, you know that this is a choice that we agreed to make together! Whatever has gotten into you to make you take a stranger into our home without talking to me about it first?"

Michael flashed me his saddest puppy dog eyes and said, "Irene, please don't be mad. When you forgot to take the cell phone and I heard it ringing, I just answered. I only planned to show her the cabin, but when she got here she gave me a real sob story about having no place affordable to live right now and how scary it was to be a woman all alone in the world. This girl is very quick, baby. She saw the indecision on my face and figured out right away what was going on in my head. She started talking about how much easier having a woman renter would be on you because she could help with the housework and maybe, eventually, even kids and pets if needed. She was very convincing, baby and well... now, as you know, she is part of our household for better or worse for the next year."

Bonnie moved in with us three days later, bright and early Monday morning. I was still a little irritated about the way things had happened, but in all fairness I really couldn't hold it against her. It was strange that a female so young was living on her own so far away from her family though. She had grown up in California, and had moved out to New York the year before. Just a few months ago a great job opportunity had landed her in Maryland. Bonnie turned out to be a very private person and that was the only information she ever volunteered to us. She looked me directly in the eyes and said, "Your newspaper ad said that you wanted someone that was open-minded. I really hope that works both ways. I may seem a little mysterious to you but I have no desire to talk about my past at all." What could I say? Right then, at that very moment, even though Bonnie and I turned out to be close in age, I felt like her mother questioning her about where she was going and when she was coming home. I decided to shut up and help her carry the rest of her boxes into her new room. One week later to the day, I came home late from the gym where I taught an aerobics class to find Bonnie naked and in Michael's arms.

Michael said that being the sole supporter in a monogamous relationship was a new experience for him. Although he had turned twenty-seven the January before we met, he had never been tied to just one woman before. But Michael knew he had no choice the first time he laid eyes on me. I was just twenty and Michael was a simple guy getting along in life the best way he knew how. A couple of friends of his had talked him into going to an art exhibit in Aberdeen, Maryland where I was living then. Back then it was considered "high class" to attend those kinds of functions. Michael wasn't really into all the snobbish stuff as he calls it, but after a lot of cajoling on the part of his friends, he figured what the hell, why not. He never expected to meet any of the artists, but after the showing was over, as Michael and his friends were just about to exit the crowded lobby I came up behind him and tugged at his jacket. He has told me many times that he will always remember the look in my hazel eyes that night, so full of fire and spice. He says that I had this quirky smile lighting up my face, giving me that innocent angel look that he has since come to know like the back of his hand.

I came straight out with what I wanted to say. "Hi, my name's Irene and I saw you admiring my work. Do you think you would like to buy me dinner tomorrow night? I'm free after seven if you are." Michael was speechless, totally blown away by my boldness. I was one pretty gal and I was seeking him out. He assured me quickly that he would be delighted to dine with me anytime and anywhere. We exchanged phone numbers that night and the rest, as they say, is history. We've been best friends and lovers for over six years now, and our relationship has moved through all the stages from pure animalistic sexual need, to passionate but caring and gentle lovers, to comfortable, playful sex with a healthy dose of all the rest thrown in for good measure. I have always been so independent that it was nearly impossible for me to trust Michael enough to commit at first. Now, since we have been living together as a married couple, we have both learned to trust completely.

Michael was working harder than ever by the time we finally found our little dream home and took in Bonnie as a boarder. It had been a week since Bonnie had moved in with us and everything seemed to be working out well for all involved. Michael came home, tired after an extremely tension-filled, stressful day at work. His latest project was way behind schedule, and the company was incurring fines every day that they ran over. Not having eaten all day, he had picked up some Tacos on his drive home, knowing that tonight I had classes and wouldn't be able to make it home until late.

Pulling into the driveway at the side of their house, Michael could see Bonnie's silhouette in the light of the front picture window. He had often thought how sexy Bonnie was over this past week. She really did look a lot like Irene, enough so that if you didn't know different you would swear they were sisters. They had the same facial features, similar slender bodies, matching hazel eyes, and nearly identical flowing, brunette hair. Michael wondered if this resemblance to Irene was why he had accepted the new renter so easily. He realized with a sharp pang of guilt that he was imagining what she looked like without the covering of her clothes. Shaking his head to clear away the disturbing thoughts, Michael walked into the house and went into the kitchen to get a diet coke to wash down his now cold fast food. He was a little disappointed to find that Bonnie had retreated to her room when he entered the house. Michael knew in his heart that he loved Irene, and their sex life was astounding, but still a man tends to fantasize about other women. It's harmless enough and it adds spice to the marriage bed. He was startled to realize that when he had seen Bonnie at the window earlier he had been looking forward to being around her.

He liked feeling the excitement, the sexual tension that a healthy, red-blooded man feels when he's around an available, sexy woman. Oh, he knew that nothing would ever happen between them, but still he couldn't hide from his feelings of disappointment that she'd gone to bed.

It was a little past 11 o'clock when Michael grabbed a quick shower and hit the sack for the night. He had an early day tomorrow and he needed some rest. His last conscious thought as he drifted off into dreamland was of Bonnie. He could see her clearly with her legs spread wide open and her hot, wet pussy beckoning him closer. He walked over to where she was laying and lowered his hard, sweat-covered body down onto her soft, inviting one. He began moving inside of her tight hole, thrusting ever so slowly at first, firmly pressing his hard cock deep inside of her, touching a spot that drove her crazy for him. That is where Michael's mind finally shut down and rested, exhaustion from his trying day winning out as he fell into a deep sleep.

Hours later Michael was having the hottest dream. Actually it was more of a dream memory than a mere dream as in it he was reliving the wonderful experience of making love to Irene on the roof top of a newly finished project. It had been one of the most intense and satisfying sexual experiences of his life. They had fucked each other on top of a building that Michael's crew had just finished constructing that morning. The rest of the crew had left for the day and Michael and Irene were the only people left in the building. Irene had the uncontrollable urge to strip completely naked and fuck Michael in full view of the neighboring buildings. That was just one more reason why he loved her so much. Michael didn't know a lot of women who would do something that wild and free in the real world. Irene was a bit of an exhibitionist and though it surprised Michael at first, it suited him just fine. He knew there were hundreds of windows staring down on that rooftop from the surrounding buildings. He found himself so aroused that he felt like he was going to explode before she had even touched his quivering flesh. His dream was so life-like that it felt like he was there again on the rooftop with Irene close beside him.

Suddenly Michael felt a warm, wet sensation engulfing his raging hardon, and he opened his eyes just enough to see a dark head bobbing over his ever growing cock. He moaned softly and reached down to hold her head and shoved himself playfully into her warm mouth. Irene had figured out how to deep throat his huge erected cock years ago, and she liked doing it because she knew how much he enjoyed it. So Michael was a little surprised when

45

she gagged and pulled off for a moment, but he didn't mind. After all, she had accomplished what she'd set out to do. She had made him horny for her! Michael lay back contentedly as she started bobbing her head over his lap once again. He could feel her lips sucking at his throbbing rod eagerly, and her tongue swirled around his heated shaft. Her mouth on him felt so good.

Irene is really going at it hard tonight he thought. They had both been so busy the last few weeks that sex had taken a back seat to other more pressing priorities. In the past couple of months they had only had sex a few times. Michael felt guilty. He knew that he should make the time to pay a little more attention to Irene. She needed regular sex, but his job had become so stressful that it had completely worn him out lately. As his hungry body responded to Irene's hot, moist mouth, his mind went back to that day on the roof with her again. He envisioned Irene's golden body lying under him with her knees raised slightly, opening her hot, wet pussy for him to thrust into her. The last rays of the sun poking through the clouds made it seem like they were under a fading spotlight. It was incredible, exciting, mind-blowing sex made even more explosive by the thought that hundreds of people could be watching them fucking like animals. The combination of that memory and the feeling of Irene's hungry, grasping lips engulfing his throbbing cock brought Michael too close to climax. Unable to stand any more stimulation he grabbed Irene's long hair and pulled her to the mattress beside his hot body.

His warm lips found her soft, sweet-smelling neck. She never needed perfumes. Her natural scent was so sexy, so intoxicating. Michael loved it. She struggled against him a little as he sucked on her neck. For some reason, tonight he felt the need to mark her as his and a little hickey wouldn't hurt her. He was a surprised that she let him do it. Normally she wouldn't let him do that to her but tonight it seemed that she was enjoying the marks of love that Michael was leaving on her soft, pale neck. After doing his damage of love to her beautiful neck, he raised himself up onto his elbows and gave Irene a deep, passionate kiss. She pulled him urgently against her body wrapping her long, slender legs around his waist. He slid down a little, taking one of her rosy nipples into his hungry mouth and began to suck on it. She was incredibly hot tonight. Even her nipples felt bigger than normal, harder, and more erect. Michael's thoughts were interrupted when he felt her small, soft hands between his thighs pulling his rock hard cock to the wet slit of her opening.

"God, Baby, you are horny tonight, aren't you! I love it when you get this way." Michael whispered the words in her ear. Irene just moaned softly, grasping at him, pulling him into her almost desperately. "Hang on, Baby, we have plenty of time," He laughed as he positioned himself over her eager body. He was really looking forward to this. The last time they had had really great sex must have been at least a year ago. She was so hot tonight it was incredible. Her hormones were working overtime! The soft, warm, wet feeling as his aching shaft sank deep into his woman's hot hole made Michael groan loudly in pleasure. God she felt sooo good.

He heard her soft whisper, "Fuck me Michael, and fuck me hard! Make me cum, Baby, please!!" He thrust hard into her, feeling her pussy swallow him to the hilt. This was going to be one of "those" nights, the ones when Irene willingly played his little whore. She made the fantasy so good for him that it was almost magical. "Yes, Baby, fuck me, fuck me till we both collapse in an exhausted heap." She whispered softly in his ear, her voice cracking just a little. He couldn't hold back his desire or his need any longer. Wrapping his strong arms around her firm, young body, he started to stroke deeply into her. The sensations her wetness gave his throbbing cock were delicious. He could hear her breath escaping in a rush every time he pushed himself fully into her, straining to make his hard cock expand and contract as he held himself deeply embedded in her perfect body. Over and over again he thrust into her hot hole, holding, expanding, pulling out, thrusting back into her, letting her feel his rod stretching her inner walls. She reacted with sheer delight, holding his shaft tightly with her pussy, rubbing her body against his in wild abandon. She was gulping, gasping, her breath coming raggedly now.

Michael could feel her body trembling under his strong pounding. Suddenly she raised her knees, keeping her feet flat on the bed, thrusting up to meet his ramming cock, to let him in deeper. She moaned loudly as he accepted her unspoken invitation and rammed into her wet pussy even deeper, pressing harder. She was cumming! Her whole body was shaking with passion under his powerful thrusts. Michael knew that he couldn't last much longer with this hot, firm little body taking in his entire aching love tool. Suddenly his essence gushed to the surface in a violent rush. Her sweet grasping pussy seemed to pull his seed from his loins in huge spurts, filling her with the moist heated cream. He was spurting hard at first, then a little less hard, and finally there was just a slow, throbbing wetness. Before long there was nothing at all but hard breathing as they lay in each others arms, dripping with lovers perspiration, cooling from a light breeze blowing in through an open window. The magic of the moment was shattered by the sound of their bedroom door creaking open and the sudden light that flooded the room when the switch was flipped. Michael jumped up to confront the intruder and found himself staring into the beautiful eyes of his beloved Irene!

The look of shock in Michael's eyes confused Irene at first. Then she saw the form on the bed behind him. Immediately she felt a wave of betrayal. Anger boiled up into her throat from somewhere deep inside her body. She was just about to lash out at him when she realized that even in her state of mind, her pussy had started to drip at the sight of his naked body. She watched as Michael turned back to the bed, a look of disbelief covering his face. As soon as Irene saw the small teasing, smile Bonnie gave him and the way she dropped her lashes, she knew beyond any shadow of a doubt that Michael had not realized he was making love to another woman. Oddly enough the thought really turned her on.

Michael ordered Bonnie to leave immediately. She stood and let the sheet drop away from her body, revealing the most perfect breasts Irene had ever seen. Irene felt her wet pussy starting to throb deep inside. As Bonnie walked past him, Michael closed his eyes, but when her body brushed his, his hot cock stood to salute her. When Irene saw Michael's cock react to the other woman, her clit twitched with excitement and she felt the wetness running down her inner thighs.

Slowly she walked over to Bonnie and took her by the hand, smiling to let the other woman know that everything would be okay. Michael still stood with his eyes closed, waiting for the click that told him Bonnie had left and Irene had closed their bedroom door. Silently he wondered what was taking so long but he was completely shocked when he found out.

Michael felt hands touching his chest -- not two hands but four! He quickly opened his eyes to see both Irene and Bonnie standing before him, totally naked. They gently pushed him back toward the bed and when it contacted his knees, Michael fell onto it. Both women joined him with a giggle. Was he still dreaming? In just a few minutes he had decided that if he was indeed dreaming, he did not want to wake up yet! Irene had moved to deep throat his iron hard rod and Bonnie had climbed onto his face, straddling him, letting him taste their mixed cum as it dribbled out of her pussy. Irene's mouth was working its magic on his cock and very soon he felt like he was going to erupt down her sweet throat. She stopped all movement and waited for the sensation to ease before she straddled his hips and lowered herself, using one hand to guide his throbbing member into her hot, wet cunt. The two women were now facing each other as one rode his tongue and the other rode his cock. They leaned toward each other and kissed deeply as they rode their little boy toy, loving the moans that were escaping from his lips. They were busy teasing each other's nipples into hard, erect statues when Michael realized that the women were moving in perfect sync. Irene rocked on his aching cock at the exact same pace Bonnie was fucking his tongue. Having two women filled by him at the same time, both of them moaning out his name and begging for him to make them cum was driving Michael crazy. He had never been this turned on before. Every time he would get too close to climax, they would stop moving on him altogether, spending time sucking on each other's rosy nipples until his urge had quieted.

Michael could feel Irene's pussy tightening and her juices soaked his balls and thighs. Bonnie had managed to cream his face until it glistened but he was lapping up every sweet drop and wanting more. The two women leaned against each other, breast to breast, holding one another tight. They were breathing very hard, their breaths coming in shallow gasps. Michael heard their sounds of pleasure, felt their quivering pussies, shared the sexual tension he felt consuming their beautiful bodies. Suddenly Irene called out, "Let's cummmmmm!" and Michael felt both gals begin to fuck him furiously, slamming their wet pussies down on him. Each one took him into her pulsing hole as far as he could go. One pussy tightened around his tongue as the other one grasped his shaft in an unmistakable grip of pure passion. Listening to the screams of lust as the two women came together was more than Michael could stand and he felt his cock erupt like a volcano, filling Irene's still throbbing pussy until his cum ran out of her.

To his surprise and great pleasure, Michael watched as the two women slid off of him and to either side of his body. Two beautiful dark heads lowered over his lap and he felt their warm tongues lapping up every drop of wetness on him. He was amazed when, after they had completely cleaned him of all signs of their sex fluids, Irene and Bonnie then took turns licking and cleaning each other's hot cunts. He watched as they made each other come and he felt his erection grow again. When both gals were completely satisfied, they curled up on the bed beside of Michael. One of them on each side of him, they leaned down and kissed his lips at the same time. The taste of all three of their cum together was incredible and Michael knew he had had a taste of heaven. Each gal slid one hand slowly down his body and gripped his once again raging hardon. They linked their slender fingers together, completely engulfing him in their joined hands, and steadily pumped at his aching cock until his hot cream started to spurt again. First one and then the other lowered her head and sucked at the milky fluid until he had no more to give them. Sighing in deep contentment, Irene and Bonnie fell asleep cuddled on Michael's broad chest, protected by the arm he kept around each of them.

When the first morning light came through their bedroom window, Irene stirred and rubbed her weary eyes. She looked over and realized that only she and Michael were in the bed and wondered where Bonnie could have gone. She hoped that her new lover had not felt like she had to return to her own room. Michael woke soon after Irene and they dressed together. They opened the bedroom door and headed down the hallway toward Bonnie's room intending to let her know that she should not feel awkward about the pleasures they had shared the night before. Reaching her door, Michael gave it a firm, resounding rap. They were both surprised when Bonnie didn't answer them. Tentatively, Irene reached for the doorknob and turned it. The door came open immediately and the couple found themselves staring into an empty room. Bonnie was gone. Not only was she gone but she was gone without a trace. No note, nothing to indicate that she had even been there. The boxes that it had taken all three of them two days to move in were gone. The room was spotless. Michael and Irene stood staring at each other in utter confusion for quite a while before he reached out his hand and slowly pulled the door closed.

Over dinner that night, Michael brought up the subject of getting a new renter to help with their expenses. Irene smiled and shook her head. She told him that she thought that she would start working full time instead of part time at the gym and with the extra income they could make the mortgage with no problem at all. Michael looked at her with eyes full of love and nodded his head in agreement.

THE WORKING WIFE

Justin sat in his usual seat at the local pub, relaxing after the long hard day at work. A red-haired beauty smiled over at him, raising herself on the barstool to let him get a good view of her breasts in the low-cut, tight-fitting top she was wearing. Justin could see everything with the exception of the very tip of her nipples. He smiled back at her half-heartedly but tonight his thoughts were more on going home and making slow, passionate love to his sexy young wife than on playing games. He slowly rose and walked over to Dena and sighed loudly.

"God, you do look sexy doll, but I am expecting my wife to come in at any moment. We always meet at this bar on Friday nights after work and go to dinner from here."

"Hmmmmm .... Really?" She posed the question even as Justin watched the confusion spread on her face, "But I thought you look like you could use a friend. And I can be a real good friend if you're lonely, mister."

After staring down into her beautiful eyes for a long time, Justin took a seat on the stool beside her. He told her that he just didn't think this was going to work for him tonight. His mood was all wrong. They had been playing out this little game way too often lately and he had lost interest in it. He watched as the dazzling smile left his wife's luscious red lips. She was clearly disappointed, maybe even a little pouty over his unexpected words. Dena was a striking young woman and seeing her all dolled up like this, pretending to be a hooker in the local bar usually had his erection raging to life.

"I did my makeup a lot heavier and darker than usual tonight," she whispered so only he could hear, "and I even bought this new bright red lipstick. I wanted to look a little trampier for you, Baby." Her voice faded away and she propped her tiny elbows up on the bar as she shifted positions. Justin knew that he had hurt her tender feelings and he felt guilty about it. He leaned toward her and, placing his arm around her slender shoulders, he kissed her softly on the cheek.

He tried to explain that the fantasy had become too routine for them, too tame, too much like work they had to do. He loved Dena but he felt the need for more excitement. His mind and body cried out for more imagination in their sex life. Dena coughed loudly to clear the tears from her aching throat. "You just think I'm not sexy enough to make other men believe I'm really a pussy-for-hire? Well I guess we'll just see about that one, sweetie! Plenty of handsome hunks check me out when you're not around, you know. Next week I'll be back and I won't even glance in your direction. Then we'll see whether I get picked up or not. When I am, hubby dear, I swear to you, I am going to fuck him!" Justin smiled as a picture popped into his tired mind -- a picture of an angry little red headed girl on the school playground yelling at her friend, "Maybe I'll find someone new to play with. Maybe I won't even want to play with you anymore!"

Being a natural red head, Dena's temper sprung into action very quickly and often she would engage her mouth before she would engage her mind. Justin knew that as soon as she cooled down and realized that her threats had been irrational he would have to find a way to let her out of them without hurting her pride. After all, that highly volatile spirit was just one of the many things he had fallen head-over-heels in love with. Justin also knew that until he lovingly let her off the hook, so to speak, those uttered threats were gonna make for one hell of an interesting week!

Day after day passed and Justin waited patiently but Dena never did take back her words. Friday afternoon found her standing in their bedroom, examining herself critically in the mirror as she applied more makeup. Dena knew she had to be very careful in planning her outfit and look or she'd never get a guy to proposition her. If she were too subtle the guy she picked to seduce would be shocked that she was expecting money. Of course if he was unsure, she could dispel any doubts he may have about her goal with her body language and some pointed comments. She inspected every detail of her look from every possible angle in the full-length mirror on the back of the bedroom door. The heels that she had picked out were much higher than what she usually wore, and Dena found them hard to walk in. The soft forest green fabric of the dress she had bought that afternoon clung to her firm, well-shaped ass like melted caramel coated an apple. She gave her reflection one last glance, noting how the deep v neckline showed off her breasts to perfection. Then she smoothed the front of her dress down with both hands and nervously headed out the door.

Dena had done a remarkable job at changing her appearance. Her long red hair was neatly tucked under her short, blonde wig. Her full lips were bright red and her fingernails and toenails were painted to match. The color was startling against the pale white complexion of her skin. Justin let out a long wolf whistle as she entered the front room. If he had not known this delectable creature standing before him was Dena, he would have thought it was really a working gal. The way she had gone all out for her appearance really turned him on and he could feel his dick jerking with anticipation. The lack of noticeable lines in her mid region made it obvious that she wasn't wearing any undies tonight. If only she would end this charade and admit that she had uttered the threat in a moment of anger they could stay home and Justin could remind her of how thrilling sex between them could be.

Dena saw the look of pure lust on his face and smiled at him coyly. *Good, let him suffer,* she thought, *and maybe he won't be so quick to laugh at me again.* She turned to her silent hubby and said in a husky voice, "Hope you are ready for all the men that will want me tonight, Baby. It's your job to play the pimp and protect me. I figure if I price my services right and throw in a few blowjobs to boot I can afford that little necklace I've been wanting from Clockman's Jewelry."

Justin leaned his head back against the wall and his eyes got a far away gleam in them.

Rethinking his position on this whole role-playing thing, he was ready to admit that the tried but true fantasy might just be working for him again. In his mind he could already see Dena with her dress hiked up to her waist, exposing her firm ass. Her beautiful tits were swinging free from her clothing, their rosy nipples hard and erect. Between her sexy lips she held the throbbing cock of some faceless stranger and she sucked him furiously while Justin pumped his hot rod into her from behind. Every time the other man would

EROTIC FANTASIES FOR ROMANTIC COUPLES

moan, Justin would ram his hard-as-rock dick deeper into her hot, dripping pussy. The scene playing out in his head was making him incredibly horny and Justin could feel the pre-cum oozing from his eager cock, soaking his silk boxers.

He figured it was time to end this little game and take his wanton wife to bed. Then again, why wait? He was so turned on now he might just take her right there, in front of the open picture window, daring their neighbors to steal a peek at them. He told Dena that they couldn't go to the bar tonight because everyone there had seen them together so many times that they were sure to be recognized. Expecting her to agree and make some flippant remark about just staying home and charging him for her services instead, Justin was surprised when she grinned at him wickedly and suggested a new bar across from the public park. He looked at her and realized that she was not ready to give him the upper hand yet and so, in a good-natured sort of way, he agreed.

Justin took Dena's arm and led her to the car. When she was seated he leaned in and reached across her chest, making sure to press her nipples hard as he fastened her seat belt. He was rewarded with a rosy blush that sprang to her cheeks and quickly spread over her body. He wondered how far she planned on taking the fantasy before she let him fuck her for real. Reaching the bar at last, Justin led the way in and took a seat at a small table. He decided to push Dena a little just to see her squirm so he picked out what appeared to be a young college student and pointed. "How about that one, sweetie?" He whispered against her ear. Dena frowned and shook her head, yanking his pointing hand down before the college boy could notice.

"Maybe you shouldn't have come in with me, Justin," she whispered with her head lowered, "Go over there and sit in the back at that table. I may point in your direction just to show a "client" that I brought protection but please don't come over here unless I signal you that I am ready to leave with someone. Let me set up something small at first like a blowjob or a hand job just to see how hard ... I mean, difficult it is. Let the men know you are watching us but don't intrude, okay?" It seemed she was going to play it out until the last point of no return. Justin could feel the sexual tension straining against his pants.

He sat beside her at the table and silently observed his sweet wife. She was totally engrossed in scanning the room carefully. Justin had never thought

55

that she would be so unflinching. He brushed his rigid cock against her creamy thigh and gasped loudly when she surprised him by stroking it. Justin felt his hardon growing beneath her soft hand and he knew that if he didn't move very soon he would cream his jeans. He stood up and moved slowly to the back of the bar, glad the lights were dim so that no one could see his jumping dick. He found himself watching Dena and hoping that she would give up soon so that they could go home and he could fuck her hot, wet pussy. Suddenly he sucked in his breath as she got up and walked over to a good-looking stranger. He saw Dena smiling at the well-built man, who was happily taking every opportunity to look down at her beautiful tits. She rubbed up against his broad chest and whispered something in his ear, giggling as his face reddened. Dena's face colored too but she didn't once waiver. As the man sat back down, Dena took a seat next to him and let her soft hand rest lightly on his thigh. After a few minutes Justin saw her hand disappear into the stranger's lap. For the first time it crossed his mind that the sweet, innocent woman he had married might actually be going to do what she had said. He raised his head again and saw the man talking softly in Dena's ear. She turned to face him and a smile crossed her ruby red lips.

The man must have asked how she was tonight because Justin heard her throaty reply. "I'm just great," she said to the stranger, "but a little lonely. Would you spend some time with me tonight?" The man turned toward her and scooted a little closer, placing his thigh firmly against her thigh, a large bulge clearly visible in his pants. Justin thought about stopping it all right now but he was finding himself more and more aroused as the scene played out before him.

Dena had put her hand on the guy's arm and was squeezing it. "I was hoping maybe you would have an idea as to how we could both have some fun. It could be a short evening or a late night. It all depends on what you want to spend." Dena slowly moved her free hand up over her tummy until it crossed her protruding nipples and slid up to her slender neck. The man's eyes followed her fingers intently. He moved closer to her.

"Maybe," he whispered, "would it be just the two of us?"

Dena had answered him calmly, never taking her eyes from his, "I do have a protection. Would you mind if my ... ummm ... friend back there stands guard while we have our "date"? Maybe in the bar's bathroom?" She waved at Justin. The man gave a little laugh. He insisted that he had to meet her "friend" before he could decide so Dena took his hand and led him toward her hubby who was, by now, looking quite concerned. When they reached his table, the strange man sat down and pulled Dena onto his lap. He wasted no time with small talk but came right to the point.

"Look mister, this is one hot gal you have here so why don't you take her home? You are not intimidating enough to scare a fly and as a pimp you really suck big time, so take some advice from me and leave before you both end up getting hurt." Justin began to sweat. Was this man joking? Dena's waist was still firmly enclosed by the man's strong arms. Seeing the undecided look on Justin's face, she started to explain that they weren't really what they seemed.

"I can see you're not professionals," the man droned on. "I should tell you that I am a police officer but this one time I'm willing to forget about what just happened if you are willing to help me forget."

Dena turned as white as a ghost and her stomach lurched as she wondered what he had meant by his comment. She was so taken off guard that when he asked her name she even forgot to use a fake one. The officer saw Justin wince and chuckled. He studied every inch of Dena's hot body slowly. When he finally spoke again it was to tell her that he thought she should really get a taste of what the life of a whore was like, and he wanted to give her that taste. Dena nibbled on her lower lip. Justin noticed that her nipples hadn't stopped pointing, and she kept unconsciously brushing them with her arms. After a long pause and several deep breaths she asked the officer where he wanted to go to give her this lesson. Justin spoke up quickly and reminded his wife that this man hadn't shown either of them any proof that he was an officer at all.

The officer pulled out a badge and handed it across the table to the nervous couple, letting them study it carefully. While they were looking at it he told them that he wanted to fuck Dena on the pinball machine at the back of the bar. Not only did he want to fuck her tight pussy but he also wanted people to watch the show. Dena's cheeks flamed red as she thought about having sex in public. Suddenly she wasn't sure she could actually do it. The cop took her hand. He slowly directed it toward his crotch and made her rub his hard cock with it. Dena glanced over at her hubby and saw that his dick was also straining for release She knew that he loved the way she looked when she came and that he had always wanted to watch her as she was being fucked hard. Justin leaned over and gently nibbled her ear. Dena felt a small flood of desire starting to grow deep inside her already throbbing pussy. She nodded her consent.

Justin and the cop stood up with her and they all went to the back of the bar room. The urgency of their pace made quite a few people turn their heads to see what the rush was. Against the back wall sat several game machines glowing eerily in the dim light. The cop wrapped his strong hands around Dena's waist and lifted her onto the biggest machine. Justin followed close behind them. Slowly, the cop slid his hands up her thighs and gently forced them apart, sliding her dress up around her waist at the same time. Dena closed her green eyes as he traced around her dripping pussy lips with his fingers, then slid his tongue in between them to flick it over her swollen clit. She leaned back against the wall and pressed herself against his mouth as he stroked her clit with his tongue and began to work his fingers into her tight hole. Dena had never looked so sexy to Justin as she did in that dark room with her lips slightly parted as she moaned her enjoyment. With one of her hands she was squeezing her erect nipples and Justin had the urge to suck them into his warm mouth. Instead he quickly unzipped his pants and began to work his already stiff cock, jerking at it furiously. He wished that he could find the courage to go over and plunge its hard shaft into Dena's sexy mouth. He found himself watching, entranced, holding back his climax and waiting to see the stranger fuck his wife.

The officer was still using his fingers to fuck her pussy. Dena reached for him and unzipped his pants, eager to get his stiff cock in her mouth. Her face turned toward him and as he realized what she wanted he started to move his hips slowly, helping his throbbing prick slide into Dena's hot mouth. She wrapped her hand around the thick base, and started swirling her tongue around the dark purple head. He responded by roughly ripping the top of her dress down so that her tits were fully hanging out. She yanked his hand back down to her pulsing pussy, shoving his fingers back inside of her hole. She spread her slender legs as far as she could. His cock popped out of her mouth with a loud wet swooshing sound and he moved to grab her ankles and slide her whole body back towards him, her tight ass now raised in the air as he hoisted her ankles to his shoulders.

Justin watched it all with growing excitement. There was his wife, legs spread high and wide, with a stranger's thick, shiny cock pressed against the entrance to her pussy. He heard someone utter something behind him, and he glanced away for a half-second, but he continued pumping his rod. Dena's face had mesmerized him. She looked like she was going to cum just from the other man's dick finally sliding into her begging cunt. Her legs were high up on his shoulders, and he bent forward to grab her tits and try to suck them as he pounded into her. She reached down and began fingering her clit. Her eyes were closed tight and she was mumbling incoherently. The cop was humping her in a steady rhythm, his groans getting louder each time he drove his cock into her tight hole. Justin could feel that he was going to cum soon. He moved quickly to her side. The sight of his wife's tits jiggling from the force of the fucking she was getting sent him over the edge, and he released spurt after hot spurt of cum all over her nipples. Dena muttered, her other hand coming up to smear his hot cream in circles on her erect nipples. Her hips thrust up to meet the cop's ramming cock. His face screwed up in a grimace and he sped up into a frenzied beat, his balls audibly slapping her ass.

Justin listened as his wife begged to be fucked and fucked hard. His fingers were now over her shoulder, squeezing her nipples, twisting them just enough to make her cry out in pleasure.

Suddenly the cop yelled out something that sounded like an animal's growl and thrust into Dena hard, holding his cock deep inside of her. Her hot body squirmed under him as they moved together, grinding every last bit of the orgasm out of their bodies. Loud clapping caused Dena to shriek and sit up. Justin tried to help her to hide herself from the group of men straining to see around him. They just smiled and left.

Dena was burning with embarrassment but she managed to stammer out her question. "Do all those men know that you're a cop?" He smiled at her and then broke into open laughter.

"I have a feeling they know, Dena. They are all on my squad and this is where most of us local cops hang out. No real hooker would ever set foot in here trying to make money. My friends and I had a lot of fun tonight. We are looking forward to the next time!"

Justin and Dena looked at each other and smiled. Both of them knew that there would never be a next time but the fantasy sure would make for some hot sex!

CHAPTER 6
ALL IN A DAY'S WORK

ALL IN A DAY'S WORK

Jeff picked up his equipment and opened the door to the brown rancher. One more routine stop on his route and then he was headed for home. His job wasn't glamorous but he owned the business and could make his own hours. Sometimes being a pet sitter was boring, and sometimes it wasn't. People often forgot that Jeff was coming and he saw things that amused him or sometimes even made his stomach lurch. Usually, he and his partner, Marc, who was working the next road over today, weren't in the homes long enough to notice or care much what was there.

He had already given his usual pre-visit phone call so that the owners could answer or at least run for cover if they had forgotten that he was coming and were in the middle of a potentially embarrassing activity. Jeff shuddered as his thoughts turned to the 500 pound plus lady that had deliberately been waiting naked in her home for him, hoping for something neither he nor Marc had any desire to help her with. It was just after that that he had changed all his business ads to read "We are experts at taking care of all your feline needs" instead of leaving them as they had always been -- "We are experts at taking care of all your pussy problems."

This particular house was much more tastefully decorated than the others. It had a minimalist theme going, and the walls were almost totally bare. The only real exception was one painting that was mounted tastefully over the small sofa. It was a gold-framed picture of a beautiful nude. She was artfully posed so that her face was hidden in the shadows, her young, firm body a graceful outline against the dark background. She was wearing a thin gold chain around her tiny waist and it entwined gracefully around her supple hips and thighs. Her dark pink nipples stood out gracefully against the pale whiteness of her small globes. It was definitely not something he'd share with his parents, but he liked it.

Jeff went into the spotless kitchen first but finding neither cat nor dog there he headed for the bathroom. Unable to locate the animal he was supposed to be walking, Jeff decided to leave a note and just go and he was almost to the front door when he thought he heard something in the bedroom. If someone was there, it wasn't his problem. Jeff had worked a long day and he was eager to get home and relax. As he put his hand on the front doorknob, he heard a loud crash from the direction of the bedroom. Suddenly it occurred to him that there could be some poor, elderly person living here all alone who was hurt and in real need of help. He called out a tentative greeting but received no response. He was thinking about leaving again when he noticed that the bedroom door was slightly open and he thought he detected some movement inside. Well, it might take an extra five minutes or so, but it wouldn't kill him to see if something was wrong.

"Hello?" he called again loudly as he pushed the door further open. "Is anyone in here?" Jeff heard a muffled sound from the bed. He tried to flip on the light but the bulb must have been blown because the room stayed an eerie blackness. Hearing the sound again he quickly grabbed his flashlight from the emergency duffel bag he always carried and turned it on. He turned in the direction of the sound and stopped dead as he realized that on the bed was a naked woman, her hands bound to the bed by some sort of ties. On her eyes was a blindfold and a small gag covered her mouth, parting her full red lips. Thin silver chains crisscrossed back and forth over her body like some kind of harness, but their only point seemed to be to adorn her beautiful breasts, and her bushy pussy. Her beautiful auburn hair fanned out on the pillow, making a very sensual frame for her face. Shocked by what he was seeing, Jeff stood there and stared at the woman restrained on the bed. Oddly, she looked like she was rubbing her legs together, trying to press against her clit. The end table by the bed seemed to have a lot of things on it and he stepped closer to see what was there. His eyes found a large number of toys and nestled amongst them, a small piece of folded white paper. He picked it up and began to read.

"Dear Stranger, Nancy is my devoted sex slave. She displeased me and needs to be punished. That's her on the bed. I tied her there and let her know that the very next stranger to enter the house would be allowed to use her sweet body in any way that he sees fit. Of course I will have to check to make sure that she is safe, but you may use her sexually in any way that you desire."

There was no signature, just a smiley face that appeared to be winking at Jeff through the darkness.

Jeff noticed that his work pants had become uncomfortably tight. He let his excited mind wander, considering how far he dared to go. He turned on the bedside lamp to get a better view of the young woman beside him. He unzipped his fly to be more comfortable. His large dick sprung free and he stroked it softly while he thought. With his other hand he reached for Nancy's thigh and softly stroked it. Startled by his touch, she jumped and tensed, but only for a split second. Then Jeff was amazed to see that she opened her thighs wider for his hand. He became braver and began exploring her magnificent body with long, slow strokes that made her squirm. She whimpered whenever his hand passed near her erect nipples or swollen clit, and she squirmed as much as possible to show him what she liked. Jeff was amused by her antics. He reached over to the end table and picked up a medium sized vibrator from amongst the toys. When he turned it on she heard the hum and again spread her thighs wide. Jeff took his time and teased her with the toy. He slid it up and down the outside of her wet lips, being very careful not to touch her swollen clit or to make her cum. Jeff had made up his mind to stay a while as soon as he saw Nancy start to respond to his touch.

Leaving the vibrator between her soft thighs, he ran to the bedroom door and locked it. When he returned he stripped and moved over her soft body as it lay on the bed. He took his now painfully erect rod and began circling her nipples with it, watching as his hot pre-cum seeped onto them and made them shine. He shoved the raging monster of a hardon between her breasts and pushed them together, fucking them hard until he was afraid he was going to cum. He pinched her nipples hard as he pulled from between her breasts. Jeff was amazed when he felt her pushing her tits up against him, seeming to want more. She had wiggled around enough that the sex toy was now at the entrance to her wet pussy. He moved it away from her, and then changed his mind when he saw how wet she had made it.. He started to push the vibrator into her hot hole slowly.

She thrust her hips up at his hand and whimpered quietly again. Jeff obliged her obvious need with several quick thrusts before he pulled the toy out of her completely. His hand was soaked by the juices that now ran freely from her cunt. The hairs of her bush were glistening in the light and the sensuality of the sight made Jeff even more horny. He could tell that Nancy was in desperate need of a good, hard fucking. Unable to wait any longer, he pushed his hard shaft slowly into her so she could appreciate the size of it. He gave her tight pussy hole a few fast thrusts before pulling out again. Nancy went wild, fighting her restraints and moaning loudly. She began pushing up hard with her pussy against the base of his cock. Jeff got off the bed and leaned down next to her ear. He whispered to her, asking her if she would like to fuck his big, hard cock with her mouth. She gulped loudly several times and then nodded her head. He adjusted the silk ties that bound her small hands so that he could turn her over onto her knees. He loved the way that her tits hung down, and her ass was perfect and tight. He reached under her to twist her hard nipples before he moved to lay cross-wise under her head. He told her that he would take off the gag if she promised to stay very quiet. Again her head nodded.

Jeff untied the gag and Nancy flexed her jaws, happy to have them empty at last. The relief didn't last very long, because he quickly shoved his thick cock into her mouth, pushing it deep into her throat as his hands pulled her head down against him. He guided her movements for a few minutes with her long hair clenched in his fist, setting a pace that sent electrical waves down his hot shaft and into his groin. He shoved his dick into her throat so hard and fast that he felt her body jerk as she gagged on it. But soon he relaxed his grip on her gorgeous tresses as she eagerly sucked him all the way in, deeper into her throat than he had ever had before. Her lips hit the top of his balls and he moaned loudly. His hand fell on the vibrator and he flicked the switch on again. She didn't even slow the rhythm of her long, powerful strokes in and out of her hungry throat as he began pushing the vibrator into her cunt. He pumped her pussy faster and faster, in time with her mouth fucking his cock. She sure knew how to use her strong mouth, sucking him hard, her tongue flickering over the head of his hard rod. Jeff could feel the heat building inside of himself and he knew he was going to cum. The sensation was so overwhelmingly satisfying that he gave up working the vibrator. He held it tight in her hot cunt, buzzing, as he grabbed her hair again and took control, fucking her mouth with fast, hard strokes until he exploded, filling her throat with spurt after spurt of his hot, salty cum. Still blindfolded, Nancy ran the tip of her wet tongue around her lips to get every drop. His cock started to stiffen again as he saw her luscious lips break into a impish smile. Jeff wondered what color her eyes were under that blindfold. He figured it was best to leave it on, though, since he wasn't sure he wanted to be identified. Her body jerked a little, and Jeff realized that he was still holding the vibrator deep inside her dripping cunt. He whispered into her ear again asking her if she wanted to cum too. She nodded and smiled a dazzling smile, moving her hips to show how eager she was for his cock. Jeff told her to suck the semi-erect shaft until it was strong and hard again. Her warm, soft lips closed around him, and her tongue carefully caressed the head of his sensitive prick. Jeff closed his eyes and enjoyed her wet massage. In only seconds, he was hard again.

Jeff moved behind Nancy and used the swollen head of his cock to tease her, rubbing it against her hard clit. He pulled the vibrator out of her hot cunt and slowly pushed it into her tight little asshole. Then he shoved his aching dick deep into her hole as hard as he could, groaning as he felt the vibrator through the walls of her wet pussy. Nancy tried her best to stay quiet but she couldn't stop the moaning as he pounded her furiously. Jeff had been intent on fucking her soft body as long as possible but he knew that his aching balls and throbbing cock couldn't wait any longer. He fucked Nancy slowly at first, trying not to cum, but as her body trembled and she began to shake in an orgasm, he sped up, fucking harder and faster with piston-like action. His balls slapped Nancy's pussy, as he buried his cock in her as far as he could, grabbing her hips to help. She kept moaning as he fucked her so hard that the shaking bed beneath them threatened to collapse. Her head was jerking from side to side as she ran her hands all over her breasts. Jeff thought he had never seen a sexier pair of tits in his life, and he slapped Nancy's ass cheeks, making her jump. Then she smiled, and he began smacking her ass in time with his powerful thrusts, knocking her body roughly against the satin sheets. The sight of her cumming over and over was too much for him and he managed a broken whisper that he was cumming, as he shot another load, this time deep into Nancy's convulsing pussy.

"I love to be fucked. Please, I want more!" Nancy cried out. Jeff wasn't getting his dick sucked, but watching Nancy beg for more of it was working all by itself. His cock rose to the occasion like a proud soldier rising to do battle. He reached for the headboard and loosed her silk ties. Pushing him flat on his back, she quickly straddled his hips. Jeff tensed and relaxed as the heat of her wet pussy tightened around his cock. She rode him for a few hard strokes and then reached down to play with his tight balls. Jeff was grateful at this point to be ridden by Nancy. He doubted whether he could even move his ass on his own, but his prick was standing tall as he watched Nancy's face and she exploded in another orgasm. Her slender body was jerking in quick spasms. Her body was still shaking when they heard a loud knocking sound from the living room.

They both froze when a deep voice called from the outer hallway. Jeff grimaced. "Oh God, that's my partner, Marc. I better go. I'll tell him I was putting your cat in the bathroom in here." He wiggled out from under Nancy, and hurriedly pulled on his clothes. As he started for the bedroom door, Nancy stopped him and pressed her soft lips against his.

"You weren't bad at all. I could see you having real potential if you tried. I'll get a kitty tomorrow and maybe next time you could spare more time for this particular house, huh?" Jeff smiled and nodded his head.

"COOKING" WITH SYRUP

CHAPTER 7

"COOKING" WITH SYRUP

I had known Johnny Marston my whole life. Okay, okay, maybe not my whole life but certainly most of it, ever since we had met in kindergarten class. We learned to ride our bikes together. We learned to swim together. We even shared our first kiss. Later I learned that Johnny's friends had been giving him a hard time over having never gone "that far" with a girl. Johnny was eleven and I was only days away from my eleventh birthday. He was over at my house and we were swinging on the two tire swings in my back yard when he leaned over and kissed me on the lips. I wasn't sure quite was happening at the time but I knew I felt something different toward Johnny after that. We never spoke about it again after that day.

As always happens, we grew up and soon we were submitting applications to the various colleges that we were interested in. Johnny wanted to be an engineer of some type and I was considering the field of teaching. We decided to spend our last summer together since chances were slim that we would both be accepted at the same college. It was great, just like when we were kids. We talked for hours on end, sometimes until the sun rose. We shared our hopes, our dreams, and our fears about the future. I was surprised and a little taken aback when Johnny told me that he had decided to get a summer job but then I started thinking that maybe he really needed the extra money for college. I realized that what upset me the most was that instead of spending all of his free time with me Johnny would now be working five hours a day, five days a week, and I would be left all alone. The thought that I would have to share my best friend with a job on our last free summer together upset me more than a little bit but I knew that we would still find plenty of time to spend together.

Only a couple of weeks into his job at The Syrup Shack, things started to change between Johnny and me. We live in Vermont and if you have ever visited our great state you know that we have little roadside buildings all over the place where they sell small bottles of the various syrups our state is famous for. I thought it was a silly job, standing out in the heat all day selling bottled sugar to tourists as souvenirs but Johnny loved meeting people so it was an ideal job for him. Anyhow, I noticed that Johnny had started making excuses not to come over in the evenings. We had gone from seeing each other every night to seeing each other three nights a week if I was lucky. After a few weeks of this I decided to go down to the shack one day and ask Johnny if I had done something to upset him and if that was why he was avoiding me. When I reached The Syrup Shack, I was surprised to find Johnny deep in conversation with a cute little dark-haired girl. She had her small elbows propped up on the counter in front of him and she was smiling up into his face. The twinkle in Johnny's eyes and the dazzling smile that he flashed her made me catch my breath. I thought back to all the times over the years when that gorgeous, sexy smile had been directed at me and I felt a strange pang of ..... jealousy, perhaps. *This is silly,* I was thinking.

After all, even though neither Johnny nor I had ever really dated in high school, it was bound to happen sometime. I mean, isn't that what people do? They date, they get married, and then they start a family of their own, and friends fade into the background as they take their place in the grown up world. Looking up, I saw him laugh at some whispered words that I couldn't quite hear from where I stood and I thought once again how good-looking he was when he let that sexy smile light up his face. I decided not to disturb them but, rather, to wait until the girl left before I went over to talk with Johnny.

I waited for over an hour but finally she left and I had my chance. When I asked Johnny what I had done, he told me that I really hadn't made him mad. It was just that he had met this girl Amanda and that he wanted to spend some time with her and maybe even start dating soon. He hadn't been quite sure how to tell me and so he had been trying to wean off our time together slowly so that I would not feel left out. I assured him that I understood and that I would always be here for him, as any true friend would be. I even told him that if he ever needed anything, all he had to do was ask and I would be more than happy to help him if I could. Five minutes later my best friend made his first request. "Amber," he whispered with his eyes cast downwards, "how do I ask her to go out with me? I mean with you things are always so easy. I just call and say meet me here or there and that's that but this is a real date and I don't know what to say to her." I told Johnny that he would do just fine but after listening to his unsure protests, I finally told him to come over to my house that night and he could practice asking Amanda out on me.

After that, Johnny practiced a lot on me. He practiced talking and joking. He practiced opening doors and holding out chairs. He practiced letting his arm drape around my neck as we walked together and even where to put his hands when we slow danced. I was having the time of my life until I realized one day that he was using me to practice his moves for another woman. I was helping not just my best friend, but also the man I had fallen in love with to romance another woman. Wait a minute ..... The man I had fallen in love with? I was in love with Johnny! Breathe in, breathe out, breathe in, breathe out, breathe in ..... The realization had hit me like a ton of bricks, sending my mind reeling, and knocking the wind from me. When had I fallen in love with him? I had absolutely no idea, but in love I was. Now what was I going to do? Johnny was falling for Amanda fast and I had to figure out how to make him see that it was me that he really wanted, that I was as much a part of his life as he was a part of mine. I decided to keep helping him with Amanda but things would be different now. I was going to use the time we had together to show Johnny that we were meant to be together forever. I was snapped back to reality by Johnny's voice. He was asking me if he could come over tonight. There was something important that he needed to talk to me about. Of course I said yes. What else would I say? I wanted to spend every minute I could with this man who I now knew I loved more than life itself, even if it was to listen to him talk about another girl.

When Johnny got to my house that night he found me out back on the swings. Giving me a playful push as he passed, he took a seat on the swing beside me. For several minutes we just sat there, swinging back and forth in total silence. When Johnny called my name and I turned to look at him I could see the embarrassment on his cheeks. He asked me if I remembered that day when he had kissed me. I nodded and blushed. Then he told me why he had done it. The blush spread over my body. Now I knew why all of the boys had wanted to visit me after that day but I had never invited any of them to play at my house. Johnny was the only boy that I had ever wanted to be with. I had been used to save my best friends pride and I didn't even care. If he had told me why he wanted the kiss I would have done it anyhow. I would have done anything for Johnny. I heard his voice as from a distance, droning on and on, telling me how he wanted to kiss Amanda but he wasn't sure how to hold her, wasn't sure which way to turn his head, and wasn't even sure that she would like his kisses. Maybe she would think he was a lousy kisser. Johnny was worried. I tried to reassure him that he would be a great kisser but seeing that the worry never left his eyes I made a suggestion. I told Johnny that he could practice his kissing on me just like he had practiced every move he had made up to this point. He stood and moved to stand in front of me. With red cheeks he whispered that he wouldn't want my parents to see and then he sprinted away and left me sitting there with a dropped jaw and a mind full of questions.

For a long time I sat there, swaying back and forth in the fading sunlight as I allowed myself to daydream about what a real kiss from Johnny would be like. I could feel his strong arms around me, his breath tickling my cheek, and finally the pressure of his lips on mine. I could feel my body responding to his touch, as my panties grew wet and the fabric of my shorts dampened noticeably. Not only did I love this man that I had already spent most of my life with but now I knew that I wanted him too, and I wanted him in a way that I had never wanted a man before. My breasts had swollen and my nipples had started to protrude through the thin material of my tank top as if they were reaching out to him, coaxing him into touching them. I decided that maybe it was time for a cold shower.

Entering the bathroom I tried to shake all thoughts of Johnny from my head but he kept sneaking back into my mind. I glanced into the mirror but it was Johnny's face that smiled back at me and my knees went weak just looking at him. I quickly took off my clothes and jumped into the shower, turning the cold water on full blast. Even the shock of the icy water hitting my hot skin couldn't chase my thoughts back to reality. As I began to soap up my body, I imagined it was Johnny's strong hands sliding over it so smoothly. I caressed my firm breasts and moaned his name softly. I pinched my nipples and pretended it was Johnny's teeth grating gently over them. My hand trailed down over my flat tummy, slowly moving further. My slender fingers touched my wet bush, teasing lightly, tugging gently. I cupped my mound and slid my middle finger inside the wet lips of my hot pussy, pretending it was Johnny's cock making the small circles around my throbbing clit. I pressed two fingers inside of my dripping cunt and fucked myself hard and fast for several minutes, all the time dreaming it was his rigid rod pumping me. Finally I closed my eyes and leaned back my head, calling out Johnny's name as my body started to tremble under my exploring hands. As the cold water cascaded down over my back and breasts, I moved one finger to push directly on my clit and felt myself explode in wave after wave of quivering climax. I felt my hot cum mingling with the cool soapsuds as they slid slowly down my inner thighs. Completely exhausted, I sank down to sit on the side of the tub, never once losing the image of Johnny with his bare skin next to mine.

When my knees were strong enough to walk on again and my breathing was almost back to normal, I wrapped the towel around my damp body and headed for my room. There I found a note on my pillow telling me that mom and dad had gone out for a special evening and would not be home until morning. Excited by this new news I called Johnny and invited him over for dinner, explaining my situation and offering to let him practice kissing Amanda on me. He accepted readily and told me that he would come around six thirty. When Johnny finally arrived, he found me in the kitchen checking on the baked chicken that I was serving him for dinner. Chicken was his favorite meal and tonight I was pulling out all the stops. He looked bewildered when I asked him to light the candles on the dining room table but he complied without comment. As soon as I had placed the food on the table I informed Johnny that I thought it would be easier for him to practice his kissing if we pretended we were on a romantic date. He shrugged but seemed willing enough so I took off the full-length cotton smock I had been wearing to reveal the dress beneath.

I knew that I looked really good when I heard the growl that came from Johnny's throat. I had snuck into mom's room earlier and carefully went through her closet to find the sexiest dress I could. It turned out to be a dark green leather like beauty with a scooped neckline that went so low that it showed all but the perky nipples of my well-rounded breasts. The sides of the dress were not connected by material but, rather, were laced together by thin gold chains that went through gold colored loops much like the ties of a tennis shoe. Down my ribs, hips, and thighs on either side, my skin was completely exposed except for the crisscrossing of the chains, which adorned my tanned color to perfection. The dress ended at mid-thigh. Because he could clearly see my skin down both of my sides, Johnny knew that I wasn't wearing a bra or panties tonight and I think he may have been a little shocked by it. When he stood up to hold out my chair, the bulge in his shorts told me that I had aroused him. Still he asked me where he should take Amanda if she dressed like that for their date. "Anywhere you want to take her." I answered but my mind was screaming, "Take me, Johnny, take me!"

We ate in almost total silence although I noticed Johnny stealing sideways glances at me often throughout the meal. I wasn't so polite. I stared openly and made overt comments, careful to keep touching his arm or brushing his thigh as we talked. When we finished eating I complained about the heat and scooped the last ice cube from my glass of water, slowly letting my slender fingers trace my neck with it and dipped it between my breasts. The heat of my body melted the ice just enough that it left a wet trail which glistened sensually in the candlelight.

After we cleared the table, Johnny offered to help me with the dishes but I told him that it was getting late and maybe we should get the kissing thing over with. I knew that if I could just get his lips on mine, I could get Johnny Marston to make love to me. Johnny was a little shy about it but he finally agreed that it was time. I turned and hopped up on the table, holding out my open arms to him and motioning for him to walk over to me. "Now, Johnny kiss me," I whispered, " and pretend you are kissing Amanda." Standing in front of me, Johnny hesitated but only for a second before he reached for me. I drew in my breath sharply as he rested one hand on either side of my face. Slowly he tilted his head to the right and his lips claimed mine. I kissed him softly at first but then I reached for his hands and pulled them to my waist so that I could wrap my arms around his neck. As I felt Johnny starting to respond to my embrace, I wrapped my legs around his waist and pulled him even closer to me, my kisses becoming more bold and passionate. The movement of wrapping my legs around him caused my dress to be pushed up above my hips and suddenly the bulge of Johnny's hard cock in his shorts was pushing against my naked pussy. His hands slid from my waist to my ass and he pulled me tighter against him, his hips moving just enough that the bulge rubbed my clit. I rocked against him slowly, enjoying the sensation his cock was causing in my throbbing pussy. My tongue slipped into Johnny's mouth and teased his, tasting every inch of his warm, wet mouth. This was exactly where I wanted to be, in my Johnny's arms, reveling in the way he was touching me. I pulled his hand down to my dripping cunt and pushed his fingers against my wetness. "I love you, Johnny," I moaned loudly, "make love to me, pleeeeeeeease?"

My voice startled him and he groaned as he opened his eyes. Looking down between us, he quickly jerked his hand away and stared at my pulsing pussy for just a second before he turned and bolted for the door. I wanted to call him back, wanted to beg him to stay, wanted to convince him to make love to me. Instead I watched Johnny leave as tears rolled down my cheeks. I thought he would love me too but evidently he was feeling guilty about what had happened. He must have really been thinking that I was Amanda before my voice had broken the spell. Why hadn't I just kept my big mouth shut?

I didn't go to the Syrup shack the next day. I didn't go the day after that either. As a matter of fact, a whole week passed and I never saw nor talked to Johnny once. Then one day when I came in from sunbathing in our back yard, the ominous green light on the answering machine was blinking away. I darted over and pressed the message button. When I heard Johnny's voice coming from the machine I almost jumped out of my skin. God, I had missed him more than I had realized. I craved his voice. I needed his company. My thoughts were interrupted by the words Johnny was saying. "Amber? Amber, are you there? Pick up, please, baby? I need to talk to you. Pick up!" Was that desperation I detected in his voice? "Amber, just listen to me, please? I love you too, baby. I think I have since we were eleven and I stole that first kiss from you on the tire swings. I am sorry I left like that the other night. Forgive me, baby. It's just that I thought I should break up with Amanda before I started anything with you. Then when you didn't come to work the next day or even call I thought you were mad that I had gone so far with you and I knew you had a right to be. But, baby, I am begging now ..... Please, don't be mad. I can't live without you any longer. I love you. I want you. I need you more and more every day! Come to The Syrup Shack at closing time tonight, baby, and I will show you how much you mean to me."

I must have replayed that message one hundred times or more. Finally, I took the cassette out and put in the spare, taking my Johnny's message and hiding it in my jewelry box beside the ring he had bought me from a gumball machine when we were seven. I had everything Johnny had ever given me with the exception of the caterpillar when we were five. It became a butterfly and we had let it loose together, laughing in childish enjoyment when it found its freedom.

The clock didn't seem to want to move that day. I kept looking but what seemed like hours to me only showed as ten minutes on the kitchen clock. I could hardly wait to see Johnny again and I wondered what his surprise could be. Eventually the clock did read three o'clock and I put on my best short shorts, my tightest halter-top, my sexiest sandals with a gold ankle bracelet, and I headed for The Syrup Shack. I spotted Johnny's head when I was still a block away. He smiled as I came through the door and quickly reached over to turn the closed sign. He shut the service window and pulled the shades, never taking his sexy eyes from mine. I felt the desire bubbling deep inside of me. When Johnny finally had the shack closed up tight and there was no way for anyone to see in, he crossed the room and took me into his arms. The kiss that he gave me left no doubt that he knew it was me he was kissing and that he wanted it that way. My body responded immediately. I jumped up and wrapped my legs around Johnny's waist so that he had to carry me across the room and set my ass on the folding table there. With one hand he quickly pushed all the papers off of it and onto the floor before he lay me back in front of him. He leaned down and teased my lips with his as he stood over me. His hands moved to my breasts but the material covering them must have been in his way because he wasted no time in raising me just enough to pull my top over my head. I should have been embarrassed I guess but watching Johnny stare at my naked tits excited me beyond all belief. He moved his strong hands over them again and I felt him squeeze them lightly. Then he turned away from me but when he heard me move he instructed me to stay where I was. I listened and waited as patiently as I could.

When Johnny turned back to me, he was holding several of the small sample bottles of syrup in his hands. He carefully lined them up in a row on the table beside of me. He leaned down and kissed me again whispering as he stood back up, "Baby, besides this syrup, you are the sweetest thing that has ever touched my lips. I've been wondering what those two incredible sweet treats would taste like together." He smiled that dazzlingly sexy smile of his and I was totally mesmerized. I watched as he opened a small bottle and began to pour the sticky liquid over my tits. Then Johnny lowered his head and I felt his warm, wet tongue as he slowly and carefully began to lap at the syrup. He placed his mouth fully over the puddle that had formed between my tits and sucked like he couldn't get enough of the taste. Then he made a wide circle around first one, and then the other firm globe, slowly moving inward, each circle of his tongue coming closer to my nipple. Finally he sucked a syrup-covered nipple into his mouth. Expecting him to lick or even suck at it, I gasped loudly when I felt his teeth. Johnny was nibbling my erect nipple and the sensation it was causing was driving me wild! Hearing my reaction, he pulled the nipple lightly between his teeth and held it there while he moved his tongue to it, caressing it over and over. My moans grew louder as what felt like electric shocks radiated from the nipple to my most inner being. I could feel Johnny's hands fiddling with the button of my shorts but I couldn't wait to see what else he had planned so I reached for them and quickly undid them, lifting my hips so Johnny could slide them off. I closed my eyes and moaned his name over and over. I never imagined he would put syrup down there but the next thing I felt was the sticky goop tickling the hairs of my pussy as it slid through them. I tried to protest but Johnny's mouth covered mine and my words were lost in his throat.

Johnny pulled a chair up at the end of the table and firmly grasped my ankles, pulling me toward him in one quick motion. He draped my legs over his neck and my heels rested against his broad back as his tongue started to lick up the syrup, slowly lapping it from my sticky bush. When there was no sign of the sticky concoction left to be seen, Johnny parted my wet pussy lips with his fingers and started to hungrily go after the syrup that had managed to seep between them and coat my aching clit. Over and over his tongue massaged it from top to bottom and then around in circles. He moved lower to the hot slit of my opening and I felt him replenish his treat by emptying the rest of the bottle of syrup there. Long, slow strokes he took. He started at the small bud of my asshole and moved forward over my hot pussy hole. Every time I would moan or whimper he would press harder, move a little faster. His mouth was driving me crazy but in a way that made me want him never to stop. When the syrup was all gone, he concentrated on my clit. The feelings he gave me were so intense that I screamed out how good he felt. Seeing me react seemed to spur Johnny on to do more. Slowly he repeated the process, using all four flavored syrups, each one bringing me a new and stronger climax. It was the sweetest torture I have ever felt. As Johnny swallowed the last drop of the last bottle of flavored syrup from off my swollen clit, he slid three fingers knuckle deep into my hot, wet, pussy whole and began to fuck me. Still cumming from the clit massages, my cunt gripped his fingers tightly. He kept asking me if I liked what he was doing, if it felt good, and if I wanted more. He asked me to tell him what I wanted. Finally, after what seemed like having a dozen or more powerful orgasms, I screamed out to

Johnny. "Oh, yesssssssss, baby! My God, you have made me cum so many times." My voice came out in throaty, ragged breaths. "I want you to cum too, baby. Cum with me. Cum in me. Fuck me, Johnny!" Hearing me begging him to ram his stiff rod into me was all the encouragement Johnny needed and he quickly dropped his clothing in a heap on the floor of the shack. At first he stood at the end of the table, holding my legs wide apart, as he moved to stroke his dick deeply inside of me. He built a steady rhythm, in and out, in and out, deep and slow. He hunched over and placed his elbows on both sides of me on the table and continued to hump me with increasing force and speed. He was moaning between gasps and I could feel the sweat dripping off of him and splashing on my body as my hips thrust up to meet him. "Pound my pussy, baby! Fuck me hard!" I screamed out loud enough that I knew anyone close would be able to hear me. The begging sent Johnny over the edge. He shoved me back to the middle of the table, climbing on top of me, and rammed his hard shaft into me until I felt it pushing against my inner walls, stretching them. I wrapped my legs around his thighs, using them as an anchor so that I could gain leverage to fuck back hard. It worked! I felt Johnny begin to shake. Then he trembled. Then he growled out loudly and exploded inside of me, filling me up with his hot, thick cum. Feeling the spurting inside of my grasping cunt, I came again, the orgasm milking Johnny's throbbing cock of every last drop of its milky cream. Johnny collapsed on top of me and together we drifted into an exhausted sleep.

When we woke a few hours later, I lay Johnny on the table and gave him a taste of what is was like to have all of his sensitive spots coated in sticky syrup and then licked, sucked, and nibbled clean by a pair of eager lips. I know he must have enjoyed it as much as I did because he came three times before I finished him off by climbing on top of him and riding him like there was no tomorrow. His hands played with my hard nipples and caressed my bouncing tits as I fucked him fast and hard. I kept pumping up and down, covered in sweat, as Johnny was moaning out how beautiful I was and how much he loved me. As we both came together one last time, Johnny asked me to marry him.

Next April we will be getting married at The Syrup Shack. We have both decided to attend the local community college and I am now working with Johnny. It gives us a chance to sample the product a couple of times a week. And as for me thinking it was a silly job? Well I have decided that maybe it isn't so bad to be hot and sticky in Vermont!

CHAPTER 8

SWEATER SOLO

SWEATER SOLO

Marlo and Thomas met one beautiful spring night in April at The Catwalk, a local strip club that Marlo had worked at for about three years. She had started as a waitress but the tips were lousy and it didn't take her long to figure out why. Night after night, Marlo watched as the dancers would leave the stage with their hands full of money. Some of them didn't even strip for it. They would just tease the men who were watching them perform, most of whom had had a little too much too drink by the time the show started. Then they would let some drunk, horny guy stuff five or ten dollar bills down their g-string or behind their bra strap and 'voila', instant car payment. After three weeks Marlo decided it wasn't such a bad way to pay your bills. Dancing she would make more in two hours than she did waiting on tables for the whole week! Of course, every once in awhile a dancer would go into the back rooms with a customer for a 'private dance' but Marlo wasn't that desperate for cash yet. She would do a lot of things for money but she was not about to let some wasted, drooling slob fuck her silly in the back of a crowded strip club. After all, a girl has to have some dignity left, even when she is poor.

Thomas seemed to really take a liking to Marlo from the very first time that he saw her dance. She made such an enticing entrance as the music started, her lithe body swaying to its beat. Her long blonde hair was gorgeous against the shiny red vinyl of the cowboy outfit that she wore. Her clothes hugged her body like the peeling of a banana and they clung to every little curve, making Thomas's jaw drop in admiration of the sheer beauty of her. She wore red fish net stockings and a mini skirt so short that he could barely see the straps of her garter belt. Her tiny feet were covered by short, red cowboy boots and on her well-rounded tits she wore a vest-like top with a plunging neckline. Thomas's prick twitched every time she made her entrance. She had practiced her routine until she could perform it perfectly without even giving much thought to the moves. Marlo would enter the stage slowly, twirling her red cowboy hat on one hand and swaying her hips as the music played... You Can Leave Your Hat On, Baby... As she reached the front of the stage she would pop her hat back on her long, golden tresses and grab the pole that was there, swinging herself around it. Then she would place her back against the pole and crook her finger at one of the patrons, carefully choosing one that looked harmless, inviting him to join her on the stage. Once her volunteer was close enough, Marlo would press her body against his in all the right places, never losing the beat of her music, sometimes causing the man to blush as the crowd commented on what each move meant. As the song neared the middle, she would get the man on stage to kneel for her and as she sang along with her theme song, she would hold up each foot in turn and let him remove her boot. Then she would prop first one and then the other foot on the man's knee and carefully unhook and roll down her stockings. At this point the men watching were usually totally enthralled with Marlo's performance. She would send the patron back to his seat and once again reach for the pole, bending down to touch its base and wiggling her tight little ass in the air. As she stood again, Marlo would loosen the snap and zipper on her skirt and allow it to slip to the floor, revealing the red satin garter and black silk thongs hid beneath it. Now the crowd would roar, begging for more. Slowly she would unbutton her vest, starting at the bottom, and working her way up to the neckline. With a sultry shake she let the garment fall from her shoulders, letting everyone see the matching black silk bra she was wearing. The club was in a frenzy at this point and Marlo had learned how to play the men to the hilt. She would pick one out of the crowd and turn her back to him, sitting on his lap and mock fucking him to the song as she let him undo her bra. As the bra would set her beautiful tits free, Marlo would raise one arm across her chest, hiding her rosy nipples while still giving the impression of stripping. All the while she was watching the crowd with a smile pasted on her red lips, looking for someone who appeared 'safe' for her big ending. As the song hit its last few lines, Marlo would straddle the man she had chosen, facing him, and plop her hat onto his head as she wrapped her arms around his neck and pressed her naked tits against the fabric of his shirt. One last line... You Can Leave Your Hat On, Baby... and Marlo would lower her lips for a quick kiss. The 'chosen one' usually gave her the biggest tip. Many nights she would go home with a thousand dollars or more in her pockets. Oh, yes, this job suited her great. It was easier than being a waitress and the pay was much better! And Marlo had discovered after her first performance that she really liked stripping. As a matter of fact, just the last few nights, she had been playing with the idea of getting bolder, of removing her thongs during the show.

Thomas never tired of coming to see Marlo dance, even though she always did the same routine. He loved the confidence that showed in her eyes, the pride that she obviously felt for her sexy body. He was impressed by the way she was able to control the men who sometimes got pushy when they wanted more of a show than she was willing to give them. Something deep inside him told him that she might become more adventurous, possibly even willing to do private parties of a slightly more erotic type. Thomas needed more women like Marlo in his company. Women who were wild and free and open to new things were hard to come by. Open-mindedness was what he was looking for, not an open body. Thomas was not a pimp, not even close. He had simply found a niche in the dance market that seemed to have been overlooked by most of the booking agents - fetishes. That's right, people with fetishes have the same wants and needs as everyone does. They want to be loved and accepted for who they are. They want to be known as unique for their preferences, not as freaks or abnormal. They want to be able to plan parties and special events that cater to their particular tastes so that they can enjoy themselves as much as anyone else can. That is where Thomas came into the picture. He had started his own business which had, consequently, grown by leaps and bounds over the last year. Thomas was the proud owner and sole manager of Fetish Fever, an adult party planning service that promised to find entertainment and/or games that were theme appropriate for any fetish-oriented party. Of course he did not deal with anything that was considered illegal but if someone had a fetish that was not against the law and needed a party planner for a special occasion, Thomas was the man they called.

Recently he had received a call from a client that had a fetish that Thomas had never heard of before. It seemed this man had a sweater fetish. He simply loved the things - all shapes, colors, materials, and designs of sweaters. What's more, the man belonged to a discussion group of people who shared his particular obsession and just the week before he had found out that one of the men in his group was getting married. Several of the men were planning a bachelor party for him but instead of the traditional stag movies that would normally be shown, they had contacted Thomas to request a stripper who would be willing to play upon their sweater fantasies. That is why Thomas had been frequenting the local strip clubs, bars, and nightclubs. He was looking for a performer that he believed could excel in the assignment. In Marlo, he thought he may have found that dancer. Thomas watched her show every night for over three weeks before he decided to approach her. As luck would have it, that night Marlo had picked Thomas for her grand finale. When she leaned down to give him the customary kiss, Thomas had grasped her long hair in his clenched fists and held her lips tightly against his. After working with strippers every day for several years now, he had not expected his body to react the way it had. As Marlo struggled to free herself from his grasp, her bare ass had rubbed his eager cock through the material of his pants. Like an obedient child waiting for its reward, his prick had jumped to life. Feeling the hardness grow beneath her, Marlo panicked, hoping that she had not picked the wrong patron to grace with her attentions tonight. She knew other dancers who had been raped after refusing a 'private dance' to a customer who had had enough to drink to forget that no means no.

Thomas sensed her growing fear and released Marlo. He leaned toward her and whispered in her ear, telling her that he wanted to speak with her privately after the club closed. He couldn't understand the look of terror that crossed her face. When Marlo delivered her stinging blow to his cheek, Thomas cried out loud in shock. What the hell was wrong with this woman and why did she slap him? Maybe she wasn't the right one after all. Suddenly she seemed unstable to him and the last thing Thomas needed was a nutcase for an employee. Still, he was drawn back and back he came night after night.

Then one night while he was sitting at the bar waiting for her show, Marlo approached Thomas. She apologized for slapping him and explained why she had been so scared. Looking over her sexy body, her full red lips, her entrancing eyes, Thomas could understand her fear of being attacked, even raped, by an unruly customer. He told her that she was safe with him and handed her one of his brightly-colored business cards. He watched as she studied the card, flipping it over like she was afraid it might have more on the back and she didn't want to miss any of the fine print. Finally she looked up at him and he could see the confusion in her eyes. "Fetish parties?" She whispered the words then cleared her throat and spoke more loudly, "You hold parties for those freaks that drink blood instead of beer and screw animals in the barnyard?" Thomas smiled. He almost laughed until he realized that she was serious.

"NO! I hold parties for people with fetishes, yes, but there are hundreds, maybe thousands of people with harmless enough fetishes." As he spoke he kept shaking his head vigorously. "I have done foot fetish engagement parties where the cake was a giant foot with painted toenails. I have done baby showers for couples with leather fetishes where we dressed little cupid baby dolls up in leather and chains. I even did a birthday party for a man who had developed a latex fetish because his girlfriend always made him wear a dental dam for oral sex. We dropped hundreds of latex balloons down on him as the guests sang Happy Birthday and he got so excited that we saw his cock push out a tent in his sweatpants before he ran into the bathroom. I still think he jerked off in there before he came back out because the tent was gone without a trace when he re-entered. Those are the harmless types of things I cater to and believe me, there is a huge market for my services. I think you would do well in my line of work. That's why I wanted to talk to you that night, to offer you a job with my company."

Marlo wondered if this was a gag or if this handsome man standing in front of her was serious. She asked him what kind of job. He explained in no small amount of detail what the customer wanted. He needed a gal who could perform a strip tease where she appeared to be making love to a sweater. He also needed one who would do the job without being judgmental or condescending to his clients. Marlo wondered why he had picked her. She didn't wonder long because Thomas went on to explain how she seemed perfect to him because he had watched her perform so many times and he had noticed that with each performance she got bolder with her actions. He also thought that she looked like a very passionate woman and so he assumed that she would be able to feign making love with no problem at all, even if it was to a sweater. Marlo couldn't help herself. She laughed hysterically at that statement. Then she invited Thomas to have a drink with her while they discussed the details of the assignment.

Hours later they ended their meeting with Marlo insisting that if she were going to take the job, the sweater could not be wool. She hated wool and she was not about to make love to it. Thomas promised that it would be a soft sweater that would not scratch her sensitive skin. They made plans to meet the next night so that Marlo could practice a new routine and Thomas could make suggestions for her. Promptly at eight o'clock the following evening, Marlo entered Thomas's office. He smiled a sexy smile at her and handed over an extremely soft, baby blue, long-sleeved sweater. Marlo set her tape player up on his desk and asked him to turn around, facing the wall behind him. Thomas did as she requested and when she finally told him to take his seat, she was wearing the sweater. It fell to her mid-thigh and Thomas's eyes were drawn to follow her slender legs. She walked over to the desk in front of him, leaned down slowly, and flipped the switch on her player. After a few seconds the room was flooded with music. Thomas had never heard the song before but he thought it sounded appropriate. It was all about being soft to the touch, I love you so much ... Baby, you are my obsession... He watched intently as Marlo rubbed first one cheek and then the other against her sweater clad shoulder. Her fingers played with the hem of the sweater, slowly lifting it up over her silk panties where she bunched it up in her hand and caressed her flat tummy with it, moaning out the song with every stroke. She continued to lift the sweater up over her firm, well-rounded tits, massaging each nipple with it until they both stood hard and erect, pushing against the silk material of her skimpy bra. The song played on as Marlo pulled the sweater off over her head and slowly placed it between her legs. She used one hand in front of her body and one behind it to pull the sweater back and forth in time to the music, riding its softness in a mock fucking that would make any man's dick rise to the occasion. Thomas could feel his own doing so as he watched, totally mesmerized by her sensual dance of passion. Suddenly he wished that he were the sweater. He managed to stay in his seat, hiding his raging hardon until Marlo finished with a loud orgasmic moan and flipped off the tape player. Afraid to let her see how she had affected him, he merely whispered that he was sure that her routine would do, and then he told her that she could go.

Marlo had one week to practice for the party and practice she did. Every day she would go over the routine, getting a little braver as she made small changes. She started to enjoy the friction of the sweater as it stroked against her pussy, causing her panties to grow wet. She was eager to meet the men that had this fetish, eager to see what they looked like, eager to know how strong their needs for the sweater fantasies went. As the day drew closer she found herself getting more and more excited until she could hardly wait for the party day to get there. She knew that Thomas would stay at the party and watch her dance and she hoped that he would not be upset by the changes that she had made.

Finally the day came and Marlo arrived early to check out the stage. As she walked into the darkly lit room she was amazed to see the weirdest stage she had ever seen. From the curtain at the back all the way down the right hand side of it, there was what appeared to be a backboard in place with pictures of the most beautiful sweaters covering it. On the left hand side were a dozen individual cubicles, each with a small table and one chair in it. Thomas explained that the cubicles were for his client's privacy. Knowing that they each had a fetish for sweaters and having seen how his own body reacted to Marlo's sensual dance with hers, Thomas had had the cubicles set up for her show to give each man the privacy he needed until his swollen cock returned to normal. Then the cubicles would be wheeled away. Marlo felt a sense of power as she realized that although she would be able to see every man in the room, each of them would be able to see only her. With a smile on her face, she went to the dressing room to get ready for her show.

Thirty minutes later the guests started to arrive and fifteen minutes after that they were all present and accounted for. Marlo took a deep breath as Thomas dimmed the lights and turned on the multi-colored spotlight. As soon as she heard the music start to play, her supple hips started to gyrate to its sensual rhythm. Marlo sauntered out onto the stage in her soft blue sweater and by the reaction she got from that small group of men, you would have thought she walked out completely naked. She heard shouts of oh babys and yeah sexys and plenty of wolf whistles. The attention made Marlo feel good, made her feel special and wanted, and most of all it made her want to do a good job. She started her routine just like she had practiced that night for Thomas but when she had the sweater completely off, her moves changed from what he had seen before to something he was not expecting to see at all. Thomas watched in awe as she undid the clasp at the front of her bra and bent over, setting free those gorgeous tits that he remembered so well. Thomas loved the way that they hung down, the way they jiggled with her movement, and especially the way that her erect nipples shined on top of them, seeming to be begging for the touch of his hands. He shook his head and reminded himself that this was an employee and that she was merely doing her job. Still, Thomas had an overwhelming urge to join her on stage and give her a show that she would never forget.

Her tits now free and clearly in a state of excitement, Marlo looked toward each cubicle in turn, making sure that she caught the eye of the man inside as she pinched her nipples hard between her sweater-covered fingers. Her tongue darted out to lick her lips as she crooned the words... I wanna taste you, Baby... I don't mean maybe. You... are my... obsession... Wow, what a reaction. Some of the men shifted just enough in their seats to let Marlo admire the bulge that she had caused in their pants. Some of them began to openly rub the growing hardness through their clothing. Marlo was amazed to find that the sight aroused her more than anything she had ever experienced before. Twelve men all with raging hardons for her!

Marlo's hands fell to her sides and she pulled at the small patches of velcro that held her lacy panties in place. Instantly it gave way and they slipped to the floor, leaving Marlo naked for all to see. She placed the sweater between her legs and started her mock sex ride to the gasps and groans of her spectators. Thomas was having a hard time not moaning out loud too. He had to remain professional even though his hot, hard, pulsing dick had developed a mind of its own. And oh the things that that mind wanted to do to the firm, sexy body dancing on the stage tonight! He definitely liked the improvements that Marlo had made to her routine. This crowd was sure to leave some big tips and Thomas knew that he would be their sole party planner from now on.

Marlo was thrilled by the men's reactions. She was getting more turned on by the minute and on impulse, she decided to see how far she could go. She caught Thomas's eye and used her fingers to make a cutting motion, letting him know that she needed a pair of scissors on the stage. Quickly he grabbed some from the drawer of a desk and darted down to hand them to her. He could tell by the gleam in her beautiful blue eyes and the wicked smile that crossed her lips that Marlo could see the effect she was having on his throbbing cock. He could also tell that she wasn't finished with him yet. Marlo wasn't finished with any of them yet. Still dancing to the beat of the music, she took the scissors and began to carefully cut off the sleeves of the sweater, one small square of material at a time. Each sleeve was divided into six sections which she then took great delight in tossing to the men one at a time. As each caught his souvenir Marlo could see their dicks jerking in their pants and suddenly she had an uncontrollable urge to cum with them - all of them. Twelve men all cumming with her at one time. What a thrill! Just the thought had Marlo's pussy pulsing. The wetness sliding down her thighs glistened brightly in the glare of the spotlight.

Marlo closed her eyes and leaned back her head, caressing her soft, slender neck with the body of her sweater. She heard moans fill the room but she kept her eyes closed and continued her fantasy. She slid one hand up inside of the sweater and let it cover her fingers like a well-fitting glove. She thought she could hear zippers being undone and the sound caused her juices to flow faster. With her sweater-covered hand, Marlo began to make love to herself, slowly stroking every sensitive spot until she couldn't stand the sweet agony anymore. She moved to her shaved pussy and could feel the wetness soaking her hand through the sweater's material.

As Thomas watched the wonder of what was going on he knew that he needed release soon or he would never be able to face his clients after the show had ended. He couldn't figure out why Marlo hadn't bothered to tell him that she was going to take the show in such a sexual direction. He tried to make himself believe that if he had known ahead of time what to expect his traitorous body would not be responding with such passionate abandon. Knowing that no one could see him from inside their cubicle, Thomas released his rigid rod from its prison. God, it felt good just to let his prick free as he watched Marlo dance but soon it wasn't enough and he took it firmly in his hand and began to stroke it. As Marlo moved two fingers inside of her hot, dripping cunt, Thomas began to pump his aching cock furiously. Watching her he could imagine his swollen cock taking the place of her fingers, happily fucking her tight little pussy hole as he reveled in the sound of her moans.

Marlo knew she was getting closer to climax as she felt her pussy begin to quiver and tense deep inside. The thought spurred her on, daring her not to quit. She had never cum when someone was watching before, preferring to make love in the dark. Now she had twelve men watching. Then she thought about Thomas and made the mental correction, changing the number of men to thirteen. Knowing that he was going to see her cum, Marlo's fingers began to fuck her pussy harder and faster with every stroke. She suddenly had the fleeting thought that she was more turned on by Thomas's presence than by all of the other men put together!

Marlo peeked at the cubicles from under her half-closed lashes. Each man had taken his part of the sweater sleeve and opened it up like a small train tunnel. They had used the sleeve to insert their swollen cock into, clearly overexcited by the feeling of it encompassing their shafts. Marlo watched the men jerking desperately at their dicks with the blue patches of material and asked herself how things had ever gotten this far. She knew that it was too late to turn back now, and she didn't really want to anyway. Her hot, wet pussy was throbbing hard and her hand was soaked by the juices running from it. She had every intention of finishing so she could hardly tell the men not to cum too. She closed her eyes and pictured Thomas standing over her willing body, ramming his iron hard rod into her begging pussy as she moaned out his name.

Watching from the back of the room, Thomas could have sworn that he had heard Marlo call out his name but seeing her writhing in ecstasy he thought that it must have been wishful thinking on his part. Still, the thought of his name escaping her lips when she was so full of passion made his thick cock ache unbearably.

Marlo kept her middle and third finger buried deep inside her hot cunt as her index finger began to rub her hard clit. She was so wet that she slid easily round and round the hard little knob until she knew that she would cum very soon. Pushing firmly against its marble-like hardness, Marlo started to scream out as she felt her quivering pussy gripping her fingers tight. In her mind it was Thomas's name that she called. Opening her eyes, Marlo watched as man after man exploded, spurting his hot, creamy fluid onto the table in front of him. The room was filled with the sounds of their moaning and it seemed to Marlo like it would never end. Finally the room quieted.

From the back of the room, Marlo could hear Thomas's deep, sexy voice crying out in passion, "Yes, Baby, cum with me! Fuck me, baby. Ride my aching cock!" She knew that he had lost himself in some unknown fantasy and suddenly she was very jealous of the lady in his dreams. No one could see Thomas but they all listened as his imaginary woman rode his erupting cock into the night. "Go, Baby, go! Don't stop. Move that tight little ass. Oh my God, you feel so good, baby, so tight and hot and wet. I love fucking you like this. Fuck me, baby, fuck me forever." Marlo could feel her jealousy growing even as his words brought her pussy to life again. She was drawing up a mental picture of the type of woman that Thomas would be attracted to when he let out his final exclamation, "Oh, God, I'm cumming, baby. Don't stop, I'm cumming. Fuck me. Milk out every drop of my hot cum with your sweet cunt, Marlo!"

Marlo's breath was knocked from her lungs. Had he said Marlo? Did Thomas know another Marlo? The room grew very quiet until the groom to be called out from his cubicle. "Miss Marlo," the satiated man yelled, "you heard the man. Go screw him until he begs for mercy!" The other men broke out into laughter, a laughter so loud and so resounding that it could be heard a block down the street. Then voice after voice joined in, coaxing Marlo to go do what she wanted to do so desperately, encouraging her to go fuck the man she loved. Marlo didn't even dress. She jumped down from the stage and ran to the back of the room where Thomas was busy tucking in his shirt and trying to look innocent.

She grabbed his hand and led him to her dressing room where she spent the night fucking him like he had never been fucked before. Her dripping pussy massaged his hot cock over and over. Her warm, wet mouth bathed it clean after every round, eagerly swallowing down their mixed cum. It was an evening full of love, an evening full of passion, and an evening overflowing with raw sexual desire. They only stopped screwing when, in total exhaustion, Thomas's aching rod and Marlo's pulsing pussy had refused to perform again. Then they lay on the dressing room table, his cock still held deep inside of her warm tunnel, and talked about their future. Thomas had decided that he did not want Marlo as his employee anymore. She wondered why until he kissed her lightly on her parted lips, turning her face up to his. That was the night that he asked her to be his partner, not only in Fetish Fevers, but in real life too. Marlo smiled a devilish smile and asked him if she would still be able to dance and do shows.

"Oh, yeah, baby," he replied with just the slightest hint of a chuckle showing in his voice, "you will be performing at least two or three times a night ..... in private dances, just for me."

CHAPTER 9
PIZZA MAN DELIVERY

PIZZA MAN DELIVERY

Joseph counted the change in his hand ..... Five, ten, thirty-five, forty-five, fifty cents. He pretended to be grateful for the tip handed to him by the young man who had answered the door.

God, how he hated this job, driving around from house to house in the hot summer air, practically begging kids half his age for tips. Oh, well, feeling sorry for himself was not going to help at all so Joseph sopped at his sweat-covered brow with a tissue and headed for his car. Maybe delivering pizza wasn't the most glamorous thing to do for extra cash but at least he could choose the hours that he wanted to work and there was no boss staring over his shoulder. Still, he couldn't quite shake the thought that 38 was a little old to be a 'pizza boy.'

The end of his shift came and Joseph was headed for the door of the Pizza Palace when his boss asked him if he would make one last delivery on his way home. The house he had to go to was right on his way and only about eight minutes from his own front door so Joseph nodded and held out his hands for the pizza box. To his surprise, his boss pointed to a couple of stacks of pizza boxes on the back counter, ten in all. Joseph carried them out to his car by twos, careful not to mash the flimsy boxes that his boss tried to pass off as adequate protection to his customers. When his car was fully loaded, Joseph pulled the magnetic pizza delivery sign off of its roof and jumped into the driver's seat. He lovingly stroked the leather-covered steering wheel and murmured words of encouragement, coaxing the engine to roar to life again. He felt almost like a traitor, knowing in his heart that by the end of the summer he would have made enough tips to put 'ole Bessie' to rest and buy the pretty silver sport car he had been wanting from the local used car lot.

As he drove, Joseph slowed and squinted at every intersection, trying to read the road signs in the dimming sunlight. There it was ..... 1499 Jersey Avenue. Wow, what a big house. It looked like a self-contained city and Joseph wondered why it didn't have its own pizza shop. He grabbed up the first two boxes and headed for the front door. Ding-dong. He rang the bell but getting no response he rang it again. Ding-dong. The pizza was burning his arm through the thin cardboard barrier and Joseph was getting more impatient by the second. Ding-dong, ding dong, ding, ding, ding, ding, dong. There, that should get someone's attention. But it didn't, and Joseph found himself listening carefully for signs of life in the house. Finally he heard a loud squeal and laughter from the back yard.

Coming around the house, Joseph couldn't find a gate on the privacy fence at the back. He resorted to hopping up and down like a rabbit, trying to see what was going on in the yard. He could hear several voices now so he wasn't surprised when he finally saw a pool full of people in the well-lit enclosure. He managed to make his voice heard over the giggles and splashes, letting them know that their pizza had arrived. Joseph was surprised when a section of the fence opened in front of him, nearly smacking him in the face. There had been no sign from his side that it was a gate.

A red-haired, freckle-faced teenage boy pointed him to a pool side table and he quickly sat down the pizza. Joseph hurriedly brought the rest of the order to the table, then scanned the patio and pool for whoever looked like they might be in charge of giving tips. He met the eyes of a beautiful carrot-topped woman who appeared to be close to his own age. She smiled and her face glowed with an angel-like beauty. Slowly, the woman got up from her chair, adjusted her bikini, and walked toward Joseph. She opened the box that was on top of the stack and nodded her head approvingly. She moved the box to the side and opened the next one carefully. She dipped one slender finger into the sauce oozing onto the crust, looking like it was trying to escape from under the weight of the toppings. She brought the finger to her lips and her tongue darted out to flick its tip before she sucked the finger into her mouth with a low moan.

"Mmmmmm, mmmmmmmmmm," she moaned, "this is great sauce." She looked pointedly at the crotch of Joseph's slacks and continued. "And it's pepperoni. I love pepperoni! It always has the best sauce. Hot and thick, creamy and salty and it just oozes to the surface, begging me to swallow it."

She said it all still looking at the growing bulge in Joseph's pants before she looked up and he saw the wicked gleam in her sparkling green eyes. Suddenly Joseph realized that this beautiful angel had sprouted some little horns and the thought was making him really horny. "I'm Linda." She continued with a devilish chuckle, "Welcome to the party." She explained that it was a graduation party for her baby brother who had just gotten his degree in accounting. Their parents had died when he was young and Linda had raised Billy all alone. He would be moving away very soon to take a job in a neighboring town. It would be the first time that the brother and sister had been apart and Linda was doing her best not to let on how sad the thought made her.

"Well, my name is Joseph, and I just delivered ten pizzas on my own time." Joseph uttered the words, trying not to let the redness show on his cheeks. He knew that he was blushing. He could feel the heat rising through his body. In his mind he kept replaying the look on Linda's face as she had studied his pants, clearly amused by the affect her burning gaze had had on his cock. And what an effect it had been. His dick had sprung up and strained against his pants, trying to get closer to the woman that had awakened it. Joseph cleared his throat and turned toward the gate.

"I guess I should go now," he said, "unless there is something else?" He waited patiently, hoping that Linda would take his hint and get his tip so that he could head home and sit in the air-conditioned study.

"I paid for the pizzas by credit card," she explained, " and I don't have any cash right now. If you wouldn't mind stopping by again tomorrow evening, I can give you a tip then." Joseph hadn't expected to be stiffed for his tip by someone who lived in a house of such size and who obviously had money. He wasn't about to come all the way back here for a handful of loose change. He uttered something about not worrying about the money and then he sprinted to his car and drove home.

The next morning Joseph was late for work because he had overslept. He had heard the alarm go off but he was lost in a dream about the sexy, red-headed imp he had met the day before and he didn't want the dream to end yet. In it, she had teased him without mercy, flaunting her perfect body with her movements and gestures. Joseph really wanted to touch her but every time that his hand would come close to making contact with her soft skin, she would dart away from him quickly, giggling like a young child in the middle of a rousing game of tag. When he finally woke up he kept telling his brain to forget the beautiful woman who had cheated him out of his tip. Maybe he would have forgotten her too, if she hadn't ordered a pizza that night and asked for Joseph to deliver it. He didn't want the assignment but Joseph knew it was silly to make another driver go all the way to a house that he would pass on his way home anyhow. He decided that he would simply ring the bell and leave the pizza sitting on the stoop so that he wouldn't have to face another excuse about why he wasn't getting anything for his troubles. Or maybe he didn't want to face the woman that had made him want her without even trying.

Joseph did exactly as he had intended, leaving the pizza after he rang the bell. He felt like the kid that rings bells at Halloween and then runs before you can get to the door to answer it. He knew that Linda would report his failure to wait for her but he didn't care. Maybe she would take the hint and start ordering her pizza from their competitor, The Pizza King. He was surprised when, not only did she not give his boss a complaint about his childish actions, she ordered another pizza the next day. And the day after that. And the day after that. In fact, she ordered pizza every day for the next two weeks, always making sure to request Joseph by name as her delivery man. Well, two could play this little mind game, and Joseph did love games. So every day after work, he would grab one large pepperoni pizza and head for Jersey Avenue. There he would set down the pizza on the small porch and ring the doorbell before he drove away without speaking a word to the devilish angel inside.

Night after night, his dreams about Linda became more suggestive and he often found himself waking to a dick that was screaming out for her touch. As he would stroke his long, hard shaft, he would close his eyes and pretend it was her giving his throbbing cock the release that it needed so much. Sometimes Joseph would get so caught up in his fantasy that only when he felt the wet heat of his own cum hitting his stomach did he realize that she wasn't in the big bed with him. He knew that he would have to put any and all thoughts of her out of his head or he was going to go crazy wanting her, craving the feeling of her bare skin against his. He had only met Linda that one time but her personality had captured his interest, her love for her brother had stolen his heart, and the bold sensuality of her actions had arrested his imagination. He realized that he wanted to see her again.

The next day, just as she had every day since the pool party, Linda ordered a large pepperoni pizza. Joseph smiled and grabbed the box, almost running for his car in his eagerness to get to her house. He made the now-familiar trip in record time and jumped from his car, running up the walkway to her front door. He climbed the steps to the porch and pressed his finger firmly on the bell. Linda gasped when she opened the door to find Joseph standing there smiling at her. She had hoped that he would realize that she couldn't possibly eat that much pizza and that she ordered it so much just to see him. Of course, she usually only got to see the back of his head as his nearly dead car puttered off down the road, taking away the object of her wanton desires. Now here he was, standing tall and handsome, a sexy smile on his full lips, and Linda could think of absolutely nothing to say. How could she tell the pizza delivery man to come in and stay for awhile, in fact, to stay forever if he wanted? With a mind of its own, her delicate hand reached out and rested against his chest. She batted her eyelashes at him coyly as she asked him if he had remembered the pepperoni. Joseph blushed and nodded. He couldn't speak. His whole body had started to burn with the fire of passion when her small hand had touched him. He wanted more, much more, and he wanted it now. His thoughts were broken by the soft words of the woman standing in front of him.

"I paid for the pizzas by credit card," she murmured, " and I don't have any cash. If you wouldn't mind stopping by again tomorrow, I will give you your tip then." Linda had only meant to break the awkward silence with a little humor but she knew immediately that she had made a big mistake. Joseph's face had shut down like a curtain had been closed over it. His sexy smile had faded away and it was replaced by a look of ...... what? Disgust maybe. Irritation, perhaps. Disappointment, definitely. She was on the verge of explaining that it was a joke, that she had the money for every delivery that he had made over the last fourteen days sitting on her kitchen table, when Joseph abruptly pushed away her hand and left.

As Joseph drove the short distance home, he vented his anger by yelling at no one. He wasn't angry with the woman who had obviously learned long ago how to use her looks, her sexy body, and her suggestive comments, to get what she wanted from men. He was angrier with himself, at his rigid rod, for responding in such a blatantly lustful salute when she had made it clear that all she wanted from him was free pizza delivery! He tried his best to talk his quivering cock into sleeping again but by the time he parked his car in the small garage connected to his home, Joseph knew that he would have to jerk off to get any relief. He hated the fact that all that entered his mind when he took his hot cock firmly in his hand was the image of a fiery redheaded angel with a skewed halo and tiny horns encasing his engorged shaft in her warm wetness. As he pumped furiously at his prick, Joseph closed his eyes and watched the red head bobbing over his lap. He felt the softness of her lips around the swollen head of his throbbing member and he moaned loudly. He knew that he should stop fantasizing about Linda but he had always stopped before he would cum and just this once he wanted to carry out the fantasy to its natural end.

He gave himself permission to let go and his mind went wild. He leaned his head back against the headrest and tilted the steering wheel out of the way of his jerking hand. He gripped his aching dick harder, using his free hand to cup his tight balls and watched the movie playing out in his aroused mind. There was Linda, sucking him like there was no tomorrow, looking up into his eyes as her hungry mouth devoured him. He felt his hot cock hitting the back of her soft throat and was surprised when, instead of gagging against his thrusting hips, she grabbed his ass and pulled him into her even further. He felt one of her hands move to play with his balls, making him moan out her name, begging her to keep going. Her throat hugged his dick tight as she swallowed in fast little gulps. He moaned louder. He could feel the wetness of his pre-cum dripping onto his hand and his pace quickened. Behind his closed eyes Joseph could see Linda as she raised her head, looking into his eyes. His hand stopped moving as he imagined the feeling of cool air hitting the wetness that her mouth had left on his cock. Totally mesmerized by the sight of her swollen lips, bright red from the friction of sucking him, Joseph listened intently when she spoke.

"Joseph, baby," the sweet, sultry voice in his head said, "I want you. I want to taste you. I need you. Please, babydoll, cum down my throat. Let me swallow all of you." She waited as if she expected him to say no but Joseph grasped the back of her head and rammed her open mouth back down on his pulsing prick. He thrust up with his hips, feeling his shaft shoving into her eager throat, filling it until she could barely breathe.

"Oh, yeah, baby," he cried out, "suck it. Suck it hard!" Without thinking,

Joseph started bucking his hips upward, almost as if he were really meeting Linda's hot, wet mouth. The fantasy was taking his mind and body to places they had never been before. He could feel her exploring tongue as it massaged the underside of his shaft and he writhed against it. He could smell the sweetness of her shampoo as her head continued to bob and suddenly he had to put his hands back in that hair. Joseph entwined his fingers in her thick, curly hair and tugged lightly, pulling just enough to make her scalp tingle. Linda groaned against his cock and the vibrations that caressed it made his legs tremble. Holding her hair firmly at the nape of her sexy neck, Joseph began to pound his rock-hard rod deep into her throat over and over again. God, she felt so good on him. She sucked like she loved doing it and the thought that Linda actually wanted his cock so deep in her throat was the final straw. "Fuck me, baby!" Joseph shouted the words out in a ragged, broken breath. "Fuck me with those luscious lips. Oh, yeah, baby, I'm gonna cum. I'm gonna, gonna ..... Oh, God, I'm cumminggggggggggg! Swallow it, baby. Swallow it all. Yeah, suck it all up!" Lost in his world of wonder, Joseph erupted like an over-active volcano. His prick convulsed in his wet hand, each spasm shooting more hot cream from its tip. He lay his head back again and gulped in deep breaths slowly, trying to bring his rampaging imagination back to reality. He was shocked by the discovery that he really wanted this fantasy to become his reality. Joseph stood on shaky legs and walked into his house, heading straight for his study and the mind-clearing coolness of the air conditioning.

He sat at his desk for a long time, reliving the experience that he had played out in the garage. He tried to convince himself that it could never become reality. A woman like Linda would never get serious with someone who was forced to deliver pizzas for extra money. He knew that she didn't think of him as an equal. To her he was merely someone who was paid to do her bidding and not even important enough to merit the common courtesy of a tip for his efforts. He wanted to make her see him as a man and not just as someone who had to serve her. Glancing at the clock hanging on the mantle, Joseph realized that he had spent the entire evening thinking about the little imp that so easily made his dick go from limp to standing proud and tall. He laughed at his own silliness as he wandered down the hallway and off to bed.

The next day was extremely hot and long and Joseph couldn't wait to get home. Linda's order came in just as he was beginning to think that she had decided to torment someone else that day. The boss was listening and smiling into the phone like the woman on the other end had some magical ability to read the expressions on his face. Joseph thought about the ability she had to make him all horny and hard without even hearing her voice. His dick had jumped up the minute that his boss had motioned for him to stay. He decided that today was the day he would put an end to little miss sorry-no-tip-until-tomorrow's head games. The boss was shocked but pleased when Joseph offered to stay and make the pizza, and lock up before he went home. Less than fifteen minutes later, Joseph's little deathmobile was chugging down the familiar route to Linda's house.

When Joseph whipped into the driveway and parked his car, he got out and pulled the pizza box to him. He shifted a little so that he was holding it in a comfortable position directly in front of his lap. He bent down and retrieved a can of pizza sauce from the small valley between his bucket seats. He opened the box quickly, fervently looking around in all directions, making sure that no one could see what he was doing, and then dumped the sauce into the box in one swift movement. Then Joseph walked carefully to the door that he had been to so many times in the last several weeks, sighing loudly as he realized that after today, he would not be coming back again. His finger hesitated only a second before he rang the doorbell. Ding-dong. No Linda. Ding-dong, ding-dong. Still no answer. Remembering the pool from that first night, Joseph circled the house and called out to see if Linda was in the back yard. The gate swung open almost immediately and she pointed to the table beside of the pool. Joseph walked around the table, standing behind it, and placed the pizza box on top of its gleaming white surface. He looked up to see a beautifully tanned Linda, still covered in droplets of water, watching him intently as she moved to place herself between him and his path of escape. He began to worry as his face reddened under her stare. Maybe he shouldn't have planned this big shock for her today. The thought was reinforced when Linda bent toward her beach bag and pulled out a rather large handful of money.

"These are all of the tips I owe you." She spoke with just the slightest tone of remorse in her voice. "I meant to give them to you before. When I made the comment about not having any cash, Joseph, I was kidding but you took off so fast that I didn't have time to tell you." Her eyes never left Joseph's beet-red cheeks and she began to wonder if offering him the money was embarrassing him. "I'm sorry that we got off on the wrong foot, Joseph. I think that we could be really great friends if we start all over again." She held out her small hand toward Joseph. "Hi, I am Linda and I have a confession to make. I don't really eat very much pizza. I just like the pepperoni. I pick them all off and eat them. Then I let the neighbor kids eat the cheese pizza that is left." She chuckled loudly; "Mrs. Simon told me yesterday that they have eaten so much pizza over the last few weeks that the kids are actually asking her for vegetables!"

Joseph enclosed her tiny hand in his big, strong one. Just like he had imagined a hundred times or more, the touch of her skin on his started a raging fire deep in his groin. His dick not only jumped in excitement, but Joseph could have sworn it started begging for some attention. "Hi, my name is Joseph and I think I should leave now." He mumbled the words so lowly that she had to ask him to repeat them. Linda's hand reached for the pizza box as she offered Joseph a slice. "NOOOOOOO!" He cried out so loudly that it startled her and her slender arm fell to her side. She looked at him quizzically and Joseph wondered how he was going to get away without letting her look into the box. The answer, he soon came to find out, was simple. He wasn't!

Linda reached for the box again and yanked up the lid. She didn't scream, or yell, or even gasp. She stayed perfectly cool as she stared down at her delivery. Then, to Joseph's amazement, she smiled broadly and nodded her head at him. She dipped one finger into the sauce and then quickly brought it to her parted lips, sucking it clean. His over-anxious cock jumped again. It's pepperoni and you know I love pepperoni!" She had such enthusiasm in her voice that Joseph could feel the sexual tension growing in him. " It always has the very best sauce. Hot and thick, creamy and salty and it just oozes to the surface, begging me to swallow it." Well, something was oozing, that's for sure, and Joseph knew that he couldn't hide what her words had done to him from her downcast eyes. He let his gaze follow hers and was filled with disbelief at what he had done. Lying there on the table was an open pizza box and inside of it, inserted through a hole that he had carefully cut from the back wall of the box, danced Joseph's sauce-covered, hard as steel schlong.

Linda pulled up a lawn chair and sat down on her side of the table. Pushing her tits down on its hard top, she leaned over the pizza box, and started to lap at Joseph's jumping dick with her warm, wet tongue. Joseph closed his eyes and moaned softly. As the sauce was licked away from the top of his prick, Linda took one hand and lifted her special pepperoni roll high so that her exploring mouth could suck all of it completely clean. "Mmmmmm, mmmmmmmm," she murmured, "this is really good, Joseph. You are the best pizza delivery man that I have ever had." Joseph was so incredibly horny that he couldn't even think straight. Linda continued in a quiet whisper, her soft finger massaging the swollen tip of his raging hardon as she spoke, "I believe in tipping according to the service I get so how about you come out of your box and cum in me instead?" Did he hear that right? Joseph thought that he must be lost in another daydream until Linda removed her bikini and stood in front of him completely naked. "Well," she inquired of the stunned man, "Do you want your tip or not?" There was that sparkle in her eyes again, the sparkle that simply dared him to refuse. Joseph was not about to refuse. He watched Linda turn and dive smoothly into the water.

Joseph yanked off the pizza box, tore off his clothes, and joined her before she had enough time to turn around and face him again. He picked her up from behind and walked through the pool, carrying her easily in his arms. When they reached the ladder Joseph told her to reach out and grab it with both hands. Wondering why, Linda did what she was told. "I have one more delivery for you," he growled, "and if you liked the last one, you are gonna love this one!"

Joseph walked backward, telling Linda to keep a firm grip on the ladder, and pulled her lower body with him until she seemed to be lying on her flat tummy on top of the water. He took one of her slim ankles in each hand and parted her legs, walking between them. As he walked closer to her firm little ass, Joseph let his hands run up Linda's legs, caressing and teasing. She felt his fingers playing with her pussy and she knew that the pool water was not the only thing making her wet. Joseph lowered his face until his chin was under the water and sucked at Linda's hard, marble-like clit until she screamed. He shifted his mouth and drove his tongue up inside of her fiery hot hole as far as he could make it go. Linda screamed out again, louder, longer. Joseph began to fuck her with his tongue as he used his fingers on her clit. Linda bounced in the water as she tried desperately to push back against his mouth, needing to feel him become a part of her, wanting to feel him driving his tongue into her.

Linda's body started to quiver and shake with passion. She could feel herself getting closer to climax as Joseph alternated between sucking her clit like a small cock and fucking her dripping cunt with his fingers and tongue. Her body tensed and stiffened as her desire climbed that mountain of sweet release. Joseph felt her body and softly encouraged her, "Cum, baby, cum. Cum on my tongue, Linda. Let go, baby." His words were cut off as he felt her body jerk and he quickly lowered his mouth to her pulsing pussy once more. As he gave his tongue one last long, hard thrust into her wet, heated hole, Joseph felt Linda's pussy muscles grip it tight. The taste of her cum on his tongue and the rhythmic squeezing of her muscles drove Joseph crazy with the need to fuck her.

While she was still in the throes of ecstatic climax, he stood and held her legs wide apart, ramming his hot rod into her in one stroke. Linda's moans of pleasure were all the encouragement that he needed. Joseph pumped into her harder and faster. "Put your feet down, baby. Fuck me back." Linda's feet slid to the bottom of the pool without her cunt ever losing its grip on Joseph's fat, hard roll. She braced herself and started to thrust back against him, her breathing ragged, her movements forceful. "Oh, yeahhhhhh, baby," Joseph called out, "work that tight little pussy. Milk me, baby, milk me!" His one hand found her waist, pulling her back harder and faster as his need for release became more desperate. With his other hand, Joseph reached around Linda to pinch each of her rosy red nipples, lightly twisting them between his forefinger and thumb before letting them go and grasping the hair at the back of her neck. She moaned out in excitement as she felt the tugging on her beautiful tresses.

Joseph fucked her pussy so hard that he was afraid he might hurt her but she just kept begging for more. "Fuck me, Joseph, please. Don't stop, baby. Harder, faster. Pump that hot pole into my cunt." God, Linda was a hot one. There was something about a woman who would use words like fuck and cunt that made Joseph's cock want to fill her up with its hot seed. He knew that was what was happening now as he felt the familiar tingling build up inside. "Fuck me, Joseph. I'm gonna cum, Baby!" Linda's excited exclamation sent Joseph over the top and, as he felt her tight, wet pussy grasping to hold his cock in, he let out a loud groan and came with her. They stood in the water as they watched the sun set, shaking in each other's arms. Joseph's lips nibbled Linda's neck gently.

When they finally emerged to dress and sit on the lawn chairs, Linda had regained the wicked gleam in her eyes. "You, know," the well-satiated redhead said, "I paid for that pizza by credit card." She winked at Joseph as he sat beside her, a sexy smile spreading across his lips. "Maybe, if you cum ..... Oooooops, I mean come, tomorrow, I can give you your tip." Joseph knew that he would come every day from now on. After all, Linda owed him a lot of tips and he intended to collect. Right that moment, in fact, he scooped her up into his arms and carried her toward the patio door as he whispered against her ear.

"Pizza delivery, ma'am." Joseph's breath tickled the skin on the side of Linda's face. "I have a large pepperoni to deliver. Do you still want it?" Linda wrapped her arms around his neck and pulled his lips to hers.

CHAPTER 10

BETTY'S BIRTHDAY SURPRISE

BETTY'S BIRTHDAY SURPRISE

Betty was a twenty two-year-old college co-ed. She had long, beautiful, raven-dark hair and deep brown eyes. Her figure was the envy of every girl in her dorm, being naturally svelte with curves in all the right places. Betty had only one real downfall and that was her big mouth. Her brother and sister had even called her 'bigmouth Betty' when they were growing up. 'Open mouth and insert foot' could have been quoted in her yearbook under words to live by. Betty was always getting herself into some sort of trouble and the night of her twenty-second birthday had been no exception.

She had been thrilled when the girls in her dorm room had offered to give her a birthday party. Nothing fancy, just friends, fun, and cake, but that was fine with her. She never had liked crowds and usually managed to find a way to avoid them. Because she had spent so much time alone or with just a few close friends in school, Betty had never been tempted to get into the vices other kids did. She had never smoked, never drank alcohol, and never tried drugs - not even marijuana.

That night Brianna, the girl that Betty shared bunk beds with, carefully decorated the small room with balloons and streamers. She hung a big banner on one wall that said Happy Birthday in rainbow colored letters. Betty had always been so sweet that Brianna wanted the night to be special for her. She set up a small card table in one corner and pulled a bright plastic tablecloth over it. On the table she placed a sign that simply read GIFTS. Her mind drifted to thoughts of what she would really like to give her sexy little roomy for her birthday. For as long as she could remember, she had always felt a sexual attraction to both men and women. The first day that Betty had walked into the dorm, Brianna had felt an attraction like never before. Her tits had seemed to swell against the fabric of the red silk teddy that she was wearing, her nipples trying to push their way out into the free world. Her matching red silk panties had grown so wet that she had to go to the bathroom and change them. Standing there, lost in her memories of their first meeting, Brianna felt the wetness between her thighs spreading. Her body felt warm and tingly, her face flushed, her pussy throbbing. She had tested the waters with Betty several times over the last few months, innocently brushing up against the other girl's crotch or tits. Although Betty had seemed to ignore her advances almost as if she hadn't even noticed them, Brianna could see the way that her body reacted. Maybe tonight would be different. Maybe tonight she would share her near-perfect body with Brianna.

By the time Betty arrived back at the dorm, the twelve or so girls that were coming to celebrate with her were already there. Most of them were wearing nothing more than tank tops and panties, their feet bare, their faces freshly scrubbed and free from any signs of makeup.

Betty perused the room full of scantily clad girls slowly. This was how she liked it. She liked having just a small group of good friends with her, none of them pretending to be someone they were not, none of them trying to impress the world with their beauty. In such a relaxed atmosphere, Betty could feel at ease with herself and others. No need to be on guard here, no need to be comparing herself, no need to think that she didn't quite measure up. She excused herself and went into the bedroom to change. She decided to do as the others had and make herself as comfortable as decency would permit, taking off all of her clothes and redressing in fresh undies and a short sleeved shirt.

The party started out much as any other birthday party. The girls sang "Happy Birthday" off key and threw confetti over their guest of honor. Betty sat beside the small card table and opened all of her gifts one by one, holding each one of them high in the air for all to see. As girls often do, some of them gave Betty gifts that turned out to be more than a little suggestive. From Sammi she got a bottle of perfume called "Sex." Miranda gave her a box of condoms in bright, glow-in-the-dark colors. With the rubbers was a hand written note that said I hope he never misses the target. It had a little sketch of an enormous cock hurdling through the air at a dripping pussy hole with the word 'bulls eye' written across it neon letters. Betty gave a nervous chuckle as she passed the paper around for the others to look at. Brianna gave her a sexy, see-thru nightie with cut out places for her boobs to peek through. Betty was almost afraid to open the big box that sat in the center of the room, afraid that her friends might have gotten her a man to use her other gifts on. With much laughter and many shouts of encouragement from the rowdy group of girls, she moved forward and tour open the package. She was surprised to find a large foam plane inside of the box. It was the cheap kind that kids would break after one day of hard play. She wondered what the toy could possibly be for until she pulled it from the box. As it cleared the side of its cardboard cage, Betty could see a pink envelope taped to the side of it, right over the sticker placed to resemble the boarding door. She pulled the envelope off and slowly pulled out the folded pink paper inside of it. Tears rolled down her cheeks as she read the note. It was to be turned in to Brianna for one round trip ticket home to see her parents. Everyone in the dorm had signed it. Betty hadn't been home in almost a year. She was working her way through college and she had to give up Christmas break and Thanksgiving break last year because of lack of funds. Now, at last, she was going home!

Someone must have spiked the punch because after a few glasses Betty found herself feeling funny. She didn't think she was drunk exactly, but then again she had never been drunk so how could she tell. All she knew was that she felt good. She felt free. She felt happy! She found herself, along with her friends, doing a lot of giggling over things that weren't even funny. She didn't care how silly they were being. She was having fun. Only when she started to feel sleepy did Betty ask Brianna to send their guests on their way.

Brianna said good bye to the last girl and shut the door behind her. She went back into the room and joined Betty on the couch where she lay. Brianna thought how beautiful Betty was as she looked down into her eyes, smiling at the goofy grin on her face. Betty's head lay nestled in Brianna's lap. She was on her back with one leg thrown carelessly over the back of the couch. Brianna felt the urge to move her hand from the girl's cheek where it rested down the length of her slender throat and across her pert tits. She wondered what it would feel like to let her hand keep exploring, venturing down that flat tummy and raising the hem of Betty's shirt to slide her fingers inside of the cute blue panties she was wearing. God, she wanted that pussy. Brianna knew that Betty was drunk for the very first time in her life and that she would probably not protest the advances too much, if at all. But Brianna didn't want to start out like that. If they were going to be lovers, she wanted Betty to know what was going on. When Betty started drifting off to sleep,

Brianna couldn't resist leaning down and placing her soft lips over the other girl's. Betty started to kiss her back gently and finally she fell asleep while enjoying the embrace.

Brianna slipped out from under Betty's head and sat on the floor in front of the sleeping girl. She picked up Betty's limp hand and pulled it against her erect nipple, rubbing herself with it lightly. As she held the soft hand against her tit, Brianna used her other hand to play with her clit, sliding it down to insert three fingers knuckle deep into her throbbing cunt. She fucked herself hard and fast, never taking her eyes off the peaceful, sleeping face just inches from her own. As her body exploded in climax, she closed her eyes and lay down on the floor, falling asleep with thoughts of sharing more than just a dorm room with the gorgeous girl on the couch.

When Betty awoke the next morning her head was pounding. It sounded like thunder rattling her brain. As she sat up, her foot touched something soft and she looked down to see her friend, Brianna, sleeping. She nudged the girl awake with the tip of her toe. Vaguely she thought of her lips pressed firmly against the other girl's luscious, full mouth, and then wondered where the thought had come from. She shook them away and rubbed the sleepiness from her burning eyes. Brianna sat up and stared at her. She made a pantomime of lifting a bottle and swigging from it before pointing to the punch bowl on the coffee table. Betty nodded her head to show that she understood.

"Did you like the party?" Brianna asked the question quietly, like she was afraid that if she spoke too loud, Betty's head might explode. Betty nodded again, finding it hard to speak when her mouth felt like she had swallowed her feather pillow in one gulp. Brianna had a brilliant flash as thoughts began to race through her over-stimulated mind. "I thought that maybe you did." she smiled. "You were getting pretty wild by the end of the night." Betty's face burned but she kept her gaze steady as she tried to remember what she had done that could have been so wild. She couldn't remember a thing ..... Period ..... Not wild, nor tame. The night was lost in a haze of confusion. She decided to bite the bullet and just ask straight out. Brianna laughed at the question. "Oh, yeah, play dumb. You are still gonna have to pay off that bet." Bet? What bet? Oh, no, what trouble had that big mouth gotten her into now? Betty knew that with money for college so hard to come by there was no way she could afford to throw her money away.

"Ummmm ..... Bri ..... What bet? What are you talking about?" Betty watched the other girl's face as she waited for a reply. She had never noticed how cute Brianna was before. Oh, she wasn't a striking beauty like Betty was, but she was definitely attractive in a cute-as-a-button, tomboyish kind of way. Betty felt a twang of attraction. She brushed it off as after effects of the alcohol.

Brianna was only going to tease her but she realized that Betty actually had no idea of what had went on the night before. She decided to keep up the charade and see where it led. "Come on, Betty," she cooed, "The strip poker game. You don't remember?" Betty shook her head. This was not sounding good and she was really starting to worry about what she might have done. "Oh my God! Betty, you were losing. All of your clothes were gone and one of the other girls suggested that we start playing for something a little more ..... ummmmm ..... valuable." Betty wondered what on earth that meant. She sucked in a deep breath. "I thought you were joking when you made the bet, especially since it was clear to everyone that you were holding a lousy hand. I mean, up until that time the bets had been fairly innocent enough, like when you lost and had to kiss me on the lips." So that's where her earlier thoughts had come from. Betty motioned for Brianna to finish the story impatiently. She had to know what she had lost. Was it her car, her stereo system, maybe her next semester's tuition? "Well, Betty, when you placed your bet, everyone was shocked. You said that if you lost, not only would you fuck two men at one time but..... ," she paused for the dramatic effect, "you said that you would have me video tape it for everyone to watch later." Brianna watched as a look of total amazement covered Betty's face. Then the other girl squared her shoulders, cleared her throat loudly, and began to speak in a calm voice.

"Who are the two men?" she asked boldly, without blushing and without flinching. She had made a stupid bet and she had lost. Now it was time to pay the piper.

"We didn't decide." Betty heard Brianna's voice as if it were coming through some distant tunnel. "That part is completely up to you." She was tempted to call the whole thing off and admit to the other girl that she had been lying. But she was thinking that the next best thing to being able to make love with Betty would be to tape Betty making love and keep the video for future fun. Of course, if Betty backed out of the imaginary bet, Brianna would let her off the hook gracefully.

"Okay then." Betty grew silent as she lost herself in her thoughts for several minutes. "My boyfriend, Craig, has to be one of them, but who else can I trust? I am not gonna have sex with a stranger." Suddenly Brianna had another inspirational thought.

"How about Bryan?" She asked the question a little too loudly, the thought of watching her fiance fucking her best friend starting her hormones raging violently. Betty looked shocked but she nodded. Brianna figured that Bryan wouldn't mind being asked to fuck the beautiful best friend of his girl. They were both very open-minded, sexually speaking, and they had talked about orgies of every kind in the past. Talked about, but never dared to participate in them. They were both afraid that anyone that they approached with the idea would think that they were some sort of perverts and so they kept it to themselves and used it in their sexual fantasies. Now they had a chance to make the desire a reality.

Craig was all for the idea until he found out that the threesome included another man. Somehow he had just assumed that he would have been making love with two women. He wasn't at all certain that he could feel comfortable touching another man's body. Bryan, on the other hand, said yes almost before Brianna had finished asking the question. He was hot, he was eager, and he was horny! Bryan had no hang ups about sex. He loved it, plain and simple. Plans were made for them to meet the following Saturday night at Bryan's apartment. No one in the small group wanted this event to take place on campus where they might be overheard or even interrupted.

The new week started with Betty rehearsing in her head the way she that she wanted the special night to turn out. She had decided that she would give both guys a blowjob, letting the camera pick it up from several angles so that the other girls would be satisfied that she had paid off her debt. No biggie, no foreplay, and no fucking. She would save that for when she and Craig were alone together. She wanted every move to be set like stone in her head so that she could perform her part like a famous movie star, playing to the audience and winning their approval. She would give them a show that would be capable of winning an Oscar! The more that Betty thought about the upcoming event, the more she began to realize that the idea excited her. Her body grew hot when she pictured it. Her nipples stood out proudly and her pussy dripped with anticipation. Maybe it wouldn't be so bad after all.

Saturday dawned much like any other day and Betty and Brianna followed their regular weekend routine of sleeping until noon before slurping down a pot of coffee between them and going to do their laundry. They passed several of the other dorm girls in the hallway and Betty couldn't help but wonder why none of them had reminded her about the night of her party or asked her about paying her debt for the lost bet. She figured that most of them didn't think that she would ever pay off so they must have decided not to bug her about it. She could imagine the shocked looks on their faces when she invited them over and showed them her video tape. She smiled as she played the whole scenario in her head. She would stand proud and tall. Maybe she would even pass around bowls of popcorn to the stunned guests. They would know that she might have a big mouth but at least she was willing to do what she said she would do, even if she were drunk when she had said it.

As the allotted time drew near, Betty and Brianna dressed carefully, applying their makeup much as they would for any normal double date. Brianna slung the camcorder bag over her shoulder and they headed for Betty's car. Betty was beginning to feel butterflies deep in her tummy. Probably just performance anxiety .... Or could it have been flutters of anticipation?

They reached the apartment, actually a small studio over someone's garage, and walked slowly to the door together. Brianna was thinking that maybe she should admit the truth and stop Betty from doing this tonight. No, she wanted to watch, she wanted to see those large, round tits bouncing up and down, and she wanted to hear Betty moan. Bryan met them at the door. Clearly he had been waiting for their arrival. They could see the huge bulge trying to escape his boxers. As they entered the front room, they found Craig already there and stripped down to his boxers also. His eyes never left the floor. His cheeks were flushed but the girls couldn't tell if it was embarrassment or excitement that lit his face in such a rosy haze. What they could tell was that he also had an aroused prick nearly jumping from its confinement.

Brianna walked over to the corner of the room and began to set up her tripod. She wanted this video to be steady and clear since she planned on using it for years to come. When everything was in order she turned to the others and asked them if they needed directions or if they were just gonna go at it on their own. Getting no answer, she took matters into her own hands and instructed Betty to place herself between the two men on the couch. Betty moved into place. Then Brianna told Craig to warm Betty up and help her to ease into things by kissing her. Craig's lips dipped to Betty's. The kiss started out slow and gentle but the couple clearly started getting into it hot and heavy. Bryan was so turned on by watching them tease and suck each other's tongues that he uttered an explosive, "Fuck!" And proceeded to drop his boxers to the floor. Betty and Craig didn't even notice. Bryan took his place back on the sofa and leaned over Betty's shoulder, his warm lips seeking out the sweetness of her soft neck. She gasped but didn't pull away. She continued to concentrate on Craig's tongue and Bryan thought how wonderful that mouth would feel on his hot, throbbing cock.

He looked over at Brianna behind the camcorder and made a little what-do-I-do-now gesture. She smiled and jerked her head, motioning him to join more actively in the couple's foreplay. Bryan's hands found the hem of Betty's shirt and he lifted it, separating the lovers' lips for just a second as he pulled it over her head and threw it to the floor. Betty shifted her position so that her tits were pressed firmly against Craig's chest. Bryan covered her back with tiny butterfly kisses and she moaned into Craig's mouth as she felt her skin starting to burn with desire. Bryan's hands went around her tiny waist and massaged her flat tummy. He could feel the other man's cock against the back of his knuckles. He heard a moan and was surprised to realize that it was Brianna and not Betty making the sound. He glanced toward her corner of the room and saw her watching the three of them as her hand furiously fucked at her wet pussy. The sight made him so urgent to be inside of a hot cunt that he pawed at Betty's skirt, almost ripping it from her body in his frenzy. Betty stood up to give him easier access and Craig stood right along with her. Bryan's hands reached around Betty's hips and grabbed at Craig's shorts, yanking them to his feet in one swift action. Now the three of them stood totally naked, Betty sandwiched in the middle. She could feel the hot, pulsing cocks pressed against her in want and need and open lust. The thought made her pussy so wet, turned her on so much, that she decided to forget about putting on a show and just fuck the hell out of both men right then and there. She took one arm and cleared the coffee table of all of its contents. Sitting on its edge, Betty lay back until she was prone and motioned the men closer. They were all startled when they heard Brianna's voice. "Wait," she called out, " I want her first. You two can watch." Then she walked over to the camcorder bag and pulled out a huge dildo. As she walked toward Betty, she strapped it onto her hips, giving it the appearance of a raging hardon. She pulled a wire from under the life-like balls and inserted a small circle between her wet pussy lips, firmly securing it over her swollen clit. "This is my favorite toy," she said softly to Betty, "The harder I fuck, the more it stimulates my clit." She glanced at the men to see what effect her words had on them and saw them both pumping their rods furiously, just like she intended to pump that lovely wet pussy being held open to her by Betty's fingers.

She walked between Betty's legs and rammed into her hard, pushing the toy as if she thought Betty's hot tunnel had no bottom. She moaned loudly as she felt her clit massaged. Betty gasped and cried out. Brianna put her arms under Betty's shoulders and her hands came from behind to grip her and hold her in place. She pushed in long, slow strokes, enjoying the feeling of the toy teasing her clit until she could stand it no longer. Betty moaned loudly and wrapped her legs around Brianna's waist, pulling her in hard and fast and both girls screamed out together as they came.

Craig and Bryan wasted no time. They were too hot, too horny, too desperate now, to care who touched who. Bryan moved to the girls' dripping pussies and quickly rammed his rigid rod into Brianna. Brianna was still fucking Betty's cunt with her toy, slowly building them to another earth-shaking climax. Craig moved to the women's heads and Brianna took his aching prick deep into her throat as Betty shifted just enough to pull his balls into her warm, wet mouth. They were so caught up in the lust and passion of what was going on that none of them even thought about the camcorder, still running, taping the whole encounter with perfect precision. Bryan couldn't believe how good Brianna felt tonight. As he pounded into her pussy he could feel the vibrations of her toy against his balls. He moaned loudly and his moan mingled with Craig's.

Craig was going to explode soon. He wondered if he should pull out of Brianna's mouth but when he started to move away a little, she reached for him and pulled him back into her tightly. His balls had grown tight as Betty was sucking them, gaining the energy to forcefully expel his milky cum down Brianna's hungry throat. The harder that Bryan fucked her, the harder that she sucked Craig's rigid rod. He watched the beautiful woman pounding the pussy of his girlfriend. He watched the man at the other end of the table fucking her cunt hard and fast. He looked down and saw the lips wrapped around his aching cock. He felt the hot mouth engulfing his balls, the tongue caressing them with urgency.

Craig screamed out, "I'm cummingggggggggg!" He felt Brianna greedily sucking down every drop of his hot cream. Her throat milked him dry before she pulled off and licked the last drops from her cum-covered lips. Betty continued to suck his balls softly until his breathing had returned to normal. She let him slide out of her mouth and he walked over to sit on the sofa.

With her mouth now free, Brianna leaned down and gave Betty a passionate kiss before she raised her head and began to moan to Bryan. "Oh, Baby, Fuck my pussy. Fill me up, Baby. Stretch my walls." His hurried pace told her that he was nearing his climax and she egged him on with her sweet lips. "Right there, baby. Right there ..... That's the spot! Oh, God, Baby! Fuck me. Fuck me hard! Fuck me Bryan!" She knew that calling his name would send him soaring and she was not disappointed. She felt Bryan's hot cum spurting into her already-wet hole until she could hold no more and it ran out of her and down onto the girl underneath. Bryan pulled on his shorts and joined Craig on the couch.

The two young women came together again with loud moans and screams of passion. When Brianna pulled out of Betty, Bryan reached for the remote, thinking the show was over. As he flipped on the television, they were all surprised as Brianna tossed her toy to the side and dropped to her knees between Betty's open legs. With her slender fingers, she spread apart Betty's dark pink pussy lips. She dove in like she was gorging on a delicious dessert, sucking and slurping, kissing and licking, teasing and tasting the sweet pussy dribbling into her open lips. Betty came over and over until her body threatened to collapse from sheer enjoyment. Staying naked, each girl climbed onto the lap of her man and nestled close, falling into a well-satiated and peaceful sleep.

Several hours later, they awoke and decided a repeat performance was in order. It went so well that they decided to have a grand finale. The four ended up staying at Bryan's the entire weekend, fucking, sucking, and enjoying each other in every way possible. It wasn't until they were on their way back to the dorms that Brianna was faced with reality again.

"Did you get the tape?" Betty asked calmly, showing no sign of the embarrassment she felt about what they had allowed to be seen on the video. "We need to show it as soon as possible and get this whole thing over with." Brianna felt guilty.

Before she knew what she was saying, Brianna had confessed everything to her roommate. She knew that Betty must be really mad because she didn't speak to her all week long. She worried that Betty might even transfer rooms. To her surprise when Saturday came again, Betty told Brianna to wear something sexy. She asked if she could borrow the camcorder and Brianna nodded dumbly. "Am I going with you, Betty?" Betty nodded at her with an evil grin on her face, the kind that makes people wonder what you've been up to. "Where are we going?" Betty didn't answer but simply motioned Brianna toward the car. They walked in silence.

As she was driving down the road, Betty stayed completely quiet, causing Brianna's mind to go crazy with curiosity. Finally they pulled up in front of Bryan's apartment and Brianna asked what they were doing there. Betty smiled again and got out of the car, walking ahead to the door. She didn't knock but walked right in as if she were expected to be there. Brianna followed. As they came to the front room, Brianna could see both Bryan and Craig sitting buck-naked watching television.

"Whaaaa ..... whaaa .....what is going on?" She stammered nervously. "I don't understand."

Betty led her to the coffee table and pushed her down on it until she was lying on her back. Then Betty turned and left the room. When she came back in she was wearing a strap-on much like the one Brianna had used the week before. Brianna gasped loudly. The men kept watching television, not even glancing in their direction.

"Well Brianna," Betty started, "First you screwed me by lying to me about the bet. Then you fucked me with your little toy. I figure you owe me big time so ..... This week, I get to wear the dildo!" As soon as the words had left her lips, the men turned off the television and gave the women their full attention.

The next week they didn't have a fuck-fest. They spent the time moving Craig, Betty, and Brianna into Bryan's apartment, where the four of them lived lustfully together throughout their college years.

SPECIAL

MEMORIES

CHAPTER 11

SPECIAL MEMORIES

Joshua sat beside the hospital bed and looked down into the face of the beautiful woman lying there, looking for any sign of life. He had not left her side since he had brought her to Memorial Hospital yesterday morning. The doctors had told him that things were not looking hopeful and that he should prepare for the worst but Joshua knew that Cindi could not be dying. If she were, he would know it, wouldn't he? He would feel it deep in his soul where they shared all their feelings and thoughts that no one else could. That's how it had been with Jordan and Lucy. He had known, even without words, and he had said his good-byes.

Cindi stirred and the movement caught Joshua's attention. He took her soft, frail hand in his big strong one and gently stroked the back of it with his thumb. Joshua wondered if Cindi could hear him when he bent down and whispered in her ear, telling her how much she meant to him and how he couldn't live without her. His mind wandered back to yesterday morning and that fateful five minutes when Cindi had been hurt.

They had been sitting in the car talking about everything ..... the past, the present, and the future, trying to decide when they would start a family. Even though Cindi was older than he by eight years, it was Joshua who was anxious to have little ones running around the house. He knew that she would stop working and stay home when she was pregnant because high-risk pregnancies ran in her family. Joshua's mind drifted back over time until it landed firmly on the memory of his first sight of Cindi. He had been a second year college student at Hastings University at the time. He and his best friend Jordan had been sitting on the commons when two of the most gorgeous women they had ever seen had walked by. Joshua was immediately taken by Cindi's beauty. Her long, flowing red hair and her emerald green eyes took his breath away. Jordan, on the other hand, loved the dark, exotic looks and almost black eyes of the other girl.

After that day, the boys made a point to be on the commons every day at that time to watch for the two women. Months went by and they began to notice something strange. Whether it was on campus or off campus, every time they saw the two women they were together, heads often tucked close, whispering in each other's ears. One day Joshua shared a thought with Jordan that made them both uncomfortable. What if the gals that they desired so much were actually a "couple?" He may never get the chance to be with the one woman who had made his blood boil and his heart pump furiously every time that he saw her. The thought was almost unbearable and Joshua decided that he and Jordan needed to come up with a plan to meet these gals and make them take notice of their admirers. Research proved helpful, providing the boys with both the women's address and their phone number. It seemed the two gals lived together too. Jordan, being the less shy of the two young college men, finally got up enough nerve to ask his dark beauty out one spring morning. He returned with a dejected look covering his face to explain to Joshua that she had said her "partner" wouldn't want her to date a college boy.

Deciding that they would never get a date with the women that they desired so much, Joshua and Jordan had made a stupid decision. They had decided that they would sneak into the gals' home and remove some small souvenirs to always remind them of their lost loves. It wasn't really stealing Jordan rationalized, it was more like creating memories of a love that may never be. Joshua knew that the reasoning was mottled but he agreed anyway, the thought of a pair of the young woman's undies in his hand making his dick leak with thick pre-cum as it nodded its approval. Silently he promised his hardened member a deep massage with the panties as soon as he had them in his possession. Anxious, the two horny young men agreed to take action the next night, knowing that both gals had late night classes and the house would be empty.

Just as darkness set over the campus, Joshua and Jordan started preparing for their late night excursion. Just in case a neighbor spotted them, they painted their faces with Halloween paint and wore dark clothing. Joshua had painted his face in a sad clown look, thinking to himself how sad he would really be if their plan did not work and he had to come home empty handed. The two men walked the three blocks to the women's house and snuck behind the shrubbery at the front door. Jordan jokingly put out a hand for the doorknob and to the surprise of both, it turned easily and the door swung open with a loud crash. They hurried inside and shut the door behind them. Joshua flipped on the light and they glanced around the room. One of their lady loves must be a little kinky because Jordan held up a pair of handcuffs that he found on a side table. Joshua once again found his cock begging at the thought, spitting its anticipation into his briefs eagerly.

Carefully, the two made their way up the stairs to the second floor. As they entered what appeared to be an empty bedroom, a light flashed on and the two men whirled in shock to find themselves staring into the barrels of two well-aimed revolvers. Behind the guns stood the women that they wanted so much, a look of anger and fear in their entrancing eyes.

"Well, well, what do we have here?" The green-eyed beauty spoke with just the barest hint of a southern drawl. "Peeping Toms? Burglars? Rapists, perhaps?" Her gaze never wavered from Joshua's eyes. "What do you think, partner ..... Should we save ourselves some paperwork and get rid of the problem right now?" Joshua could have sworn that he heard Jordan sob but he couldn't turn his head to look. He was totally consumed by the fire in her eyes mixed with ..... What was that he saw? Amusement! She was laughing at them, amused by their obvious fear.

"Maybe we should let them explain why they are here, sis." The darker gal spoke with an accent too though Jordan was not quite sure what kind it was. She glanced at him from the corner of her eye. "They could have a good reason for breaking into our home, scaring us half to death, and ruining the first night off either of us has had in weeks. On second thought, I think I like your idea better, sis, let's just ....." She let her voice trail off into thin air, leaving their over-active imaginations to do the rest.

Joshua had considered running but he knew he wouldn't get far on his shaky legs. He watched as the other woman directed Jordan into a bedroom and closed the door behind them. Joshua closed his eyes and hoped that a gunshot would not be the next sound he heard. A few minutes later he heard Jordan's confused voice screaming out, begging for mercy. Then he heard his buddy's words dissolve into tears and sobs.

Once they were alone together, Jordan's guard had led him to the bed and pushed him down onto its satin cover. She had made him lay back and swiftly locked his wrists to the headboard with handcuffs that were waiting there. She gagged his mouth with a pair of thong panties from the bedside table before she unbuttoned his shirt and proceeded to tickle his skin with a large feather that she also pulled from the drawer of the table. "My name is Lucy," she whispered as if it were some great secret. "I think you need to be punished for breaking in here tonight." Jordan's fear was overrun by lustful excitement as she reached down and gently pulled at his balls through the material of his pants. "I need some time to think about what your punishment should be. Until I come back, you can lay here and ponder why you did something so stupid and, just in case you try to get away ....." She picked up a pair of scissors and quickly cut off his pants and briefs, laying the cold blade on top of his hot cock for just a second. The unspoken threat scared Jordan into submission. He closed his eyes and waited for her return as soon as he saw the door slam shut.

Joshua had received similar treatment from his captor. He had found out that her name was Cindi. She and Lucy had been roommates, lovers, and partners on the police force for four years now. Cindi had taken all of his clothes off before cuffing him to her bed. Then she had given him the feather torture, careful to cover every inch of exposed skin from his head to the soles of his feet. He was humiliated when his prick stood tall and proud, oozing hot cream from its tip, at the soft touches of the feather. Cindi reached her forefinger out and massaged the liquid into the swollen head of his cock. "Mmmmmmmmm ..... Nice. Does it work as good as it looks?" Joshua just stared at her. He didn't answer because he didn't know. At twenty years old, he was a virgin, always having been too shy to even ask a girl for a date. Cindi chuckled. She dipped her head and ran her tongue around the tip of his cock. "It definitely tastes as good as it looks." She stood up and walked briskly from the room.

When Cindi re-entered the bedroom, she was wearing only her uniform top and a matching cap. In her hand she held a small black baton which she slapped against the open palm of her other hand. Behind her was Lucy, similarly dressed and smiling with her full, sultry lips. They walked over to the bed and Cindi started to speak softly. "Look, sis, doesn't he look delicious?" She moved her baton and ran it from the base of Joshua's quivering dick all the way to its swollen, throbbing head. She held the baton out toward the other gal. "Look what a mess he made on my nightstick. I think he should be punished for that. What do you think?" Lucy nodded and chuckled under her breath. She leaned over, her full, round tits swinging free below her as she took the baton deep into her throat, sucking it like a cock. Finally she raised her head and smiled again. "Time to pay for your crimes young man." Cindi spoke in a voice that showed a sense of authority. She started to pump at her small bat, her tiny hands holding it firmly, and Joshua started to worry as he wondered what she might be thinking of doing with it.

Without speaking another word, Cindi climbed onto the bed with him, her hands on his right side, her knees on his left, and her body crossing over his like a soft bridge of flesh. Lucy came to the edge of the bed right behind Cindi's firm ass and gave her a resounding slap on it, leaving a red hand print on the white skin. Cindi moaned loudly as Lucy brought her nightstick to the wet entrance of her hot pussy. "Fuck me, Baby." She moaned the words softly as she leaned back against the probing baton. Joshua watched as Lucy slid the rod fully into Cindi's wet cunt, fighting to hold back the eruption he felt growing inside of him. "Yesssssss, Baby. Fuck me with that big, thick rod. Harder, baby, faster, fuck me!" Noticing the way that his prick twitched every time she moaned, Cindi inched her body around so that she was parallel with his body, her hot, moist breath teasing his iron rod and her dripping pussy just inches from his face. From his angle, Joshua could see the rod disappearing into her tight hole over and over as her moans grew more and more urgent. "Yeah, Baby, pound my pussy. Pound it hard!" He watched as she shoved her pussy back against Lucy's hand, meeting every stroke with a powerful thrust of her own. Suddenly, Cindi started to yell loudly. "Fuck me, Baby. Don't stop. Don't ..... Don't ..... Don't stop, Baby ..... I'm cumminggggggggggg!" Cindi's body shook like it had been overtaken by some great seizure, the sweat dripping from her body and splashing onto Joshua's. The whole scene frightened him a little but it also made him very horny. His dick was screaming for attention now and he tried desperately to think thoughts that would force it into peaceful submission before the more-than-likely insane women saw it and decided to punish him further.

He waited for Cindi to get off the bed but was surprised when she reached back and removed the gag from his aching jaws. Before he had time to form words, she had pushed her wet pussy firmly against his lips. "Lick me!" The tone of her voice left no room for argument. After a few minutes, Joshua found the sweet, salty taste of her pussy becoming more and more appetizing and he was starting to lick with gusto when she spoke again. "Suck my clit. NOW!" He sucked and was rewarded with her loud moans. "Stick your tongue inside my hot cunt. Deeper. I said deeper!" She practically bellowed the command and Joshua drove his tongue into her as deep as he could go. "Good boy. Now keep it there." He thought ..... Keep it there? For how long? Joshua was beginning to wonder where all of this torture was leading. Cindi held out her hand to Lucy and helped the other girl to straddle Joshua's rigid rod. She held it straight up as Lucy lowered her warm, moist, cave onto it, swallowing every inch until she rested on his balls. "Now, buddy, fuck my baby. Make her moan. Make her scream. Fuck her!" Apparently Cindi liked giving commands, liked having control over others, and liked being the one in charge of every situation. Joshua realized that his fear had faded away and in its place he felt wonder, excitement, and amazement at all the new sensations his body was experiencing. He had masturbated in the shower before but his wet hand hadn't given him the same overwhelming electrical tension that Lucy's hot pussy gripping his cock was giving him. She sat with her back to Cindi, her face pointing toward the foot of the big bed. Cindi's hands wrapped around Lucy's middle and she cupped the full breasts with careful intent, pinching the erect nipples between her thumb and fingers. Lucy groaned. "Fuck her now!" Cindi barked out the order loudly and Joshua began to move his hips.

Cindi began to ride Joshua's tongue with wild abandon, fucking him harder with every bounce. Before long her movements mirrored those of Lucy who was fucking his huge, raging hardon with her hot, wet cunt. Joshua closed his eyes and listened to the moans as he found himself fucking the women back, his tongue diving deeply into the warm cave of Cindi's pussy, his rigid rod drilling Lucy's tight hole with forceful strokes. He could feel the familiar sensation of building excitement deep in his loins. His body begged for release, the urge getting stronger as he heard each woman cumming with groans and gasps. Cindi stayed planted firmly on his tongue, her pussy muscles gripping him over and over as his body tensed, jerked, and exploded with a force that threatened to propel Lucy right off his pulsing cock. Finally Cindi climbed off of his cum-drenched face and stood beside the bed peering down at him. She put her hand out to Lucy and pulled her off the exhausted man's body. Joshua closed his eyes ..... Peace ..... Rest ..... Sleep. But these things were not meant to be for the cuffed captive just yet. To his surprise, Cindi stood and walked to the door, picking up her handgun as she went. She never lifted it, never pointed it at Joshua, never threatened him in any way and yet he felt that he had no choice other than to obey when she spoke.

"Lucy, Baby, uncuff him." She smiled with a look of total satiation flooding over her delicate features, lighting her face with a dazzling brilliance. "Okay, man, walk into the hallway." Joshua walked. "Faster! Move it! We have work to do. Good boy. Now, go into the bedroom at the end of the hall." Joshua knew that was the room that Jordan had been taken to and he began to move more reluctantly, not knowing what to expect behind the big, brown door. Lucy walked ahead of him and slowly pushed open the door. Cindi nudged Joshua's back and as he stumbled into the dimly lit room he saw his best friend lying naked on the bed, his mouth gagged, his eyes wide with fear, and his hands cuffed to the headboard. Joshua started to speak to him, to tell him not to be afraid, but Cindi quickly tied a gag around his slightly parted lips and pushed him into the chair at the side of the bed. His hands were bound by what appeared to Joshua to be silk bathrobe belts and his ankles were secured to the chair legs by fuzzy-covered cuffs. One girl took each of his knees and they spread his legs wide, tying his knees to the side rails of the chair and leaving his prick standing proud, refusing to bow its head even when in this state of confusion.

Joshua wondered what was going to happen now but he didn't wait long to find out. As soon as they knew he was tied securely, the two women took off their uniform tops and climbed onto the bed with Jordan. Joshua tried to close his eyes, tried not to watch, tried not to let his dick jump and jerk in anticipation but he was totally enraptured by the show these two women were giving him. He sat there staring openly and with growing ..... Enjoyment ..... as his best buddy was treated to an earth-shattering, mind-boggling blowjob. Cindi sucked and lapped at his tight balls and Lucy swallowed his cock until there was nothing left outside of her warm, moist mouth except the balls that Cindi was sampling with her soft lips. Jordan writhed and squirmed under their exploring hands and lips. He moaned so loudly that the gag fell from between his lips. After what seemed like hours of sweet torture but actually was only about fifteen minutes, Jordan had erupted over and over as each woman swallowed her fill of his hot, thick cream.

Cindi left the bed and came over to where Joshua sat. "Have you learned your lesson yet, bad boy?" She almost sounded like she was serious but Joshua definitely detected a lilt of amusement in her words. He nodded his head vigorously. "No, I don't think you have, wicked man." She dropped to her knees in front of Joshua and wet one of her fingers in her mouth. Quickly but gently she slid it into his ass where she proceeded to massage his prostate with considerable pressure until she felt his balls starting to tense. Then Cindi sucked his balls deep into her mouth and the sensation of the warmth and wetness mingled with the sucking motion pushed Joshua into another riveting orgasm. She let his breathing return to normal and then she untied him and instructed him to climb onto the bed. Joshua moved slowly, careful not to let his naked body touch that of his best friend's, knowing that neither of them would ever feel comfortable with each other again if anything physical happened between them. All of his worries were brought to rest in the next few minutes.

Both women joined them in the bed and positioned the men with such precision that they could have been re-enacting a crime scene. Joshua's hands were tied to the foot of the bed with the robe belts that had kept him in his seat earlier. His legs were lifted high to allow Lucy to stretch out Jordan's legs beneath them. Then Joshua's legs were lowered over Jordan's, each one crossing one of the other man's and forming an x where their flesh met. Joshua thought about lifting his head enough to look down at his friend but his view would have been quickly cut off. Cindi climbed onto his lap, facing away from him, and lowered her dripping cunt onto his hard, willing shaft. Joshua moaned and heard it echoed as Lucy mounted Jordan in the same way. Now the two young, hard dicks were nestled warm and wet inside of the women's tight holes. The two women sat facing each other as each began to move her hips in a sensual dance of sexual want.

Soon Joshua and Jordan had forgotten the uncomfortableness of the situation they found themselves in, as the pleasure being given to their bodies grew stronger. Lucy and Cindi were both moaning loudly as they each tried to fuck their partner harder than the other. The two women were leaning toward each other, Cindi sucking one of Lucy's marble-like rosy nipples into her hungry mouth. Lucy leaned her head back, her long hair swaying against the skin on Jordan's thighs, tickling it and causing shock waves to engulf his heated groin. Her hands went around Cindi's back, holding the other woman close, then slowly slipped between them to caress Cindi's swollen tits. Joshua and Jordan were so excited by the sight of the two women making love to each other, the feeling of their wet pussies engulfing them, the sounds of their moans and groans of passion, that the two men started to participate fully. Every time one of them would shove his rigid rod up deeper into his rider, the other one would feel the thrust through the tension in his legs. Even feeling that tension and knowing that he was feeling Jordan drilling into Lucy made Joshua feel more and more horny.

"Fuck me. Fuck me hard!" Cindi yelled out the words just as she released Lucy's nipple and offered the other girl hers to taste. Her hand came down with a light, stinging slap on Joshua's outer thigh but instead of hurting, it made the young man want to shoot his hot load deep into her cunt. "I said FUCK ME!" She screamed out the words this time and Joshua found his hips thrusting up so hard that she almost bounced off his throbbing dick. Cindi leaned back and reached behind herself, loosening Joshua's ties and setting him free. Lucy must have done the same because soon the two women were on their backs side by side with the men pounding their pussies from above. The bed was soaked with the sweat of passionate bodies fucking and sucking. Joshua could feel Jordan's shoulders as they brushed his own and soon the contact led them to move in perfect time with each other. Each man pushed into his woman's grasping pussy hard and deep, pulled out slow and easy, and then rammed his rod back in with a moan. Cindi and Lucy had their heads turned toward each other and kissed passionately as they were being fucked, each of them playing with the other girl's tits. The sight was too much for the young men and soon both of them were shooting hard, their thick cum filling up the hole that was offered and running over onto the sheets.

Joshua groaned and collapsed on top of Cindi who wrapped her legs firmly around his waist and whispered in his ear, "Not yet, Baby. I want you to keep fucking me." Her hips began to grind against him and his tired cock, which had been softening inside of her, stood up and paid attention. "Oh, yeah, that's it Baby ..... Fuck me again. Drill me hard. Shove that hard, hot dick in as far as you can go. Do it NOW!" Her words had the desired effect and soon Joshua was growling like an animal with the effort of shoving deeper and deeper into the demanding woman. He felt the bed move but he didn't pay much attention until he felt soft hands massaging his ass as he fucked Cindi hard. Looking over he saw Lucy, once again on top of Jordan, her eyes smoldering with lust as she fucked his hard-as-a-rock rod. She had one hand behind her playing with Jordan's balls and with the other hand, she caressed Joshua's ass. When they came this time, the four young people all came together in one terrific climax.

Lying all curled together in a satiated heap on the bed, Joshua's thoughts wandered to the future, imagining where things would go from here. He also wondered why tonight had happened to begin with.

"Oh, Baby, that was great. It was everything we had hoped. My pussy is so happy now, I swear its purring!" Cindi spoke in a soft drawl, like a sleepy, contented kitten after a warm bowl of milk. "Where did you get these two at, Baby? More importantly, what did this little dream cost us?" Jordan was confused by her words until he heard Lucy speak.

"Wait!" Lucy almost shouted. "Do you mean you didn't set this fantasy up, Cindi?" Cindi shook her head, a look of fear starting to etch its way onto her lovely face, replacing the joy that had been there a few minutes before. "Cindi, this is no time to joke, Baby." Lucy's voice took on a panicked, pleading tone. "You know these guys, right?" Again Cindi shook her head hard. "Oh my God! Baby, if you didn't do it and I didn't do it then ....." Lucy's voice trailed off into a small sob. "Cindi, these two were really robbing us and we just fucked them all night long!"

Then the whole story tumbled out and Joshua and Jordan listened with growing fascination. Cindi and Lucy had been discussing a special fantasy for several months, even joking about one of them setting it up with a couple of her male friends so that they could live it out. In the fantasy, the two girls were home alone when a couple of male robbers broke in. Instead of taking them to the police station, the two women would hold them captive and use them sexually for the night. That night when they had heard the loud crash right at their front door, each woman had assumed that the other one had set something up with her friends and left the door unlocked for them to "break" in. Because they each thought it was a surprise from the other woman, each played along, willingly doing her part as convincingly as possible to make the fantasy work. And it had worked with only one little fault ..... These were real robbers and not friends helping out!

Joshua almost dissolved into laughter as he watched the look of horror cross the women's faces. Their guns were out of reach and here they lay, totally naked, held in the strong arms of the two men who had come to rob them. Unable to let them fear anymore, he and Jordan explained how they came to be there. He held nothing back, even explaining how he was only hoping to steal some of Cindi's undies to keep to always remind him of her. The sun rose to the tinkling laughter of the two beautiful angels in the bed. It wasn't the only thing that rose that morning. The men each sported a raging hardon, evidence of their raging hormones and their devilish horniness for these gals.

After that night, they had acted out many fantasies together until yesterday morning just after breakfast. They had been riding down the road, talking about their futures together, and trying to decide when they would marry, when they would start a family. Both Lucy and Cindi wanted kids and they had everything all worked out in their heads. A double wedding sometime in the spring, two years of love and lust and fun as a foursome, and then they would settle down and concentrate on making babies. Everything fit into a nice, neat little package. They were so busy making plans that no one saw the big truck that decided the stop sign wasn't really meant for him. He plowed into the side of their car with enough force to send them spinning across the road. They finally stopped after they skidded against a mailbox. Unfortunately, the box's wooden pole had been broken off and pushed through the rear window, stabbing through the back of Lucy and running her through to impale Jordan's heart as the two sat embraced. One look in the back seat and Joshua knew that his two friends were gone forever. Moaning from the passenger seat reminded him of Cindi and he looked over to find her bruised, cut, and breathing hard, but at least she was breathing.

Joshua's car had been badly smashed but when he put it in gear, it moved jerkily. Afraid to wait for an ambulance, he had driven to the hospital as quickly as his damaged car would take him and that was where he had been ever since, at Cindi's side. She had awaked once, just long enough to ask about Lucy and Jordan. Joshua had held her tight in his strong arms as he told her the bad news, their tears mingling together as they grieved for their lost loved ones. Then she fallen back into a deep sleep and she hadn't opened her beautiful eyes again.

Joshua came out of his reverie with a start. He thought, just for a split second, that Cindi's hand had squeezed his. Was it wishful thinking? He wasn't sure at that point but he lay his head on her chest and was comforted at the steady rhythm of her heartbeat and the smooth sounds of her breathing. He must have fallen asleep there because when he opened his eyes again, the room was in total darkness. He felt Cindi move beneath his head and wondered what made her stir so restlessly. When she coughed, Joshua jumped up, afraid that she might be choking until he realized she was just clearing her throat.

"Hey college boy." She sounded so frail that Joshua knew he never wanted to let her out of his sight again. "Lets get married as soon as I get out of this prison, okay?" Her voice was still thick with tears for the friends they had lost. Joshua nodded, forgetting that Cindi couldn't see him in the blackness. He wanted to marry her. He wanted to hold her. He wanted to comfort her and share her sorrows. He wanted to love her forever. Cindi reached deep down inside herself and listened to Joshua's unspoken words. Tears ran down her face as she felt what he had felt ..... the fear of dying, the horror of losing two of his best friends, the overwhelming terror of the possibility of losing the one person he couldn't live his life without.

Joshua turned on the light and saw Cindi crying on the bed. She looked up at him and smiled through her tears. "Baby, I think its time we give up our fantasy life and start to live our real life. I love you, Joshua, yesterday, today, tomorrow, and on into eternity ....." She stopped and gulped, swallowing away her emotion before continuing, "On second thought, Baby, we have it all already. You are my reality and you are the only fantasy I will ever need. Joshua walked over to the bed and hugged Cindi tight against him, wondering if she ever fantasized about fucking in a hospital.

HOSPITAL - "ITY"

CHAPTER

12

HOSPITAL - "ITY"

We were on a road trip when it happened ..... the hottest sex I had ever had in my life. My boyfriend, Marshall was traveling with my brother, George and me. We were visiting several states, trying to see what wonders this wonderful country of ours held. George had always been clumsy, even as a child, and so it came as no surprise to me when he stumbled while climbing out of the backseat of the van and landed flat on his face in the dirt. He laughed and made some lame joke as he jumped up and dusted himself off, apparently no worse for the wear.

It was three days and two states later before I noticed that George was moving slower than his usual break-neck speed and that he seemed to be sporting a slight limp. When I asked him about it he hung his head and pulled up the right pant leg. His ankle was an angry black and purple mixture with spots of red, blue, and green thrown in here and there. It was swollen to nearly twice the size of his other ankle and clearly it was hurting him badly. When I asked George why he hadn't said anything he told me that all of his life his little "accidents" had managed to ruin my plans for doing things that I wanted to do and he was not about to let that happen this time. He can be so sweet sometimes that I forget he is my brother and actually start to think of him as being human.

When Marshall found out what was going on he looked for a local person and got directions to the nearest hospital. As we pulled up to the emergency room door I read the bright sign out loud. "WELCOME TO GOODFEEL GENERAL HOSPITAL it read, where we make sure everyone goes home feeling good." I chuckled in amusement at the clever name of this small town medical center. Marshall and I helped George from the van and practically dragged him into the emergency room. We expected to be waiting forever but the intake nurse met us at the glass doors. "Oh, you poor baby." She almost sang the words with a cute little lilt to her voice. "What happened to you?" George's face screwed up in an expression of exaggerated pain. I know its amazing but my wonderful little brother, who had not shut his mouth for one second of the drive to the hospital, suddenly lost the power of speech. The pretty, dark-haired, musical nurse reached over and put her small hand against the side of his cheek. "Don't worry sweetie." Again she spoke very softly. "We will take extra good care of you here, I absolutely promise." She led us into a large room with shelves of books at one end and a roped off area full of toys. She sat beside George, one hand casually lying on his upper thigh as she asked question after question, carefully writing down the response to each. When she had a thorough medical history on George, as well as all of his insurance information and current address and phone number, the beautiful nurse stood up and walked toward the door. Reaching it she glanced back and beamed at George, who immediately slouched in his seat and let a look of overwhelming pain take over his face. "We will be with you in just a few minutes. Try to relax and think happy thoughts."

Then to my amazement, she brought her fingers to her lips and blew a kiss directly at George's face. With a swoosh of her hips she disappeared through the door and we were left alone in the room.

We didn't have long to wait. Less than five minutes later, a breath-takingly handsome orderly came in with a wheelchair and lifted George into it without speaking a word. I stood to follow but the orderly shook his head at me, motioning for me to sit again and wait. I wanted to go with my brother but I knew that the injury wasn't life threatening and that we would most likely be on our way within a few hours so I sank back into the overstuffed chair I had been occupying. I lay my head back, closing my eyes for a little rest. No, a little rest certainly wouldn't hurt any of us I thought as I drifted off to sleep. I was startled awake by an unfamiliar voice. Marshall must have been sleeping too because when I opened my eyes I saw him rubbing at his, a dazed and confused look on his face. We looked up at the doctor now standing over us.

"Miss Hanson, I presume?" He offered his hand. I nodded and let him engulf my own hand in his, giving it a friendly shake. "Your brother was lucky in a way. While he did somehow manage to put several hairline cracks in his ankle, he didn't break any bones so with a little caution and common sense, he will heal very quickly." My eyes were glued to his full lips, taking in every word as if it were a national emergency we were discussing. "He will have to spend the night so that we can make sure the ice packs and splint help to bring the swelling under control and I have already given him a mild pain reliever. If the pain doesn't go away soon, we may have to give him something a little stronger." I found thoughts racing through my head ..... *Forget George, you sexy doc, give me something a little stronger, like you!* I had no sooner thought it than he looked directly into my eyes and said, "And, of course, if you need anything, anything at all, don't hesitate to ask." I nodded dumbly. "You can go in to see your brother for a few minutes now if you would like to."

Marshall and I tiptoed into the room so that we wouldn't wake George. He looked so frail lying there, his hurt foot propped up on a pillow. He moaned a little in his sleep and we hurried out to let him rest. A nurse met us in the hallway. She told us that there was no need for us to leave, no need to hunt a motel close by, and no need to sleep in the van tonight. The hospital had "special" waiting rooms for visitors who needed to spend the night and she had reserved one for us, knowing that we were from out of town. We thanked her profusely and followed her happily down the hall. She stopped in front of a small door marked Visitor Room #1 and swung it open.

As she flipped the switch, light filled the room and I gasped at what I saw. This room was nicer than most of the motels we had stayed in over the last few weeks. Against one wall were a mini refrigerator and a microwave. There was a large screen television, a radio, a tape player, and a cd player. There were two beds and they sat one on either side of an alcove, looking inviting with their soft, puffy comforters and numerous pillows. There was a small table in the middle of the room with stacks of games on it and there was a bookcase full of books against the wall between the beds. Wow, too bad George was only going to be here one night! I didn't know then what a night it was going to be. The nurse said for us to sleep well and to enjoy our visit. "We like everyone who comes to our hospital to go home feeling good, whether it's a patient or a visitor."

After she left us alone, I fixed Marshall a tuna sandwich and helped myself to a cheese one. We found an adequate supply of soda cooling in the bottom of the fridge and so we sat at the small table and enjoyed our meal in silence. When the last crumb was just a memory, Marshall suggested we move to the beds and watch some television. He handed me the remote and I flipped on the set to find a young couple in the middle of some pretty passionate sex. I turned the channel and found an older couple, not quite as frenzied with need, but still hot enough to make my panties grow damp. After the fourth channel I gave up, tossing Marshall the remote. It seemed like all I could find on this set was sex stories. I mean, I love sex, but how embarrassing would it be for one of the nice nurses to return and find us watching smut on their TV? Or maybe we would be excited enough by then to actually be screwing when she opened the door. The thought probably wouldn't have bothered me so much if I hadn't noticed right away that this wonderful room that had everything else had no lock on the door.

I took off my clothes and pulled back the heavy comforter, climbing under the spring-fresh scented sheets beneath. They felt so cool and crisp against my skin. I fell asleep with Marshall's voice echoing in my head. "Ohhhhhhh, yeahhhhhhhhh, baby. Free food, free beds, and all the free porn we can handle!" I pulled the sheets over my head.

I'm not sure exactly how long I had been asleep. I'm not really sure what woke me either but the room was dark so I closed my eyes again, thinking some unremembered dream had probably startled me awake. Again I was nudged awake. This time I knew what had done it. The sheet had been pulled away from my body and I could feel moist, heated breath tickling the skin of my lower abdomen just before I felt soft lips touching my neatly-trimmed mound. I couldn't believe that Marshall was willing to have any kind of sex here, knowing there was no lock on the door, knowing that anyone could walk in and catch us at any time. The possibility of getting caught with my pussy quivering in his eager mouth brought me wide awake and filled every pore of my body with sexual tension. I have never been an exhibitionist and I didn't really want anyone watching my most intimate encounters but I have to admit, the thought that it could happen excited me more than I would have ever imagined it could.

Warm hands slid up my thighs and two thumbs pulled my swollen pussy lips apart just seconds before I felt his stiff tongue drive deep into my throbbing hole. I tried not to moan, not to bring attention to the fact that we were not sleeping. I didn't want someone passing by to hear us and open the door, breaking the magical spell of sensuality that we were living in. His hands felt so strong, so urgent. They were everywhere all at one time, massaging and caressing as his mouth and tongue eagerly sucked and fucked my dripping cunt. I lifted my hips, pushing my pussy into his face. He grabbed my ass and pulled me closer, fucking my hot hole with his rigid tongue, going in deeper and harder with every thrust. I couldn't hold back my passionate groans any longer and I moaned loudly, "Oh, Baby, I didn't know you liked to play doctor." I chuckled at my own remark but my breath caught in my throat as I heard Marshall reply ..... From the other side of the room where his bed was!

I reached out and fumbled around, searching for the lamp on the bedside table. I switched it on and looked down between my legs to see the handsome orderly from earlier. He never raised his head. He never even acknowledged that he should stop. He just kept fucking me with that wonderful tongue while he slid his thumb over my throbbing clit and pressed gently, starting to rub in tiny circles. I thought Marshall would kill him but looking over, I could see my sexy boyfriend was already occupied. His hands were buried in the long, blonde hair of a young woman in a candy striper's outfit and his cock was buried to the balls in her slender throat. She was sucking his dick like there was nothing else she liked to do better in the world and he clearly did not want her to stop. Watching him disappearing between her swollen lips over and over made me hornier than I had been in a long time and, catching Marshall's eye from across the room, I indicated that I wanted to continue. He nodded his agreement just before I saw his whole body tense. I knew that he was cumming by the way the little blonde had to keep swallowing over and over as he held her head down tight against his lap. My own hands slid to the back of the orderly's head and pulled his mouth tight against my aching pussy as I shoved my hips up hard, slapping against his face. He rolled his eyes up to look into mine without ever moving his head. I saw a look of pure pleasure cross his face as he drilled his tongue deep into my hot, dripping pussy hole, sending me into crashing waves of sweet release. I looked over and saw that the young candy striper still held Marshall's now-limp dick gently in her mouth. Her lips were shiny with his cum. She didn't move but watched the orderly that had been pleasuring me until at last he pulled his tongue out and stood over me.

I wasn't quite sure what to expect next. I guess I was kind of thinking they would probably leave now and I would wake up the next morning to find it had all been the erotic dream of my emotionally and physically exhausted mind. It wasn't a dream. The orderly nodded at the candy striper and then dropped his pants to the floor, revealing the biggest cock I had ever seen in my life. He was hard as steel and I was almost afraid that if he touched me with that rigid rod, he would hurt me ..... Almost. But I was also very turned on and curious to know what being pumped by a piston of that size would feel like. I followed his gaze and saw the blonde poised gracefully over Marshall's raging hardon, holding the swollen head of his saluting prick at the wet entrance to her pussy. The orderly positioned his huge member against the open lips of my cunt and, with a nod toward each other, he began to push into my hole as she swallowed Marshall into hers. God, I was so hot, feeling his prick filling me up, stretching out the inner walls of my pussy, pounding into me hard and fast. I watched as the slender woman rode Marshall, building a rhythm as she fucked him, her hands resting on his broad chest.

Marshall was moaning louder as he started thrusting his hips up to meet the wet pussy pounding down on him. His hands slid around her slender waist and pulled her down hard as he shoved up into her. She lifted her hands slowly to her bouncing tits and started to play with her rosy nipples. As I watched them fucking together, I found my own movements getting more desperate and more frantic. I wrapped my legs around the orderly's waist and used them to pull him into my begging cunt. He dropped his weight on me and I felt my tits smashed against his hard chest, the springy hairs tickling my nipples as they slid against me.

"Fuck me. Fuck me hard!" I moaned out the words and heard Marshall's animal-like groan in reply. He was grunting with the effort of holding back his orgasm and I wondered why he didn't want to cum. I looked over and saw his hand reaching across the small space between us and suddenly I knew. Since Marshall and I had become a couple, we had never cum with anyone besides each other until tonight. He still wanted us to cum together! I held out my arm and entwined my fingers with his, watching as a brilliant smile lit up his sexy face.

"Cum with me, Baby!" I shouted out the words as I felt myself getting closer to climax. "Fuck that pussy until you cum!" I could feel the tension in his outstretched arm. I could see the jerking movements in his thrusting hips. "I'm gonna cum, Baby. Cum with me, please, cum with me!"

My body tensed and started to quiver under the vigorous drilling of the orderly's large dick. The man fucked like a machine on ever-ready batteries, long and hard and deep. I knew I was about to explode and from what I could see, Marshall was almost ready too. I nudged him one last time to join me, "Cum with me, Marshall. Now, Baby ..... I ..... I ..... I'm cummingggggggggg now, Baby!" My grip tightened on Marshall's fingers and he made some kind of animalistic grunt as he also reached his climax. The pretty candy striper collapsed against his chest but made no effort to remove his satiated cock from her dripping hole.

The orderly waited until the grasping spasms of my cunt came to a full stop before he climbed off of me. He sat between my legs and started to rub my over-stimulated clit until it swelled into a hard marble again. I could see the candy striper between Marshall's legs, her slender hand coaxing his cock back into action as her lips caressed his tight balls. I thought that these two must really love sex and I wondered how many times Marshall and I would be sucked and fucked by these two people who as of yet had not made a single sound. I felt the warmth between my legs growing again, shooting its electrical shocks throughout my body. I watched as Marshall's cock grew hard and stood tall under the soft hands of the other woman. To my surprise, when she had him fully erect, she dropped to the floor beside of his bed and held his shaft straight up in the air. Then she turned her face toward the orderly and smiled broadly, nodding her head. He immediately stopped teasing my clit and stood up. He stooped and lifted me in one fell swoop, carrying me over to where Marshall lay on the other bed. As he lowered me to sit, the candy striper guided Marshall's hot cock into my dripping pussy hole.

His dick slid into me easily, filling me until I thought I would burst. God, he felt so good. The orderly's hands gripped my waist and started to lift me up and down on Marshall's cock. It didn't take long before my newly excited body took the hint and started to move on its own, falling into the rhythm of a sensual dance we had shared many times before. The orderly took the candy striper by the hand and they walked toward the door, stopping to smile back at us over their shoulders before they finally left.

Marshall and I spent the next hour fucking each other until our bodies finally gave out and we fell asleep in each other's arms, his semi-hard cock still held comfortably inside my overworked pussy. As I slept, I kept dreaming about different kinds of sex with the two mysterious visitors who had brought us so much pleasure.

The next morning we woke to the beautiful sight of the sunrise shining in the open window. I looked at Marshall and he looked at me. "Baby, did what I think happened really happen here last night?" I whispered the question. "Or was I just having an extremely erotic wet dream?"

The very corners of Marshall's sexy mouth started to turn upwards and he whispered back, " Well, Baby, if you think we had one hell of a night full of incredible sex ..... If you think we were fucked by two gorgeous strangers oozing passion from every pore of their bodies ..... If you think we fucked like wild animals until we collapsed from exhaustion ...." He stopped and drew in a deep breath before he continued, "It happened, Baby. Believe me, it happened!"

Just then we heard a knock at the door and a small, sweet voice told us that George was being released from the doctor's care and we could pick him up in the lobby in fifteen minutes. Marshall and I straightened the beds, cleaned the room, and headed toward the lobby. George was sitting in a wheelchair, a bewildered look on his face. He was no longer in pain but he did seem to be lost in his own thoughts. He smiled up at me kind of half-heartedly as I started to push him toward the glass sliding doors. As I walked, I glanced down the hallway and straight into the eyes of the orderly from the night before. He never acknowledged that he knew me but merely smiled a little smile and started to whistle as he continued pushing the cart full of trays in front of him.

We were almost to the door when the young, blonde-haired candy striper ran over to Marshall. She pushed a note into his hand and stretched up to place her lips on his cheek in a soft kiss. George really looked befuddled now and I knew he was wondering what that little scene was all about. Maybe some day we would tell him ..... maybe. For now it was a night for Marshall and me to remember, a night for us to savor, a night for us to replay in numerous passionate fantasies. It was a night to be kept private, a memory to cherish, a secret to further bond us together as a couple.

Marshall pulled the van around to the curb where George and I were waiting for him. As we lifted my dear brother into the back seat, a nurse that I had not seen before came out to retrieve the wheelchair. She stepped quickly up into the back of the van and kissed George full on the lips, then just as quickly hopped down and was gone. "I know I was on a lot of painkillers last night." George began talking to no one in particular. "But I had the hottest, wildest dream. You wouldn't believe how real it was. In it I was sleeping peacefully on my hospital bed when something woke me up. When I was finally wide-awake I realized that this hot nurse was having the time of her life sucking like a Hoover on my candy stick. I mean, she really got into it and she had me cumming in no time flat." George stopped and started to talk more softly. "I guess that sounds really silly, huh? Well, anyway, she obviously wasn't done with me even after I came because she climbed onto my chest and masturbated until she came, soaking my chest with her hot juices. I got so excited that my cock stood up begging for more of her attention. She finally climbed on top of me and fucked me until I nearly passed out. Then she just left. Funny thing is this ..... She never spoke a single word. Not one word, sis, can you believe that?"

"Coming from your warped little brain I can believe anything, Georgey porgey. You always have had a great imagination."

I slammed the sliding door shut and climbed into the front seat beside Marshall. As he revved the engine, he reached down to the console between our seats and picked up the note he had been given by the cute blonde. He read it and chuckled before handing it to me. It was an invoice for the services of the night before marked paid in full. On the bottom of the paper, in bright fire-engine red ink, were neatly printed the words ..... Thank you for choosing Goodfeel General Hospital for all of your medical needs, where we make sure everyone goes home feeling good.

CAN'T BEAT THE FEET

Martin and I met for the first time when I was on a photo shoot in Florida. The second day there our regular photographer, Gail, had gotten a bad case of sunstroke and had to be rushed to the hospital. Samson's Shoes, the client that we were doing the ad for, insisted that we either finish the assignment on time or else they were going to take advantage of the "out" clause in our contract and take their business to another advertising agency. Being a small, family-owned business, and knowing that Samson's was one of our biggest clients, we decided that we would hire an outside photographer for just this one shoot.

Dad had stopped by that morning to tell me all about the new guy. I guess I kind of pictured him in my head as some sweet old gentleman who loved taking pictures and was feisty enough to refuse to retire. I don't know why I had built up that picture of him but when he arrived on the set that morning I was very surprised. In front of me stood one of the handsomest men I had ever seen. He looked close to me in age and he was just short enough that I could look directly into his gorgeous brown eyes. I know, I know. Models are supposed to be tall with long, slender legs, but I am a different kind of model. I am a foot model. Don't laugh. It's true. I model things like shoes, socks, toe rings, and ankle bracelets. If it decorates the human foot, I have probably modeled it for someone's catalog. In our town alone we have three billboards with my feet on them.

I stumbled, no pun intended, into the world of foot modeling when I was about seventeen years old. Marie, a close friend of mine since kindergarten, had wrangled me into going with her to an audition for a local television commercial. I sat waiting, rather impatiently, on the edge of the stage with my legs crossed and swinging one bare foot. One of the young men in charge of attempting to maintain some sense of control during the auditions came over to ask me to take a seat in the audience and, quite by accident , I kicked him hard. He let out a little yelp of pain and doubled over. I was afraid I may have hurt him but in just a few minutes he had grabbed my foot and lifted it high, exclaiming loudly at its perfection. I laughed at his silliness but it didn't take him long to convince me that he was not joking and soon I found myself with a new career. When Dad saw how well things were going for me, he changed the specialty of his advertising agency to hands and feet and we have been partners ever since.

Anyway, there we all were, standing around a giant beach ball and sipping lemonade when Martin first came on set. He didn't even look into my eyes. His gaze went straight to my feet. I remember thinking how much this man must put into his work. He did however, manage to offer his hand for a quick shake and to mumble something that may have been a greeting if I actually could have heard it. I decided right then and there that I was not going to like him. He was too withdrawn, too different from Gail and her bubbly ways. Still, I couldn't help being drawn to his sexy eyes like a moth to a flame.

Working with Martin was a new experience for me. He didn't just bark out orders and expect me to fall in line. He would carefully lift my foot and put it where he wanted it, tilting it and checking the shadows and light to make sure it looked its best. Every once in awhile he would call a short break and drag a chair over beside me, pulling my aching feet into his lap and massaging them gently. I began to look forward to seeing him on the set every morning. Maybe we had gotten off to a bad start. Maybe working with him wasn't going to be so bad after all.

Toward the end of the week, I realized that the shoot was almost over. I felt an unfamiliar sadness deep inside at the thought of not seeing Martin again. When he asked me out to dinner the last night to celebrate a successful shoot, I said yes before he was even done the question, then reddened at how eager I must have sounded. It was the first time that I let myself admit that I was eager to spend time with Martin, both on and off the set.

He took me to a cozy little restaurant along the beach and we watched the sun set from the balcony before we took our seats. We both ate very light, just fruits and cheeses, and I knew that he was here for the company just like I was and not for the food. I felt warm inside knowing that Martin wanted my company in more than a professional way. After dinner we walked hand in hand along the beach, gentle waves lapping at our feet as we strolled. We moved just far enough away from the restaurant that we could still see the lights shining like little fireflies but the noisy din of the diners had faded into the background. Martin took off his jacket and laid it out on the sand, sitting and pulling me down to rest beside him. I felt his hand resting on my thigh and I sighed in contentment.

After several peaceful minutes, Martin's hand began to slide down my leg and I wondered with some nervousness if he was heading to explore more ..... private ..... areas. To my surprise, he passed the hem of my skirt and continued to move downward until he had my foot in his strong hands. Slowly he removed the sandal I was wearing and lifted my tiny foot to his lips. I felt him kissing the back of my heel, his lips burning a trail around my ankle. I had never thought of my foot as an erogenous zone before but the more he fondled, caressed, and kissed it, the hotter I got. My whole body was responding enthusiastically to the attention he was giving my feet and I gasped out loud at the wetness I felt growing between my thighs.

Martin's tongue teased the tip of my toes and I opened my eyes, looking down into his beautiful brown ones that were smiling up at me. I watched as he sucked each toe into his warm mouth before covering the top of my foot with kisses. I had never had a man pay attention to my feet before unless it was the client inspecting the merchandise. I was rather enjoying relaxing, the wind blowing through my hair, letting Martin treat me to these pleasures I had never known.

I lay back in the sand as his lips moved slowly but steadily upward. My hands slid down across my tummy and grasped the top of my skirt, inching it up to show more of my creamy white skin, tempting his lips to keep exploring. At least I would have one night of passion with this wonderful man before I had to head home in the morning. From his position, Martin now had an enticing view of my upper legs and ass. In between the cheeks of my tight ass he could see my cute little hole and just a hint of my pussy opening. The very sight caused his stomach to turn somersaults as his imagination and extensively tested library of fantasies took over and instructed his cock to rise to the occasion. He seemed uncomfortable to me and I thought that maybe I was pushing for more than he was willing to give at this time. I stood and was about to thank him politely for the wonderful dinner when I noticed a very slight bulge in his dress pants. Determined to reap the rewards of this encounter after all, I feigned a possible sprained ankle by grimacing and holding out my hand for support. Ever the gentleman, Martin showed genuine concern on his face as he allowed me to put my slender arm around his shoulder and limp slowly toward the gleaming lights of the distant restaurant.

Martin suggested that I should sit so that he could gently massage my ankle. I wasted no time complying. My ankle, receiving expert attention from Martin, who had never of course treated a sprained ankle in his life, felt fine but he had to be sure I was okay, and so I let him continue to kneel in front of me, playing with my foot. Gradually, I hiked my skirt up inch by inch, revealing more leg than Martin had ever seen, except at work on various shoots of course. Occasionally, I would lean over, closer to Martin than necessary, to inspect the damage and make sure that the bulge in his pants was still there. Finally, I raised my tiny foot as though to test it and allowed it to brush heavily against Martin's raging erection.

"My, oh, my, what have I done?" I drawled innocently.

"Don't worry, I think you're okay now" said Martin, embarrassed by his obvious lack of control over his body's responses.

"I would like to thank you" I whispered in a thick, sultry voice, pulling Martin towards me, still keeping him kneeling between my open legs.

I leaned forward and pulled him against my chest, letting my shirt fall open to reveal my swollen breasts and rosy, taut nipples. I kissed him on the lips and ran my hands over his firm ass, slowly moving my fingers round to the side of his pants. Martin's eyes bulged in his head at this sudden change of events, and his cock jerked up even straighter against his stomach. Encouraged, I pulled him tightly to me so that there could be no doubt that I could feel his hard cock against me. Martin looked down and his gaze fell on my naked breasts. He marveled at their shape and beauty. He was convinced that he was going to cum in his pants in no time flat at this rate. He pushed his strong body hard against my soft one , again smashing my tits between us. I looped my thumbs into the belt hoops on either side of his pants and pulled them down to reveal his towering cock. It was far bigger than I had imagined.

Slowly, as I watched the expression on his face, my hand inched closer to his stiffened shaft. Triumphantly, I wrapped my hand around it to get an idea of its size and pulled down roughly. Martin made a squealing sound which I took for pleasure, so I continued to move my hand up and down, gripping his cock as tightly as I could. Faster and faster my hand traveled up and down the length of his red hot cock until Martin grabbed it and made me stop.

"That feels great but can we try something a little different?" Martin asked hesitantly, keen to ensure that I continued my ministrations but wanting and needing a different pace. Taking my soft hand in his, he placed it lightly towards the top of his rigid cock and moved it up and down slowly, showing me how he moved his thumb over the top in a circular fashion now and again. I learned quickly how to bring him the greatest enjoyment. I took time to look at his cock, noting the way the skin moved over the inner body of it, and how it seemed to be particularly sensitive around the top. I looked at his tightened balls, quickly moving my free hand to cup and cuddle them lightly.

His bulging red weapon looked ridiculously big with my tiny, delicate hand wrapped firmly around it. I continued my rhythmic stroking. Martin seemed to enjoy having his engorged cock stroked but things didn't seem to be getting anywhere. My hand was fast tiring and the way Martin moved now and again suggested that his knees probably hurt from kneeling for so long. I slowly pushed Martin back on the sand so that he could lay down, his stiff cock still rigid and standing straight at attention like a small soldier waiting for his orders. In so doing, I managed to lose the last of my clothes and lay down beside him naked. I noticed several small hairs around his erect nipples and down the center of his chest.

Martin's hand slid over my newly-exposed chest, exploring my firms tits and tweaking my nipples with gentle force. My gaze was still fixed on the first live cock that I had ever seen as it bounced against his taut stomach. I grasped his hard cock again, raising my leg to allow him to move his hand from my tingling tits to between my open legs. The feel of a hard cock in my hand and a man's fingers teasing my wet slit persuaded me that it was time to let him try and enter. Martin needed little encouragement, and as I shifted into a more comfortable position, he placed himself between my trembling legs. Trying to look like a natural-born stud, he plunged deeply into my dripping pussy. I marveled at the strength and thickness of his plunging piston, and noticed that it was quite difficult for him to aim it into my small, tight hole. I used my hand to reach down between us and spread my soft pink pussy lips. Martin had a stupid grin on his face as he slowly pushed forward under my eager guidance and let his purple knob rest just inside the dripping entrance to my hot cunt. He stroked gently for almost a minute, entering further each time until he had all of his enormous cock buried deep inside me.

"I think I'm going to cum," he growled looking down at me with a look that was begging for permission to release.

"Pull out then and I'll do the rest." I whispered shakily before I moved away, releasing his cock from my pussy's grip. I sat cross legged in the sand as Martin knelt in front of me, bringing his oozing cock about mouth level. I held his cock and moved slowly up and down as he had shown me earlier, my soft hands gliding smoothly over his tool due to the lubrication from its dive in my hungry tunnel. Martin looked at me for some time before his gaze moved downward to the dark triangle of hair that covered my enlarged slit. He lifted my hand off his stiff shaft and instructed me to watch him. I think he wanted to help me learn the right way to do things but he also hoped that a brief pause for my much needed education would calm him down and make him last a little longer. He held himself with four fingers towards the top of his manhood. Rubbing up and down slowly, he showed me that gentle movements focused around the sensitive purple head were the most effective. Then he let me try for myself, guiding me tenderly until it felt right. While I practiced, he sneaked a look at my well-shaped legs, and the beckoning area that existed between them. His cock jerked and swelled involuntarily, releasing a little blob of white cum as my tongue darted into its tiny opening.

Then Martin held the tip of his cock with his thumb and index finger, and moved the foreskin backwards and forwards, no more than half an inch. I watched fascinated as clearly his cock stiffened again, turned a deeper shade of red. The dark veins bulged along the length of his weapon. He let go and I gently grasped his harder-than-steel cock, slowly running my finger around the wet head. He moaned loudly and I took my cue, moving my hand further down, and began gently stroking. I could smell his pre-cum on my hands and took a moment to record the smell in my mind for future fantasies. It dawned on me that this was indeed one of my most played out fantasies, that of Martin and me making passionate love together. I felt Martin place a hand on my shoulder, steadying himself as I slowly increased in speed and my pussy lips parted to reveal my inner folds and marble-like clit.

"Is that good for you?" I asked Martin, looking for reassurance that I was indeed pleasing this man I had come to love so much.

"Mmm hmmmmmm" he replied, taking my left hand and placing it under his balls. I was surprised but didn't make a move to take it away. In fact, I explored a little, finding out that his balls were quite squishy and could be moved around easily. I took my right hand away from the tip of his cock, beginning to fully stroke his shaft from top to base. Martin's breathing became heavier and I noticed tremors running through his stomach and legs. His cock looked as though it was getting thicker and longer, and certainly the head seemed to be bulging more. He grabbed hold of his ass as his hips started to buck gently back and forth. His breathing became shorter and shorter and I instinctively responded by increasing my stroking. I gently squeezed his balls causing him to buck hard and grunt loudly as he came in an earth-shattering orgasm.

I saw something fly over my head, and then felt something land in my hair. I continued to pump up and down, and more and more creamy cum spurted over my tits and into my face. I didn't stop, but just kept pumping as the liquid continued to rain down on me. Eventually, Martin took away my hand with a deep moan. He slumped back onto the sand, facing away from me. I giggled quietly to myself, thinking what a sight I must have been. I had cum in my hair, and traces were running down over my tits.

I swiped my finger over my wet breast and put it in my mouth, tasting his salty seed. I quickly picked up my clothes, covered myself, and knelt down to kiss Martin on the cheek.

"It hurt a little because it was my first time, but I was just worried about getting pregnant." I whispered the confession to his turned back. "Anyway, it was fun to see it shooting out." I continued with a little giggle. Martin didn't respond and I thought for awhile that I must have disappointed him. Then I heard him mumbling incoherently and I realized that he had drifted into a peaceful sleep. I sat for what seemed like hours listening to his exclamations as he lived out a dream that obviously excited him as I saw his cock spring to life and look for a willing partner. Mostly his quiet ramblings were indistinguishable but occasionally a word was clear and I started to detect a theme to what he was saying.

Apparently Martin had a thing for feet, especially delicate, well-manicured ones. I listened as he told his dream lover how to use hers to bring him the most pleasure. Unconsciously his words excited me all over again. I could feel the wetness seeping from somewhere deep inside me and my pussy began to throb with a definite desire. Looking down at the sleeping face of the man I loved, so peaceful as he lived in his little dream world, I determined to make him as happy as he had made me earlier. When he rolled onto his back, I carefully positioned myself between his slightly parted legs. I lifted my own slender legs and placed my feet squarely on his broad chest, just inches below his face. With my toes, I stretched and started to caress Martin's cheeks lightly. He stirred and leaned into my caress. Getting bolder I began to run my feet down his chest, using my toes to tease his nipples. He must have thought he was still dreaming because he started to give me directions in an unsure voice.

I listened carefully to each request, doing my very best to fill it perfectly. I slid my feet down his firm stomach, around his engorged cock, and to the inside of each of his thighs. Martin moaned and sighed. My toes massaged his tight balls, squeezing them gently, pushing them from side to side. His legs parted further and I scooted closer to his raging hardon, placing the arch of each foot on either side of the swollen shaft. I clasped my feet together, holding his hot cock firmly between them and began to stroke him with long firm strokes. He groaned loudly and I glanced up at his face, calling his name softly to see if he was awake. I received no response so I assumed he was still in the throes of his dream. My hands moved to run my nails lightly over the sensitive skin of his inner thighs and he jumped perceptibly at the sensation. His response encouraged me and my touches became bolder.

After several minutes of my touching and fondling his thighs, my feet still stroking his cock rhythmically, I bent down and used my warm wet tongue to eagerly lap up the cum seeping from him. His voice whispered, asking me to lean back and use one hand to rub my clit as I fucked him steadily with my feet. I did as asked and was rewarded with more thick precum that dripped onto my freshly painted toenails and made them glisten in the moonlight. I began to notice that I was stroking myself with the same intensity and speed that I was fucking Martin. I closed my eyes and lost myself in the sheer joy of the feeling of my fingers entering my wet pussy hole. I could hear Martin's moans and groans growing louder and I knew he was close to exploding. With every sound he made I pushed my fingers into my pussy deeper and harder. My feet gripped him tighter, now sliding easily over his swollen purple cock because of the wetness of his thick drops of cream coating them.

I pumped furiously at my cunt, unconsciously squeezing Martin's hot rod over and over in a mock orgasm. From the sounds he was making I knew that the real one would follow soon. I felt his legs tense and his body begin to tremble just as he moaned out my name and his hot seed spurted over my feet. I opened my eyes and looked down to see that Martin was wide awake, his face twisted into a mask of pure pleasure. When the spurts slowed, before his cock decided to sleep again, he quickly grabbed me and pulled me on top of him. His hands roughly gripped my hips and slid my pussy up and down on his still rigid rod. I could feel him deeper in my depths than he had been before and my own climax built with amazing speed and force. The heat consumed me and before too long I was crying out.

"Martin, I'm cumming, I'm cumminggggggggggg!" My words spurred him to thrust his hips up at mine, meeting every stroke with an equal force and need. I could tell by his expression that he was cumming again and I let my head sink to his chest, keeping him deep inside me as my pulsing pussy milked out every last drop of his hot cream.

Later, we walked hand in hand back to the car. As we strolled we discussed our future together. Martin had assumed that his little fetish would turn me off and that this had been nothing more than a one night escapade. I, on the other hand, had learned that it's not always what we do but who we do it with that brings us the greatest pleasures in life. Martin gave me pleasure. He made me feel special, wanted, and needed. He made me happy and if playing "footsies" made him happy, then I was willing to play the game. I hugged him close and whispered all of this into his ear, feeling his strong arms tighten as he felt the full impact of my words. We stood for a long time lost in each other's embrace, knowing tomorrow morning I would be leaving and not knowing how long we would be apart.

As it turned out we weren't apart for long. Gail made the painful decision not to come back to work and dad found himself in need of a replacement photographer. Luckily for him, I was able to give Martin outstanding references. More luckily for me, he took the job when it was offered and we have been together ever since with Martin "shooting" at every opportunity.

NOT JUST
ANOTHER
CLOSE
SHAVE

CHAPTER 14

NOT JUST ANOTHER CLOSE SHAVE

Mary watched the convoy of cars and trucks winding their way from the lush green valley a few hundred feet below. They slowly snaked and sputtered up towards the mountain pass, bound for a world as yet unknown to her.

She envied the tourists their freedom to explore beyond the closeted environment of the picturesque mountains she called home. Recently, her own need for adventure had driven her to hike up the steep mountain when she should have been in class. She had walked one colorful autumn day up through the dark, steeply sloping forest to emerge again into the shimmering sunshine of the early afternoon. The weather had been perfect, with just a hint of a breeze that cooled her tanned face and rippled the soft down of her young arms. There, lazing on the deserted mountainside, she had gazed down at the people in their tiny town below, amazed by how small their community looked from such vast heights. Occasionally, more so recently, she had felt cramped and concerned that while time marched on in the world at large, it passed over Jacksonville with abandon, choosing to concentrate on the more receptive larger towns.

Mary was not one of the town's beautiful girls, but her features were distinctive. She had a boyish face, deeply set hazel eyes and a strong, straight nose. It was a face that people would find pleasant rather than beautiful. Her skin was perfect and unblemished . Her wavy red hair normally fell to below her shoulders, but was constrained presently by a cheap, dime-store barrette.

A loud pop brought her back to the present, as Mary realized that some optimistic team-mate had passed the ball to her.

"Mary Lewis, for goodness sake pay attention! Look around you!" shouted the gym teacher, umpire, and part-time sadist Miss Gable. She was a tiny woman who in Mary's estimation was about twenty-three, not much older than the girls she taught. Her body had evidently given up adding inches to her stature during her teen years to concentrate on providing a mane of thick dark hair that hung down to her waist. Miss Gable wore sweat suits mainly, making it difficult to judge her physical build. Mary had seen her undressing in the locker rooms a couple of weeks ago and had remarked to Jenny at the time that she could have passed for one of the senior girls.

"I don't think so," Jenny had said, "She looks like a virgin". Mary smiled at the memory. She looked up towards the hoop and threw the ball in her hands. She was surprised to see it sail through the air at great speed and; moreover, in the direction that she had wanted it to go. The flow of adrenaline and the rush of expectation subsided as quickly as it had begun, as the ball fell safely just to the left of the net. Mary determined that she had spent the past thirty minutes walking, trotting and running around the cement rectangle that was the school's outside basketball court to little advantage, the ache in her legs proof of her exertion.

Recent months had replaced her gangly features with a recognizable feminine form. There was a hint of shape in her long brown legs, accentuated by her bright white shorts. The final whistle sounded, and so she spun on her heel and headed for the locker rooms.

As she trudged toward the door, she looked across the field and down again into the valley. She admired the beautiful colors of the autumn leaves as Mr. Widner , who owned the Five and Dime Store in town, cut a plot of very tall grass in his garden. Mixed in with the grass were various wildflowers, and the scent drifting up to the school was sweet and comforting. In contrast, Mary thought, to Mr. Widner's one and only little girl, Bertha, who was in the same class as Mary and had recently become a thorn in her side. The animosity had started, as far as Mary could recall, in this spot, when Mary had accidentally knocked Bertha down on the cement while making a shot. In revenge, Bertha had hit Mary across the back while Miss Gable was repeating commands for the linguistically disadvantaged students.

Despite Mary's lack of exertion on the court, she was hot and sweaty from the limited exercise and small beads of perspiration clung to her forehead. She looked forward to the end of term, only ten days away, when she wouldn't have to run up and down in the heat, and could lay by the YMCA's pool with Jenny, speculating on the many guests and their lives.

Mary entered the changing area of the locker rooms. At the far end of the room she could see Miss Gable standing by the entrance to the showers, waiting to catch some poor girl who tried to leave without showering. Noise echoed around the room as girls laughed, lockers banged, and the showers hissed. Mary sat down to remove her shoes. She pulled down her socks, discarding them by her side. She walked over to her locker to retrieve her white towel and clothes. A couple of her classmates darted past her on their way to the shower, their young bare asses showing a hint of shape.

Mary returned to her reverie, remembering her fascination when she had discovered two or three soft hairs growing above her vagina. She had wondered how long they had been there and that night had taken a long look at herself in the mirror. Returning to bed, her hands had explored every conceivable source of interest, finding evidence that her pert tits were starting to mature. She had pulled her nipples and discovered that they did indeed get hard and elongated, just as she had hoped they would.

Mary stood up and saw the steam billowing through the doorway of the showers. Miss Gable inspected each of the girls as they made their way to and from the stalls, trying to be the model of supervision and discretion. Mary pulled her shorts down past her knees, bringing each leg up in turn to allow them to drop to the floor. She gripped the hem of her shirt and tugging upwards, removed it in one swift movement to reveal her small tits. She was very proud of them even though she had nothing to do with their shape, size or circumference. She hung the shirt on the hook above her head, and quickly pulled down her cotton panties. Mary now had a thin layer of light hair growing above her vagina, which scarcely concealed the lips of her pussy. Then came the walk she dreaded ..... past Miss Gable on the way to the showers, feeling her eyes taking in her shape and mentally comparing her to the other girls. The return journey, for some obscure reason didn't matter to Mary. Miss Gable could look at her tight young rear all she wanted.

Mary took her towel and strategically moved it as she walked down the aisle, using it to shield her most private assets from prying eyes. Few of the other girls looked at her, although Mary glanced at Shari sitting naked on the end of the final row of benches. She noted that Shari had large tits, much larger than her own, and a thick patch of black hair between her parted legs. Shari's head leaned to one side as she toweled her hair dry and talked to her neighbor, Bertha. Mary quickly averted her gaze, deposited her towel on a hook outside the showers, and entered carefully.

The shower room was completely white, tiled from floor to ceiling. It was much warmer than the changing room area, and had a smell that reminded Mary of wash days when she was a child. A small half wall ran along the center of the room with the exception of about two feet at either end to allow all-round access. Mary took a bar of soap and moved under a vacant shower. Two of the girls were shrieking in the corner of the room as they tried to rub soap into each other's hair.

Mary smiled, peering through the steam. She recognized Kathy and Marlene who had become very good friends in recent months. Kathy deftly moved to position herself behind Marlene with her arms around the other girl's slender waist. She rubbed a soapy hand across her face. Marlene squealed with delight as they play fought. As Mary watched, she realized that the whole class was growing up quickly, including herself, making the transition from childhood into womanhood. A year ago there were only a few girls who showed signs of physical maturity. Now all the girls in her class were blossoming. The two girls continued to giggle and mess around. Mary noticed that they both had huge tits that swayed and bounced as the girls frolicked in the spray. As she continued to stare, she realized that she had been watching Kathy's hands roaming over her Marlene's tits. She was unsure whether the girls were aware of being watched, but Mary was slowly coming to the conclusion that while their movements would have been considered horseplay a year ago, it could only be described as mild petting now.

Mary turned quickly towards the wall as thoughts raced through her mind. She lathered up her hands and soaped herself under her arms, then stretched her arms up high to allow the water to rinse her off. Glancing at the two in the corner again, Mary caught a glimpse of a hand between Marlene's legs moving quickly backwards and forwards. Marlene had closed her eyes and was leaning against the wall. Unable to contain her curiosity, Mary turned her back to the shower, and ran the bar of soap across her legs while watching the action in the corner, convinced by now that the mystery hand between Marlene's legs belonged to Kathy.

The misty fogs of steam lent a surreal backdrop to the erotic show, as the girl's activities drifted in and out of focus while the showers hissed. As the water rinsed Mary's legs, she took the bar of soap and let it lazily slide over the contours of her firm tits. Unconsciously, she paid special attention to her hardening nipples, running the corner of the bar of soap around them in small, firm circles. They responded, growing and crowning her small white globes.

Kathy's hand was moving faster now, and Marlene gripped the shower head for support, giving her tits a classic shape and preventing them from bouncing so violently. The steam momentarily parted and gave Mary a shocking view of a number of soapy fingers flashing in and out of Marlene's vagina. As the picture faded back into steam, she saw Marlene's mouth slowly open and heard a low moan from the corner as though she had been hurt in some way. As Mary's young mind processed the information she had gathered, another part of her was more concerned with mimicking the action she had observed, and her hand had now found it's way from her small tits to between her own legs which were parted further than necessary for standing up in the shower. Again, she used the corner of the soap to massage her vagina, while her thumb trailed behind adding further pressure to the exploration, the whole action causing her to lean forward slightly. The outer lips of her pussy soon parted and bubbles of soap ran along the delicate virginal skin.

With the middle finger of her right hand, she ran over her wispy pubic hair and down along the length of her slit, exploring and probing as her clit became enlarged and stood to attention. Mary felt a strange tingling inside her stomach. With unconscious abandon, her middle finger slipped into her tight little hole while the palm of her hand rubbed over her clit. Slowly she extracted the finger, reveling in the pleasure that emanated from within her pussy. Her pussy lips fought to retain their hold on her finger each time she pulled it out, giving up their little prisoner with increasing reluctance.

"Is it clean enough down there for you, Mary?" said Abigail as she moved under the adjoining shower.

"What? " said Mary as she fumbled with the soap. , "Oh, ummmmm, some really hot games today."

"Yeah, I caught the tail end of their little show too. It's not the first time you know." Abby whispered with an air of confidentiality.

Regaining some of her composure Mary left the shower room, grabbed her towel from the hook, and skipped around the ever-watchful Miss Gable. She was aware of an unusually warm glow between her legs, and she determined that as soon as she had the chance, she would play with herself and a bar of soap again. She moved to a bench and stood with her right leg on the seat, toweling herself as she replayed the action in her mind. Only as she dried between her legs did Mary realize that she was still very aroused, and immediately dropped her leg back to the floor to preserve her modesty. Confused, she reached for her white panties in the pile of clothes and quickly stepped into them and pulled them up. It sounded like Kathy and Marlene were still fooling around as cheers resounded from the shower area. Mary remembered that she had promised to invite Jenny for dinner at her house, so she hurriedly slipped her blouse on. She checked her panties to make sure that she had not put them on the wrong way round, and sat down on the edge of the bench to pull on her white socks. She stuffed her bra into her skirt pocket and pulled her skirt on quickly. Finally, she jumped into her shoes, grabbed her towel and duffel bag, and practically flew out the door.

Turning left into the main hallway she breathed in the fresh, cool air. Mary pulled off the barrette holding her hair and let the red waves cascade over her shoulders. She took a hairbrush from her bag and quickly ran it through her damp hair giving it some semblance of order. Her pleasure from the anticipated dinner with Jenny was evident as she hurried out the school's door.

Jenny was leaning against the wall of the school just outside the main gate, watching the traffic coming up the hill from the bus stop. As Mary approached, Jenny smiled and started to walk slowly down the hill waiting for her to catch up. From behind, Jenny looked like any other average high school girl.. Her legs had more shape than Mary's, but were shorter, giving Mary a height advantage of a couple of inches. Jenny's blonde hair was parted in the middle with a fringe over her eyes, falling loosely down either side of her head to her shoulder blades. As Mary caught up with her, she noted that Jenny's breasts were at least a couple of inches larger than her own, and recalled that the last time they had been in the showers they certainly jiggled a little. Her face was impish, cute and rounded with a small nose and shining bright blue eyes. In a similar fashion to Mary, she was only average in the beauty department.

"What kept you, I thought you were just behind me?" said Jenny loudly.

"Hey Jen, you'll never guess what happened, it was so weird," whispered Mary, looking cautiously around for unwanted eavesdroppers.

"Tell me, tell me, please?" said Jenny, genuinely excited. Given Mary's usual inability to be the carrier of idle gossip, this had to be world-class information. And so Mary recounted the story of Kathy and Marlene and their fun in the showers . Mary continued the story with the arrival of Abby, and explained that there had been some misunderstanding about her washing herself.

"Hey, big deal! So you did it in the showers, everyone's doing it somewhere or other, silly!" said Jenny, treating her exposé as an unimportant embellishment to the fabric of the story. Mary didn't try to argue that it was a misunderstanding. Jenny knew her too well and Mary realized that there was no sense prolonging the facade, so she just turned to Jenny and grinned wickedly at her. Jenny smiled and nudged her in the ribs like a fellow conspirator as they turned to walk, side by side, to the bus stop.

Mary felt a mixture of relief and excitement. She was surprised that not only did Jenny confirm that she played with herself too, but that she thought everyone else did as well. Mary felt that more experimentation in the bath tonight was called for in the name of self-awareness. As she reflected on the nature of the conversation with Jenny and her light treatment of the subject, Mary couldn't help wondering why she hadn't talked to Jenny about it before since it wasn't such a big deal. It would certainly be easier to talk to her than her mother. She considered herself very lucky to have such an open-minded and mischievous best friend as Jenny Wagner.

"Oh, and I think I have some of my clothes on inside out, I feel funny," mentioned Mary as they arrived at the newspaper stand. "Hang on, I need to get a magazine for my mom. Come on," she said, pulling Jenny into the shop.

"Where do you feel funny? Perhaps you've got your period." said Jenny, picking up a men's magazine from the shelf.

"No, it was last week. Hey, you can't look at that!" squealed Mary, grabbing the magazine and returning it to the shelf where it had previously rested. She showed a copy of "Women of Tomorrow" to the curious girl beyond the counter and offered her the correct money. Leaving the shop, they crossed the road and waited at the bus stop. The daily ritual of traveling by bus meant that they only had two minutes to wait and then a twenty minute ride as the bus looped around the town before crossing the valley and heading back up the hill to where both Mary and Jenny lived.

They boarded the bus and made their way to the back seat as usual, sat down and flicked through the magazine until they found the problem page. Silence reigned as the two girls read about a woman whose husband wanted her to invite friends to their house to watch them have sex. One paragraph that received prolonged attention was concerned with how a woman's husband wanted his wife to masturbate him, including orally. Mary and Jenny were delighted that the letter contained graphic detail of what the husband wanted her to do.

"Can you imagine, having sex while people are holding you? I wonder what it's like?" whispered Jenny, rhetorically.

"Come on, next, next!" answered Mary, turning the page.

The next letter was a long one from a young girl in a university who wanted to know why she had started her college a virgin and now felt it was compulsory to have sex with as many different boys as possible. The girl was sure that her requirements were abnormal and went on to say that she didn't think she had ever truly orgasmed.

"Did you orgasm in the showers?" inquired Jenny in a curious tone.

"Of course not, I told you." Mary responded with a hint of indignity surfacing.

"Relax, you would know if you have. I know I haven't ever, not if it's like it is in the books and movies." Jenny shared this secret as if it were public knowledge and nothing to be ashamed of.

Now this was news to Mary but today was getting out of hand and making her very nervous. Her calm little world of day-dreaming had been shattered by revelations and conversations that were both graphic and personal. On one hand, she felt uneasy with herself and on the other she felt reassured that Jenny was there to defend her emotions as needed. The warm glow from between her legs convinced her that further investigation was definitely warranted in this case. Mary sat quietly, staring at the magazine.

For the remainder of the journey, Jenny related the contents of an adult movie she had found in her dad's VCR, leaving out some of the action that she found difficult to explain or where she thought that Mary wouldn't believe her. At the end of the ride, Mary's cotton panties had a tell-tale damp patch as a measure of the potency of Jenny's narrative.

The bus pulled up about one hundred yards from Mary's farmhouse, and the girls walked up the hill together. The house stood back from the road, with a line of pine trees forming a border around the side of the ornate garden. A wooden porch stretched around two sides of the house. The windows had black wooden shutters either side. A small pathway led from the low garden gate up to the door on the right hand side of the building.

By this time, Mary had decided that she had to get out of the restricting clothes and find out what was annoying her. The feeling was becoming a nuisance. She opened the door with her key and passed through the kitchen into the wood-floored hallway. Traditional prints hung on the facing wall with a large mirror at head height. The paneled walls made the room dark and the large light hanging from the ceiling was needed most of the day. To the left of the hallway were the stairs to the bedrooms and bathroom, while further at the end was the entrance to the living room. Visitors could hardly miss the numerous photographs on the hallway walls of Mary from her early years, playing on the mountainside and paddling in the freezing cold lakes. Mary wished they could be exchanged for something, even more recent pictures, but her mother always said that she was such a sweetie at that age, and the pictures were her treasured memories.

Mary bellowed "Mom" at the top of her lungs making Jenny jump. They received no reply. "Good, should be a note from her about dinner somewhere. She always leaves a note when they are going to be really late," said Mary looking around. Both girls dumped their schoolbags on the floor, and went back into the kitchen. Mary left the magazine on the table for Jenny to read and found her mother's note stuck on the 'fridge. In summary, it warned against opening the door to strangers, had emergency phone numbers, return times that night, and finally a request to take something from the freezer and heat it in the microwave. Mary left the note with Jenny and went upstairs.

Jenny could hear Mary walking on the creaky floor above, heading into her bedroom. Just as Jenny flicked the switch on the wall, a blood-curdling scream echoed through the near-empty house, followed by another and then another. Then absolute silence.

Jenny raced out of the kitchen and bounded up the stairs two at a time. She burst into Mary's bedroom to find her face down on her pink bedspread, sobbing into her pillow. Jenny noted that she had all her clothes on and there seemed to be no obvious reason for her distressed state. She looked across the bed and saw that the pink curtains around the window were open. The white dressing table, desk and bookcase around the room were all in order. The top drawer of her dresser was open, revealing her collection of underwear.

"Mary, what the hell's wrong? Speak to me!" Jenny screamed as her panic rose.

"Bertha" was the only response in between sobs. Jenny could see tears running down Mary's cheek. She sat down on the edge of the bed and put her hand on Mary's back. Jenny knew only too well of the simmering feud between the two girls, but didn't understand how Bertha could have hurt Mary in her own bedroom. Jenny's hand gently brushed her cheek and the sobbing subsided slowly as she ran it through Mary's hair. Mary raised her head and rested it on Jenny's lap, allowing a tide of tears to trickle onto her skirt.

"The little bitch put gum in my undies, it's everywhere!" moaned Mary. Jenny looked down to Mary's skirt and couldn't see anything. "I can't get my panties off because of the stupid gum. That cow is going to die for this." screamed Mary. Jenny had never seen her friend so angry. Inwardly, she thought it was a clever prank that she would have to remember.

"What are you going to do? You'll have to get cleaned up somehow." Jenny asked quietly not wanting to chance turning that anger on herself. "How much is there?"

"How much can she get in her fat mouth? It's the size of the Grand Canyon!" shouted Mary. And with that, the clouds lifted and the tears slowly subsided to a drizzle ..... or at least enough for Mary to look up at Jenny and smile.

"Is it really everywhere? I mean, is it on your blouse and skirt as well?."

"No, I don't think so" answered Mary as she looked down at her clothes. "I hate that fat bitch! I really, really hate her!"

"OK, so take off your other clothes before it gets on them as well. Then we'll think about your underwear." Jenny tried to be the voice of reason in the storm of discontent.

Mary was surprised by her authoritative tone and the assumption that this was going to be a joint venture. However, there was some logic to what she said and there was nothing new in being half dressed in front of Jenny so she sat up and undid the buttons on her blouse, letting it fall open, making no attempt to cover her naked tits from the gaze of Jenny who remained sitting on the edge of the bed.. As she sniffed loudly, she knelt on the bed and unzipped her skirt, rolling onto her back so she could get it down her legs and off. She then sat up again with her legs curled under her and looked at Jenny.

"Let's have a look. Stand up" said Jenny, as she sat with both legs over the side of the bed and Mary perched between her knees. Jenny took hold of the elastic waistband of her friend's panties and slowly pulled down. Whimpering sounds and the look on Mary's face confirmed that the gum had well and truly stuck to her panties and the small patch of pubic hair just above her pussy. Jenny looked up at Mary knowingly. "We'll have to cut the material off, then get rid of the gum with a razor. Let's go to the bathroom, there must be something there that your Dad uses" said Jenny, getting up off the bed.

"Are you crazy?" cried Mary in astonishment. She shook her head and looked down at Jenny, thinking hard about the suggestion. Again, there was logic in the idea, but having someone, even Jenny, so close to her pussy, not just touching, smelling and probing but being able to see inside and change the appearance of her most personal and private place was the most outrageous proposal. Mary thought quickly, hoping that there was a more palatable solution to her dilemma. Eventually, Jenny's obvious care and concern for her friend persuaded Mary that she should agree ..... at least until it became too embarrassing. As she arrived at the conclusion, a genuine warmth was born inside Mary for her friend, and she looked on her with a new degree of friendship. The image of schoolgirl buddy and giggling little classmate diminished as one of companion and fellow young woman of the world took its place. Mary wanted to hug Jenny, but chose to refrain, at least until this was over.

"Any better ideas? Perhaps your Mom could do it, or maybe even your Dad?" teased Jenny, taking her hand as she moved towards the bathroom. "Come on, I've used a razor before on my armpits, it's no sweat." Mary followed reluctantly, pleased to have had the decision made for her but apprehensive about Jenny's ability with a razor. "Where do you keep the scissors, and what about your Dad's shaving cream?" Mary replied that the scissors were downstairs and her dad didn't use shaving cream as he used only an electric razor. She disappeared down the stairs to have a look and see what she could find.

The gum was beginning to hurt, and was no doubt responsible for the itch between her legs. Mary sat in the kitchen while she waited for some water to boil, one foot dangling towards the floor while the other was tucked up on the chair, giving her a good view of the problem area. She leaned back onto the kitchen counter and rubbed her mound with her hand through her undies, trying to reduce the itching. She concluded after a minute or two that it was only rubbing the gum deeper into her pubic hair, so she crossed her legs tightly and tried to forget about it. She ran her hands over her firm tits, feeling the tightness of the young nipples that perked up in response to her caresses. She smiled naughtily as she ran her finger lightly around each small globe, noting the warm feeling inside as she massaged the creamy orbs. She hadn't really thought about wandering around the kitchen in just her underwear in broad daylight. She glanced out into the back yard to confirm that nobody was there watching. She wondered if she had seen a curtain move in the neighbor's house, but there was certainly nobody there now. That would have given them something to gossip about, seeing a teenage girl with only her panties and socks on in the kitchen, apparently playing with herself.

Mary opened the fridge and took out a can of pressurized whipped cream just as the kettle whistle screeched. She returned to the bathroom with two cups of hot chocolate, the scissors and the cold can of cream to find Jenny sitting on the edge of the bath. She had placed a towel on the woodwork that surrounded the half-full basin, and had obviously found two or three disposable razors as they were floating aimlessly waiting for action. Jenny directed Mary to sit up on the basin, and positioned her so that her right leg dangled over the edge, and the other leg was pulled up onto the woodwork, much like the position she had adopted for in the kitchen earlier. Jenny took the scissors and cut the material at its thinnest points, allowing the underwear to fly apart, leaving a small scrap of cloth in Mary's lap.

"I hate her, you know. I'm going to get her back for this!" said Mary, the words hissing between her clenched teeth. It was now easy to see the way that the gum had adhered to the inside of her undies and matted into her dusky pubic hair. Tugging gently at the material, Jenny was able to pull another inch away from Mary's sore pussy before Mary's hand on her shoulder told her that this was becoming too painful for her friend.

"OK, I think we'll have to cut from here" said Jenny, snipping off the material below her pussy that wasn't stuck too badly. This left a small patch of white cloth between Jenny and the very center of Mary's sex, giving Jenny a close-up view of the rising mound of her friend's vagina. Jenny looked closely, and noticed the little valley between Mary's pussy lips through the material. If Jenny had studied even more closely, she would have seen a small damp spot towards the bottom of the cloth, confirming that while Mary had superficial control of her emotions, other forces inside her had responded to the contact. Jenny inhaled the sweet stickiness of the chewing gum wafting up from Mary's warm pussy until she realized that she had been staring at her friends mound without doing anything for too long. She was about to grasp the material when Mary grabbed her face and tilted it upwards to look at her.

Jenny smiled and crouched back down to resume her work. She rested her left arm on top of Mary's leg so that she could hold the cloth and scissors without tiring too much. Starting at the top, she pulled gently at the cloth, snipping between the panties and Mary's delicate skin, releasing a little each time. After a few seconds, Jenny could clearly see that Mary's pussy had opened to reveal the pink folds of her inner lips with the hood of her clit standing proudly above her young virgin tunnel. After a couple more cuts about half of the material had been removed, and Jenny was well aware of the rich musky scent coming from between Mary's legs. Whether this was as a result of her escapade in the showers, or their discussions about the problem page, or Jenny's tale of the erotic video or Jenny's ministrations or even a culmination of all was hard to tell. However, Jenny was quite sure that Mary was aware of the view she presented to her friend, and decided that she would make this experience one of the utmost pleasure, making up for the discomfort and embarrassment that she had been forced to suffer that afternoon. Jenny moved her left hand down so that her fingers moved over Mary's clit and into the ever-widening valley between her moist lips. She kept her fingers there while pretending to attack a particularly stubborn lump of gum. Mary stiffened noticeably, involuntarily increasing her grip on Jenny's shoulder.

Jenny quickly decided that there was still some work to be done, and that sitting up there on the bathroom sink was not the place for a girl's first orgasm. Snipping more quickly now, she moved her hands back to the cloth and had the whole piece off within a minute.

"There, that wasn't too bad, was it? Now I'll get rid of the rest and you'll be back to normal. Chocolate break, I think," said Jenny, offering one of the warm mugs to Mary.

They drank in silence, remaining in their respective positions. Mary noticed that she could clearly see Jenny's nipples through her school blouse, and was convinced that she had not seen them in such an aroused state before. The thought vanished from her mind as Jenny started to shake up the cold can of cream. Jenny squirted a little onto her hand and rubbed the cream over the patch of stubble above Mary's vagina. Mary gasped and shuddered as the coldness touched her sensitive pussy mound. With a smile, Jenny used the tips of her fingers to massage the cream over Mary's pussy lips, bringing her fingers back up to Mary's mouth.

"Have a taste" said Jenny, enticing Mary with a mischievous smile. Mary's tongue slowly curved up as she lowered her head towards the cream-covered hand and licked Jenny's middle finger, from the bottom to the top, to the bottom, and then all around as she took it in her mouth. Once the finger was cleaned of cream, Mary leaned back on the medicine cabinet and giggled in an almost drunken fashion. She smiled, her head inclined slightly to the right as she looked at Jenny through half open eyes.

Jenny sprayed a little more cream and administered it to the stubble again. Taking one of the razors from the sink in her right hand, she checked Mary's posture. She was still sitting how she had been earlier, but Jenny pushed her left foot tightly in against her bottom to make sure that she had the best possible access to her pussy hole and the patch of cream that seemed to have covered much more skin than necessary. Mary's right leg continued to dangle over the edge of the surface, while she propped herself up with her right hand, and again placed her left hand on her friend's shoulder. With a cautious sweep from left to right, Jenny removed a swathe of cream and a little of the stubble. Mary was pleased to note a number of things, namely that she still had two legs, she hadn't screamed and that the razor seemed to have cut through cleanly. Jenny continued for a couple more strokes until the majority of the upper stubble had been removed. She rinsed the razor in the basin and stood up to survey the scene. It looked as one would have expected. There was a young woman with a smiling face and firm, beautiful tits, sitting on the sink, legs apart with her pink pussy lips covered in dairy cream. Jenny saw Mary looking down at the area where her pubic hair had been, and noted the angelic face with such a look of sweet innocence in her eyes. The little mound of cream over the entrance to her vagina looked so inviting, and Jenny felt her own body trembling slightly as Mary again ran a finger through the cream and tasted it with her tongue. She would have loved to do the same, but there first came a real test of dexterity where she had to shave the tiny amount of hair that usually covered the upper reaches of her friend's young pussy.

Changing razors, she bent down and pulled Mary's right pussy lip across her moist tunnel entrance using the thumb and forefinger of her left hand at the bottom and top. Slowly, she ran the razor down shaving the lip. She repeated the process for the other lip. Taking a wash cloth, she wrung out the warm water and very gently placed it over Mary's vagina.

"Hold that in place. Go and lie on your bed and I'll finish it off and clean you up," she said, watching Mary's little bottom wiggle as she left the room. Jenny took a towel and placed it on the counter top. She opened the medicine cabinet and helped herself to some small scissors and a bottle of Baby Oil, wrapping them in the towel. She went quickly next door to the toilet, and lifting her skirt, pulled down her panties and sat on the toilet. Looking down, she could see a large damp patch in the crotch, clear evidence of her afternoon of fun. She took the Baby Oil and dispensed the smallest amount onto her fingers, guiding them to her pussy and around her clit. She wiped her fingers on the toilet roll, flushed the toilet and left with her toys.

She found Mary lying face up on her bed wearing a new blouse although she had not bothered to button it yet. The fading sunlight of the early evening flooded the room, causing Mary's tan to be contrasted even more strongly by the whiteness of her blouse. Her small tits pushed at the material on either side, and her nipples were barely visible underneath the fabric. Her legs stretched to the end of the bed. Her now-hairless pubic mound sat between them beckoning invitingly. Mary's head was inclined towards the door, her lips were parted in the beginnings of a smile and her eyes looked longingly at her best friend. Jenny placed her towel on the bed and sat on the side as she had done less than an hour ago, facing Mary.

"I'm going to make sure that all the little bits have gone, then I think we had better make sure that when I put your panties back on they won't irritate you," said Jenny, glancing up and down Mary's body. Her gaze rested on the smooth, hairless vagina of her friend, and moving Mary's legs across to the far side of the bed, she indicated that she wanted to lie down alongside her to get a closer view. Mary lifted her bottom off the bed, pushing her pubic mound way into the air and then letting herself down again, giving Jenny enough room to join her on the small bed. Jennie guessed correctly that Mary's sole purpose for the rest of the evening was to reach orgasm - a desire that was growing into an obsession as evidenced by the natural parting of her pussy's outer lips and the display of her pretty pinkness. A copious quantity of lubrication had already seeped out of her pussy, glistening in the evening sun.

Taking a small flashlight from the bedside table, Jenny bent Mary's legs and pulled her knees apart. She flicked the switch on the flashlight, took hold of the small scissors and positioned her head between Mary's parted legs so that Mary had to drape her right leg over her shoulder. She trained the beam of light on her friend's newly shaved pussy, noting that in fact she had done a remarkably good job. There was no chewing gum to be seen, but she had missed some small hairs above Mary's clit , which were easily accessible thanks to her aroused state. Moving Mary's right outer lip to the side, she gently snipped a couple of hairs, making a few little noises to ensure that Mary appreciated the effort involved while preparing her for the stimulation that she was about to receive.

"There are some tiny bits of gum that we ought to get rid of if possible. Hang on, I'll see what I can do" lied Jenny, putting the scissors out of the way. Very lightly, and very slowly, she ran her middle finger along the outside of Mary's wet pussy, caressing her inner thighs gently , teasing with the suggestion of more intimate caresses to follow. Down the right side and up the left, then around the bottom. Jenny repeated the movement a number of times, until she was both convinced that Mary's orgasm was gathering momentum and that Mary realized that this was pure sexual arousal rather than anything to do with the gum anymore. Mary understood what was happening, and her senses focused on the light touch of Jenny's young fingers as she caressed the smooth skin of her inner thighs. Her vagina felt heavenly as she anticipated that longed for touch between her legs. The fingers drifted slowly closer, moving from her thighs to just above her clit, moving so gently around the outside of her pussy as Jenny teased, aroused and excited her, promising to touch the very center of her being in a way that nobody had ever touched her before. Mary thought she would scream any minute as her need to feel Jenny's fingers on her swollen clit overtook all sense of rationality she may have possessed. She moved her whole body forward to engage her fingers only to sense Jenny moving away, prolonging her foreplay as she began to tremble slightly, her legs wobbling. Jenny watched as Mary lifted her legs, desperate for deeper stimulation.

Jenny reached beside Mary for the Baby Oil and flipped the cap. She let a small quantity drop onto the fingers of her right hand. Resuming her position, she pulled the hood of Mary's clit up and exposed the little bud in all its splendor. She allowed a drop to fall over it and again, delicately, massaged all around it. Taking a few more drops, Jenny ensured that both inner lips were coated in the magic potion causing them to glint in the beam of the flashlight. Slowly, but absolutely surely by now, Jenny inserted her index finger between the folds of Mary's skin and into her hot tunnel. She withdrew her finger and again returned to massaging her clit, waiting to discover whether this would be a shock or a moment of intense pleasure. Mary's legs began to tremble.

Jenny felt a small, soft hand exploring the area just above her own knee. She bent her right leg, allowing instant access to the undies inside her open skirt. She took the wandering hand and pulled it gently up, allowing Mary to feel the wetness from her vagina, and to run a finger between her pussy lips to give the other girl a sense of her arousal. Shortly, she kissed Mary above her pussy and slid her legs around so that she was sitting facing Mary, directly between her legs and just out of reach. Jenny reached over Mary's head, took a pillow and placed it doubled up under Mary's bottom. This extra-exposed view afforded all the access she needed. Lubricating her right hand again, she placed her left hand on the top of Mary's pubic mound, and gently, slowly, inserted two oil-covered fingers into the depths of the girl's pussy, pushing firmly in all the way until her little finger lay along the hot sweet valley of Mary's pussy. Mary let out a gargled groan as new sensations flooded her body, registering the two fingers exploring deep inside her pussy. Jenny was convinced that Mary needed very little artificial lubrication, given the thick, slick tunnel that she had encountered. With all the thoughtfulness of the caring friend that she was, she allowed Mary to grow accustomed to the sensations between her legs, before pushing slightly harder into her, increasing the rate of stroking with her fingers as she employed her other hand over her engorged clit. Jenny marveled at the tightness of Mary's sweet pussy, and the tight grip on her fingers with every stroke, which coincided with a now regular moan from the other girl. Slowly, she withdrew her slippery fingers and took a swollen outer lip between her thumb and finger, running up and down the length of it. She swapped to the other lip, gently squeezing as Mary twitched on her bed.

Looking up at Mary, she saw her running the palms of her hands over her tits, pinching the nipples occasionally and massaging the small cones in fevered activity. Her face was contorted seemingly in pain, possibly because she felt she might not achieve orgasm, but hopefully because the feeling of lust and sexual abandon had now swept away her modesty, inhibitions and reserve in a tide of unbridled desire for release. Jenny slipped two fingers back inside her friend as they both reveled in the new experience. She took a good look at Mary's pussy, the position of her little brown hole, and the secret folds of skin that were now fully exposed to her view.

Mary raised her bottom in time with Jenny, and although the synchronization was less than perfect, the effect when they did connect served to provide deep penetration inside Mary's pussy. Jenny looked down at her fingers moving quickly in and out of her friend, and parted her own legs in sympathy for her own pent-up passions. She felt the walls of Mary's vagina suddenly relax and then contract just as Mary screwed up her eyes and brought her hands from her tits down to between her legs, resting her palms of her hands on either side of her virgin pussy. Mary grabbed her feet and pulled them wide and back above her body, giving Jenny maximum room to access her tight pussy. Her thrusting was curtailed by her position, but her whimpering gave Jenny the timing cue she needed, understanding from her own efforts how close her friend must be at that moment. Deciding to take her the rest of the way, she increased the depth and rate of her finger fucking, turning her fingers on the way in and out to stimulate every conceivable surface inside her beautiful friend.

"Oh, God!..... Something's happening!" panted Mary, a look of shock across her sweaty face. She bucked violently on top of the pillow, pushing herself high off the bed, maximizing the power of the thrusting fingers that penetrated her. Sensing the final hill, Jenny pushed deep into her and put her free hand underneath her bottom, grabbing her cheeks while she maintained the rhythm of her finger fucking, pushing hard on each down stroke to enter as far as possible. Mary started to say something, but no words followed, even though Jenny could see she was trying to speak. Her orgasm engulfed her as she felt the walls of her vagina pulsing and gripping the fingers rhythmically at first, giving way to random seizures of pleasure in sympathy with contractions of her vagina. After what seemed like eternity, Mary exhaled loudly and took in a deep breath, releasing her vice-like grip on her feet and allowing her knees to bend slightly into a more relaxed position. Jenny slowly removed her fingers, and helped Mary to lower her legs onto the bed. She then pushed Mary onto her side and arranged her in a fetal position. Laying now the correct way on the bed, she maneuvered herself alongside the other girl and put her right arm around her waist. Jenny kissed the back of Mary's head and pulled her tightly to her, cupping her right breast. A faint smile passed across Mary's lips as she drifted into a peaceful sleep.

It was over an hour before Mary woke up, finding Jenny still cuddling her and breathing gently. She carefully moved her arm, and slid off the bed. From a drawer she took a pair of panties and slowly pulled them up and into place. She was relieved to discover that there was no particular pain or chaffing as she could have expected. She buttoned up her blouse, picked up her skirt off the floor and made her way to the bathroom. Jenny had evidently cleaned up before they went into the bedroom as it was perfectly neat and tidy. Mary was aware that while she could feel her now hairless pussy, she really wanted to know what it looked like. The bathroom afforded no means of discovery, and so she padded out down the passageway into her parents room. The largest bedroom was also the brightest, and even in the late evening sun was bright enough for her purposes without switching on the light. Mary walked across to the wardrobe and looked at her image in the big mirror that covered one of the doors. As she parted her legs she concluded that superficially there was no difference in her appearance. She watched her right hand move across her stomach and down between her legs, searching for any new feelings or sensations that might be found as a result of her misfortunes. Mary considered that she was very lucky to have been able to get rid of the gum so quickly, but even as this thought passed through her mind, her attention was grabbed forcefully by the memory of the intimacies that had taken place with Jenny. There was definitely, in her mind, some rationalization that was required with respect to their love-making.

While for someone ten years older the act of masturbating with a friend would have been a major turning point in that persons life, Mary had no such considerations. She knew that other school friends were doing something similar, and moreover, there was no long-term agenda attached to their playing. And so her feelings towards Jenny were separated from the afternoon activities they had enjoyed. Mary felt inwardly reassured that she was simply growing up rather than embarking on a course into dangerous territory. Mary put her thumbs into the sides of her panties and pulled them down. She kicked them over into the corner of the room, and sat down in front of the mirror. Sunlight streamed through the window, illuminating her legs and providing her with a perfect opportunity to view Jenny's efforts. She bent her legs and parting them to expose her vagina, put her feet up against the mirror and leaned back on her left hand. Strangely, the first thing that Mary noticed was that she had a freckle just above her clit. She rubbed her thumb over it and proved to herself that it was real. Looking at the view in its entirety caused her to grin widely. What a fabulous sight she thought, noting that yet again, her pink inner lips were pushing their way out allowing a view of the inverted V of the hood over her clit . Mary noted that there was probably some of the Baby Oil inside her as it glistened still in the sunlight. As she ran her finger over her inner lips, she quickly gasped. Mary realized that she was a little tender. She dressed and went back into her own bedroom to find Jenny still asleep, but now curled up tightly facing away from her. She put her hand on her thigh and gave her a little shake. Jenny stirred, and rolled over onto her back.

Mary didn't bother to move her hand, which was now in between Jenny's legs. Jenny slowly opened her eyes and smiled at Mary. She followed Mary downstairs into the kitchen, noting that it was now seven o'clock. The other girl's parents were still not home and Jenny had decided she should probably go before it got too dark. As she moved toward the door, Mary reached out and grabbed her, pulling her into a tight embrace. As Jenny began to relax, Mary leaned her back on the kitchen table, spreading her legs to expose her pretty pink panties. Mary pulled up a chair and pushed Jenny down until she was laying flat before taking a seat between the other girl's legs.

Jenny knew what was going to happen, knew that someone could be watching, knew that Mary's parents could return unheard at any time and catch them. All of the could haves just excited her even more and her panties started to darken with the wetness they were absorbing from her dripping pussy. She gasped as she felt Mary's soft hands pulling the undies down and slipping them off her feet. She held her breath wondering what to expect next but she was unprepared for the shock waves that assaulted her body as Mary's mouth started to move over her inner thighs, her tongue tasting and teasing the soft white flesh.

Jenny moaned and squirmed as Mary's tongue wasted no time but zoomed directly in on its target. She pushed firmly but gently on Jenny's small marble-like clit, grabbing her bottom and pulling her tighter against her hungry mouth. With long, firm strokes Mary quickly built up the tension in Jenny's over-stimulated pussy. As she felt the other girl's body quiver and tighten in preparation for the explosion to come, Mary drove two fingers knuckle deep into the now dripping hole. Jenny let out a scream of passion and her tight young pussy muscles grasped at the fingers hungrily. Mary lay her head on Jenny's tummy and the two friends stayed that way until both had caught their breath and were ready to talk.

"So, whatever will we do about Bertha and the gum trick?" Jenny posed the question without really expecting a reply. She looked at Mary with a devilish grin spreading across her face and gave her friend a quick wink. Mary smiled in response and shrugged her tiny shoulders. "I know," Jenny continued, "Let's return the favor tomorrow in gym class. She will never expect it so soon." Mary's face lit up at the thought of perfectly dull Bertha experiencing what she had been through because of the gum. Her friend's voice broke into her thoughts. "Maybe we should be nice and leave her the whipped cream and a razor in her locker, just to make things easier for her. You know, so she won't have to waste any time looking for supplies."

Mary couldn't contain herself any longer. Looking at the almost genuinely concerned look on Jenny's impish face she burst into sudden laughter. Jenny joined in and soon the two were rolling on the floor in tears. When they could calm their raging hormones and out-of-control humor, they made serious plans for the next school day, stopping to play occasionally. Before Jenny started out the door for her own home, the two girls carefully placed several packs of bubble gum into each of their schoolbags.

The next morning, as the two girls walked down the sidewalk to the bus stop, Jenny turned to Mary with a mischievous wink and asked, "What do you think, my friend, shall we learn to blow bubbles next?" Oh yes, this would be good for Bertha they rationalized ..... And as for Mary and Jenny ..... They would never look at a pack of bubble gum the same again.

CHAPTER 15

HUBBY'S HOBBIES

HUBBY'S HOBBIES

It was somewhere near their eleventh anniversary that Jessica noticed Jeremy becoming more and more withdrawn. His daily ritual was pushing the snooze button on their alarm clock four or five times before jumping up and hurriedly showering. He would then dress without a word and grab a cup of hot coffee as he rushed for the door. Occasionally he remembered to give her a quick peck on the cheek as he darted for the car. Jeremy worked until long after dark every day and when he finally did return home, he usually ended up secluding himself in his study until the wee hours of the morning. Jessica wondered what he could possibly do in there behind the large door all alone for so long. Whenever she ventured to question him on his activities, commenting on how much she missed the time they use to share with each other every night, Jeremy merely said that he was engaging in new hobbies and urged her to find pastimes of her own. Day after day he followed the same routine until Jessica became so lonely she was almost desperate to know what hobbies he had taken up in his private den. One day when Jeremy went for a quick walk she decided to have a look. To her surprise, she found the study door would not budge. Jeremy had locked her out!

When Jeremy arrived home, Jessica was already in bed. She could have been anywhere for all he had known. He didn't even bother to look but went straight into his secret hide-a-way and shortly after the door slammed behind him, Jessica heard the strains of music drifting throughout the house. She determined to find out what could so hold his interest that his wife of eleven years faded into the background and apparently disappeared. She also determined that whatever it was, she was not losing her husband to this wonderful "hobby." Tomorrow, one way or another, Jessica would find out what he kept hidden behind the locked door. Tomorrow, life as it had once been for them would return. Tomorrow ….. Tomorrow faded into the mists of a restless and toss- filled night.

Jessica woke at 7 o'clock, switched off her alarm and went through her daily routine of preparing for the many tasks of daily life. Over breakfast, she mentioned a visit to the doctor's and said she would be a little late that evening. Jeremy never looked up but merely nodded his head to show that he had heard her and understood that he was to start supper that night.

As soon as he rushed from the house, Jessica ran to the door of his study, not even waiting to hear his car pull from the driveway. She was eager to see what had kept his attention so faithfully these last two months or so. Her hand reached tentatively for the doorknob and she took a deep breath as she turned it. Just as she had expected, it refused to give her entrance despite her feeble attempts to twist it first one direction and then the next. Jessica tried to remember where they had put the extra key. She knew that they had one for every door in the house but she never kept track of them because neither she nor Jeremy ever locked doors. They believed in respecting one another's privacy and so the need to lock the other one out had never really arisen before. If Jeremy had simply asked her to stay out of his hobby room, Jessica would never even have thought about going in but somehow knowing that he was placing a barrier to her entrance instead of requesting his privacy made her feel very uneasy about what she would find when she finally did get that door open. And she would get it open... even if it was the last thing she ever did.

At first she tried to force the door, using a kitchen knife and trying to slide it between the lock and the face plate, but soon she noticed the scratches and flakes of paint that would be all too noticeable to her husband's keen eyes. She thought about taking the doorknob off but wasn't completely certain she would remember how to put it back on and she didn't want to have to explain what was so important that she had to go in that room before Jeremy got home. As a last resort she decided to take the door off its hinges, knowing that even she could replace a hinge pin. It was while she was in the garage looking for the flat head screwdriver that Jessica remembered where Jeremy kept all the extra keys. Smiling to herself, she headed to the upstairs hall and the small plastic shoebox on the top shelf where they kept miscellaneous junk. Rooting through the many items inside, she was able to locate a key ring marked "house keys" in just a few minutes and was quickly jogging back down the steps.

Gripping her newly found keys in her hand, Jessica approached the door which seemed to her as if it were daring her to enter the darkened room it shielded from her view. She tested first one and then the next key, inserting and withdrawing each one until she heard the unfamiliar click of the lock giving and the knob turned freely in her hand. When she swung open the door she was surprised to find a study, everything in its place, everything neat and tidy. It looked much the same as it had the last time Jessica had ventured in this room almost six months ago. She walked around the room slowly, perusing every nook and cranny but unable to find any sign of a hobby.

Jessica shook her head, trying to clear it of the numerous thoughts she had allowed to gather there, and started for the door. Just as she turned the lock, intending to pull it closed behind her and return the room to its guarded state, she saw the blinking yellow power light on her hubby's computer. Curiosity drove her to take the mouse firmly in her hand. The moment Jessica moved the hand-shaped curser, the screen saver gave way to a full screen shot of her, totally naked and beckoning the viewer with a crooked finger to come closer. Jessica turned up the volume and heard a remarkably accurate simulation of her own voice purring, "Welcome Sexy, cum in and stay a little while."

The words and the innuendo in them made her blush despite the fact that she was completely alone in the room. She saw no files to click on and was beginning to wonder how to get into the computer when the small speakers crackled loudly and her virtual self continued to talk. "Go ahead, baby. You hit the right spot and my world will open to you." Jessica thought that she had never sounded so sexy before. Jessica had always been the prim and proper one with Jeremy being the one who craved diversity, begged for adventure, and tried to gently nudge her into participating in his many fantasies. There were times when Jessica thought that it might be fun, might add some spice to their marriage but then her strict religious background would kick in and she would remember the endless hours of instruction from her health teacher and her mother on the "proper" way to have a sexual relationship with your spouse. She knew that what she had been taught must be right because Jeremy came every time and often drifted off to sleep in a satiated glow. Jessica was happy to know she had performed so well but there was also a twinge that invaded her tummy sometimes, a twinge that hinted that she herself might be missing out on something. Jessica always wondered what the something could be.

Pulling herself out of her thoughts and focusing on the naked image of herself on the computer screen, Jessica began to randomly click the mouse over spot after spot. "Oh, yeah, baby, that's good." The mechanical voice appeared to be willing to help her find the right spot. "Mmmmmm, lower baby, lower." Jessica moved the pointer on the screen directly down the image's center.

"You are getting sooooooo hot, baby." Jessica stopped just short of touching the mirror image on its most private of spots but then, reminding herself that it was just a computer, she quickly clicked over the thick patch of dark hair covering her photo pussy. The hand opened and two fingers disappeared into the curly jungle. Just before the screen changed, Jessica watched herself as she threw back her head, screwed up her face in a look that almost seemed to indicate pain, and screamed out loudly, "Yes, baby, yes! Cum in to meeeeeeeeeee!" Then to her shock, the computer Jessica spread her long white legs wide and gave the real Jessica a very close up and in-depth view of her wet pussy. Moving the fingers of the curser over the giant cunt's clit elicited all sorts of moans, groans, and ragged panting from the computer's speakers. Jessica dared to move the fingers over the dripping entrance to the pussy and was immediately rewarded as the screen began to move and took on the appearance of something sliding through the black pussy hole. She landed with a thump on a clean computer page, all signs of her video self gone. It looked like any other page with files and icons peppering the whiteness. Jessica looked over every file carefully until she came to the one marked "hubby's hobbies." She clicked on it without hesitation and waited to see what her boldness would reveal.

The folder opened and revealed another page which was neatly organized. Abby, Beth, Corinne, Debbi, Elaine, Frances, Gail ..... She found a folder for every letter of the alphabet, every name belonging to a woman. Jessica wasn't sure whether or not she wanted to see what the files held but at this point she felt there could be no turning back so she let her curser click on the file it was covering. "Nikki," the file she had chosen, opened immediately.

Jessica wasn't quite sure what she was reading at first but as she continued down the page she realized that it was a story about a young girl named Nikki and a slightly older man named Miguel. About halfway through page one the story became very sexual in nature. Though the graphic words shocked her at first, Jessica found her eyes glued to the page, unable to pull them away from the scene playing out before them.

Jessica read every word slowly ..... Miguel heard Nikki turn on the bathwater in the upstairs bathroom. He gulped down a mouthful of orange juice and waited for the sound of her footsteps, anxious to go upstairs only when she was ready for him He sat on a kitchen stool, his cock bobbing slowly as the blood coursed hotly through his veins. The dull ache that had been simmering previously now became true pain. His rock-hard manhood throbbed with every heartbeat, sending signals each time as though some sort of overload had been reached.

He took his hard cock firmly in his hand and his thumb searched out its sensitive head, playing for a while with the stickiness that he found at the tip. He realized that he had never been this aroused before, and wrapped his hand around his shaft to record its size. He returned his attention to the tip of his cock, spread the sticky liquid around with his fingers, and tasted it to satisfy his curiosity before wiping his fingers on his bare leg.

He understood what she wanted, had no doubts about what it would lead to, and as he walked to the kitchen door and out into the hallway toward the staircase, he could find no wrong in their intentions. Within a few minutes, he was sitting in the warm bathwater, his back to the taps, looking at Nikki as she washed her hands in the bubbles.

"Stand up and I'll wash you first, then you do the same to me, okay?" Miguel loved the way that Nikki's voice sounded so musical, like the tinkling of beautiful wind chimes swaying in a gentle breeze. He stood up slowly, his cock jutting out proudly from his stomach, his balls hanging loosely down beneath. Nikki took the soap and knelt in front of him, pulling his foot onto her thigh. She soaped in between his toes, up to the back of his right knee and around the back of his shin, noticing how firm his legs were. She turned her attention to the other foot, repeating the ceremony and then continuing up his thigh, around to his firm ass and finishing with his balls in her hand. She rinsed him down, pleased to see the veins in his cock thumping as the blood provided the strength her soft body craved.

As she soaped the other thigh, she took his cock and rubbed the bar of soap over the engorged head, pulling his foreskin down gently and running the soap all the way around. Miguel held on tightly to her head and the wall, willingly moving his left foot onto the edge of the bath when guided by her soft touch. She pushed the soap between his legs, lathering his anus until the soap felt sticky and dry.

Wetting her hands, she dropped the soap and took his cock in both her hands, rubbing slowly the slick length of his hard shaft. She continued for several minutes as Miguel moaned softly with his eyes closed. Nikki turned him around and asked him to kneel down, bottom raised high to expose his anus. He willingly did as she asked, and she massaged the area with soap, ensuring that he understood her intentions. Very slowly, she inserted her wet soapy finger into the hole, pulled it out, rinsed it and repeated her actions. His muscles reluctantly relaxed, allowing her slippery finger unimpeded access to the tight chamber. Nikki was careful not to take him too far, and sensing that he must be somewhere on the way to cumming, she stopped and whispered to him, "Now it's my turn. Very slowly and very gently."

Miguel turned to face her, pulling her up as he found the soap and lathered his hands. He washed her feet in turn, moving up to her thighs and covering her pubic area generously with soap. Nikki was pleased that he was in no rush, and that he was taking care to feel his way around her body and explore every avenue of pleasure. He made no attempt to push a finger into her vagina, but instead turned her around to face away from him.

Nikki leaned on the side of the tub, her swollen breasts flattened against the cold surface, her rear up in the air, demanding attention. Miguel rubbed the bar of soap through the valley between her cheeks, dropped it and massaged the area to ensure the hole was slippery. He placed his right hand on her back and slid his index finger in. Nikki gripped the tub, turning her head to one side, eyes closed, and mouth open as she murmured words of encouragement. He pushed harder, watching his finger disappear into her in a wondrous sight that caused a little cum to appear on his cock. He copied her actions exactly, cleaning his finger and making sure it was slippery before reinserting it, feeling the walls of muscle inside her gripping him so tightly that he thought he might be trapped.

Stepping from the tub, Nikki took a clean white towel and draped it over the side of the bath. She turned and leaned back, watching his cock glistening with soap as the water gurgled away. She instructed Miguel in a husky voice, telling him to pass a bottle of baby oil from the counter top of the nearby basin. Miguel flipped the cap and passed the bottle to her. As he sat back down between her feet and faced her, he pushed his own legs alongside her. She squirted a little oil over each breast, massaging it over her skin with the palm of her hand. Then she led a thick trail of oil from her tight tummy to her soft thighs and back up over her pussy, allowing it to dribble between her legs, down over her marble-like clit and into the pink folds of her inner lips.

Her fingers moved sensuously from her erect nipples, over her tummy to disappear with the lovely liquid between her long legs. She passed him the bottle and closed her eyes, her stomach trembling as she waited for his touch. Miguel sat up, allowing Nikki to part her legs slightly more. He held the bottle over her pussy and squeezed as the clear oil drenched her curl-covered mound, collecting around her rear, making the floor of the bathroom slippery. He rubbed the oil over her inner thighs, moving slowly towards her wet pussy as his fingers ensured that every inch of her skin was slippery and oiled for action. She looked at him through half-opened eyes, ordering him to allow her to caress his hard cock with her oil-covered fingers. Happily obeying her orders, Miguel got to his knees, held the bottle at the tip of his cock and squeezed, watching a little river run from its purple knob to the underside of his sensitive shaft and finally disappear into the hair around his balls. After another squirt, he took his cock in his hand and pulled the foreskin down, rubbing the knob again with his thumb, noting the wondrous shine and the way the veins bulged at the heightened sensitivity of his tool. Nikki moved to sit on the side of the tub, placing her feet so they were resting lightly on the cold floor. She reached out for his cock as she slid slightly lower on her perch. She guided him towards her gaping pussy, allowing the tip of his cock to rest at her entrance for only a second before she slid further on it.

Miguel dropped the bottle and carefully balanced himself as he withdrew almost all the way and then pushed back in. Nikki held his arms as she stared at him wide-eyed, his powerful cock filling her with warmth beyond all her wildest fantasies. He thrust even deeper and she felt the ribbed veins of his cock meet the tiny ripples inside her.

Smiling, Nikki sighed and slid quickly down as her feet firmly met the floor. She felt the slightest twinge as he plunged hard into her, the pubic hair from his balls covering most of her pussy. He took up the rhythm again, without any rush, stroking in and out as he looked at the expression on her face changing from surprise to pleasure. The oil spread over their limbs as their excitement grew, and Nikki wrapped her silky legs around his back, pulling him tighter into her, his cock growing and stretching her warm tunnel.

Nikki braced herself as the thrusting increased in pace, her face now sweaty and her legs aching from their task of helping Miguel to thrust deeply into her pussy. She was moaning now, as Miguel plunged in and out, changing the length and intensity of each powerful stroke. He was driving into her deeply before withdrawing until he was nearly fully out and then spearing her again unmercifully, as he lowered himself, pushing her knees toward her chest. Pounding rapidly, Nikki felt her orgasm building, felt him growing again and heard their breathing becoming quick and ragged and in time with the cock that ground into her relentlessly. Miguel leaned forward to kiss her cheek softly and as he worked his way around to her lips with his tongue she came, screaming as patterns of light sparkled behind her eyes and her legs muscles became weak. Her throat and mouth went dry as her lungs refused to draw air. She saw Miguel still thrusting into her, faster and harder. As the wave of orgasm passed over her, he came violently, jerking so hard that she was shoved against the side of the tub. She felt the flood of hot cum shooting inside her as he stopped, his arms holding her so tightly that she thought he would crush her ribs. He started pumping slowly, moaning as he came over and over again inside her sweet hot body.

Nikki carefully unwrapped her legs and noticed the pain in her muscles as she released her grip on his arms. Miguel lay heavily on top of her, still nestling into her ear as they both rolled onto their sides, his cock continuing its pulsing inside her hot cunt. Their hair was matted in sweat and oil, and stuck to the sides of the tub as they caught their breath and savored the warm glow within. Nikki reached down between her legs as if to confirm that there really was a cock in her pussy and wrapped her fingers round the base of his shaft. She noted that his balls had disappeared inside him, leaving crinkled skin where they had been hanging just minutes before.

Miguel took her hand and steadied her as she stood tentatively, trying to ensure that her legs would hold her weight. She wrapped a towel around herself and stood on the bathmat as Miguel cleaned himself off quickly, sensitive to her body language that asked to be alone. He left as she stared at the mirror, anxious to see if she looked any different. With the exception of a sweaty face and messy hair, Nikki decided that there was no difference that anyone would notice.

The insistent ringing of the telephone finally managed to break the computer's hold on Jessica's attention and she ran to catch the caller before it was too late. Jeremy's voice crackled on the line, telling her to pick up some wine on her way home from the doctor's office. She agreed, constantly looking around herself, feeling shame and embarrassment at the snooping she had been indulging in.

Despite the guilt that was plaguing her, Jessica returned to the office and slowly read file after file, each one more sensual and sexual than the last. She noticed with some amazement that her pussy had grown damp, and then wet, drenching the pure white cotton undies she always wore.

She was on the verge of shutting down the computer when she saw the file marked "Jessica" and curiosity drove her to open it. She was disappointed to find it empty except for one sentence ..... "Maybe some day Jessica will loose the wild woman inside and allow herself to find pleasures that as of yet she has always denied herself." Jessica felt a heaviness flood her heart as she shut off the computer and relocked the den door. Looking at the large clock in the hall, she noticed that she had only about ten minutes to reach Dr. Mercer's office.

When she arrived for her appointment, Jessica slipped into the bathroom and attempted to dry her dripping pussy. Her thoughts were running wild and she tried to coral them back into the box where she had always contained them until today.

The doctor's office was glistening white. Everything, even his desk in the corner was white. A padded table covered in white paper sat against one wall. Above it was a light and various tubes which Jessica didn't recognize. There was an eye chart next to the door and a big poster of the heart and blood system. Food and diet information alongside the poster completed the charts on the walls. Dr. Mercer was probably fifty years old and had a great shock of snow white hair. He asked her how she was in a friendly voice, motioning to the seat next to his desk. He read her medical history in silence, all the while nodding as if agreeing to the terms of her visit with him.

"Now, we're going to make sure you're okay on the inside Jessica," the old doctor droned, " Has anyone explained the importance of these little check-ups?"

Jessica nodded and the doctor launched into his well-rehearsed speech about female health, the need for regular check ups and the fact that there was nothing to worry about. He mentioned the actual internal examination that he would do, told her that it was very quick and painless and completely confidential. Jessica relaxed slightly until she heard about the internal examination. Dr. Mercer proceeded to take her blood pressure and temperature.

Jessica stared at her white socks and little black skirt, feeling the pressure of the band around her arm as she heard him pump up the bulb and then let out the air. He nodded approvingly at the reading and then instructed her to undress completely and climb onto the table, covering herself with the paper sheet that was offered.

"We'll have a quick peek and have you home in no time" said Dr. Mercer.

Jessica obligingly turned away from the doctor and slipped off her clothes. She dropped them to the floor, kicking them once when she noticed damp signs of the day's wear on the crotch of her undies, and then she climbed onto the table. Dr. Mercer took his position at her head and slowly moved the end of his stethoscope over her chest. The cold end made her jump slightly and the doctor apologized with a smile. He pulled the stethoscope from his ears and proceeded to knead her breasts, circling around the white mounds. He brushed the slightly erect nipples with his fingers and felt around her armpits. Jessica watched his fingers wandering over her for several minutes before closing her eyes and starting to relax. As soon as her guard was down, memories of the erotic stories she had read earlier flooded her mind..

"Any pain from your nipples, or strange feelings from your breasts?" The doctor's soft voice barely registered but it did bring Jessica's attention to where his hands were traveling. His fingers probed and prodded around her stomach, descending slowly towards her most private of areas. Jessica felt herself tensing.

"Deep breath, please. And out again. That's fine, now scoot down to the end here and bring your knees up," Dr. Mercer said as he moved round to the foot of the examination table. He felt his way along her thighs, and parted her legs slightly as he probed closer to her sexual center. He brought up the stirrups, placed Jessica's feet into them and dropped away the end of the table. She had been maneuvered into the position so quickly that she had little time to react. The sheet covered much of her pubic region, although as the doctor adjusted the stirrups further apart, it rode silently up her thighs until Jessica knew that even though the doctor was standing, he could see every intimate part of her. She tried to relax and let her mind wander back to the stories.

"Now, I'm going to open you up a little and take a quick swab. It might tickle," Dr. Mercer said as he sat down again and trained the light in between her legs. Jessica strained her head upwards to see if there was any expression of disgust on the doctor's face. He continued to nod and mutter to himself, and Jessica assumed that he had probably done this thousands of times and was bored seeing the private parts of women. She certainly hoped so as she stared at the ceiling and braced herself for the intrusion.

Dr. Mercer had a view from Jessica's anus all the way to her head, with the sheet hiked up to reveal her pubic region. Her pussy lips were now slightly open and in a very mild state of arousal. He moved closer to her thighs and pulled on a pair of latex gloves. First he carefully spread her outer lips wide apart and touched all along them. He gently pushed the hood of her clit back and forth before pushing it all the way up to fully expose her hard pink knob. Jessica jerked involuntarily and squirmed under the touch.

"Does that hurt?" he asked.

"No, it's just a little ….. Well ….. I'm sure you know" stuttered Jessica, thinking that of course it damn well affected her. Her body had so much sexual tension from her morning excursion into her husband's private life that she couldn't force her body not to respond. She began to lose herself in a fantasy, pretending that Dr. Mercer was Jeremy.

"Do you have a boyfriend?" her fantasy doctor asked, returning his fingers to the sweet valley of her wet pussy lips and the little treasure beyond. Jessica shook her head.

Taking a tube of KY Jelly, the doctor spread copious amounts around her lips, softly caressing them a bit longer than was necessary, ensuring that there was sufficient lubrication at the entrance to her vagina to ease the path of the speculum as it entered. He whispered for Jessica to relax.

"This will feel just like it does when you put your own fingers inside you. Do you do that?" he asked. His words made her body feel hot. Jessica nodded, unable to answer verbally because of the rising heat coming from her lower regions.

"Mmmmmm ….. That's okay. I know you find it quite pleasant. Some day you must let me watch you play, won't you? All healthy young women experiment, you know" he added, presenting the KY-covered device to her entrance and pushing it gently into her.

"Ohh" she squealed as she felt it entering her. She was expecting the steely hardness of cold metal but found herself caught her by surprise as she felt instead the steely hardness of a hot cock pushing into her well-prepared pussy. She closed her eyes and held her breath. Her hands gripped the side of the bed tightly as the dream doctor plowed into her. Turning, he quickly spread her opening wider with his jelly-covered fingers and then rammed his throbbing cock inside the warm wet hole.

Jessica was not enjoying the sensation of being examined, but in the back of her mind there was something about it that fascinated her, something that gave her run-away imagination fuel for her fantasy. She felt the strangest contrast between the softness of her insides and the hardness of the rigid rod filling her. Jessica felt an indescribable stirring deep inside.

"All done!" Dr. Mercer's exclamation brought an end to her dreaming, releasing her mind from the fantasy fucking it had been enduring as surely as if he had grabbed the throbbing cock and pulled it forcibly out of her. He took a box of tissues and wiped her carefully, removing as much of the lubricant as possible from the swollen lips of her pussy. He took a second tissue and wiped the area from her vagina to her anus, ending with a swift circular motion around her little brown hole. Jessica wiggled uncomfortably as she realized that her body was still responding sexually to the doctor's business-like touching. He probed her hole with his gloved hand. He inserted his finger very slightly, and removed it, watching the muscles dilate. Jessica's mind flew back to the anus play between Nikki and Miguel in the first file she had seen that morning. Her tight ass hole contracted repeatedly with the excitement of the memory.

"You can jump down now and get dressed. Use more of the tissues if you need them," Dr. Mercer said, removing his gloves and dropping them into the trash bin. Jessica was sure now that she must be obviously aroused, especially after her thoughts about Nikki and Miguel and the attention the doctor had paid to her pussy and ass.

Jessica swung her legs over the examination table and jumped to the floor. Turning away from Dr. Mercer, who was now busy writing in her file, she wiped herself clean with the tissues as best she could. Jessica was more anxious to get her clothes back on than to completely get rid of the remainder of the KY jelly from her vagina.

Flamboyantly tossing his pencil onto the shining white surface of the desk top, Dr. Mercer stood up and smiled, indicating the door.

Jessica left the doctors office and went out into the street. She was confused as to how she ended up fantasizing about Nikki and the story that she had read. But she also felt reassured and comforted by the old doctor's obvious kindness and consideration for her state of discomfort. She hopped into her car with every intention of heading home.

Jessica was just a block from home when she remembered Jeremy's request that she pick up the wine for dinner. She drove to a nearby liquor store and chose a particularly good year. As she shopped, she could feel the wetness between her legs and she knew that this was no longer the lubrication from her medical examination. This was her hot pussy begging for a release that it desperately needed. When she leaned to hand the clerk his money, Jessica's breasts brushed his arm and she was shocked at how quickly the nipples jumped to attention. She blushed, sure the man had noticed her highly aroused state.

In the car, Jessica found her mind living a life of its own. She felt free, like someone who had been given permission to go outside after years of not seeing daylight. She was overloaded by images of herself fucking the doctor, the local bus driver, the clerk who had waited on her, and hundreds of other men she had met in her life. In every fantasy she knew who the man was but when she looked at him, it was Jeremy's loving face smiling back at her. For the first time in her married life Jessica realized that fantasies could be fun.

She made one more stop before she went home that night. Jessica pulled up to the local pharmacy. She went inside and quickly purchased a box of latex gloves, a blood pressure kit, and a stethoscope. Tomorrow, she determined with a smile, the folder marked "Jessica" would not be empty.

CHAPTER 16

PAINT ME PERFECT

PAINT ME PERFECT

Donna knelt in the bath, and with the soap, cleaned her tight tummy and moved lower, her hand settling between her long slender legs. Her soapy hands roamed over the roundness of her rear, her fingers running freely between her cheeks. She parted her legs as far as the bath would allow and introduced her anus to the pleasures of a soapy finger. She was so surprised by the effect that it shocked her into wondering why she had never really experimented before with her small tight hole. Gradually, and with a finger renewed with soap, she slowly pushed into the crinkled opening. She wavered between feeling excitement at the new sensation and shame at what some would consider to be a dirty deed.

It was clear which emotion won her over as Donna stood in the bath and, holding onto the medicine cabinet with her right hand, she placed her leg on the side of the tub. The view between her legs would have been stunning to anyone who walked in right then, the cheeks of her firm ass separated by the position of her legs. Her curl-covered pussy lips parted to reveal not just her inner folds of flesh but a wonderful view inside her as her whole tunnel opened up, begging for attention. Her clit stood proudly out from underneath its normally protective hood as her fingers slid over her slick skin. Taking the soap, Donna explored every possible source for new feelings and sensations, again coming to rest at her anus. She dropped the soap into the bath and massaged the hole, probing slowly but firmly. She entered further and further, deeper and deeper until she was sure that she was not doing herself any damage. The feeling of guilt subsided into one of pleasure, and Donna found the probing to be very satisfying. After a couple of minutes, she made her mind up that she would bring herself to orgasm, and she let most of the water out of the tub and sat down again.

The room was warm as she leaned her head against the towel she had placed at the end of the tub. Her fingers again found her swollen clit and ran around the delicate little bud in slow, light circles. Her legs involuntarily parted to make room for her soapy fingers and she pushed at her anus more forcefully now, a warm glow emanating from her newly discovered source of fun. Donna really wanted to use both hands, so she moved the towel to the side of the tub and turned to face the wall, causing her legs to lift and her body to squash up into the width of the tub. Now she could rub her clit with the fingers of one hand while pushing firmly against the entrance of her tight ass with her other.

Her legs were stretched pointing to the ceiling, and her head was laying back on the towel so she would have had a view of her raised feet if she had opened her eyes. Instead, she had visions of Matt as she fantasized and masturbated wildly. She felt the signs of her orgasm approaching as her stomach muscles tightened and her face scrunched into an almost pain-like mask. Her finger was now pushed as far as it would go into her anus, while her other hand continued to flash across her clit. Now and then her fingers would disappear into her wet pussy, only to re-emerge with a slight slurping noise, covered in thick creamy cum, before returning to their duty of keeping her clit sensitive and alert.

Her fantasy finally conjured up a picture of Matt cumming over her naked body as his hot spurts mixed with the paint covering her and ran downward in streaks of fabulous colors. As the orgasm reached her, she had the presence of mind to keep quiet just in case anyone could hear without her knowing it, but the sound she might have made with her open mouth was exchanged for a violent jerking of her head in time with a final push into her anus with her soapy finger. She lunged forward and fell back again, smacking her head on the side covered with the towel as she grunted. Although she was dimly aware that she had banged her head, she was not going to stop as the waves of pleasure took control. She stopped rubbing her clit to place her hand over her pubic mound as though to grab it all and squeeze it together. Her leg muscles ached badly, but there was a rapidly increasing warmth as her slender body jerked and spasmed in the throes of ecstasy for what seemed an eternity. As they subsided, she slowly pulled her finger out of her anus, causing another wave of pleasure to ripple though her as beads of sweat formed into rivulets and trickled down her face.

Eventually, she turned and stretched out fully in the remainder of the water, soaking up the last of the magic, eyes closed again. For nearly half an hour she remained motionless in the water, as waves of pleasure subsided and a feeling of calm and contentment carried her to a lofty plateau of peace and tranquility. At last she returned to reality and stepped carefully out of the bath, noting that she felt a little light-headed as she wrapped the towel around her shoulders. She saw in the mirror that her hair was matted and feeling the ends confirmed that it needed drying. As she explored her hair, she encountered the bump she had sustained, and marveled not at the slight pain to her touch but at the tremendous energy released during her orgasm. Donna wondered if it felt the same way during sex and decided she would probably never know if she couldn't find a way to make Matt notice her as more than just his subject. She had been posing for Matt for over six months now, mostly nude for his paintings, and Donna wasn't even sure if Matt knew she was a woman yet. He was always totally engrossed in his work and seemed not to be affected when he touched her, positioning her this way and that, and making sure that she reflected the light in the most favorable way. Donna, on the other hand, had begun to take note lately that as his fingers brushed her pussy or his arm pressed against her tits, her nipples would stand to attention and her cunt would grow hot and wet.

She dried her hair and directed the hot air stream across her tits, legs and pubic mound. It tickled slightly and she stopped when she realized that it was making her uncomfortably dry between her legs.

Taking a little Baby Oil, she remedied the situation by rubbing the tiniest of amounts onto her parched pussy lips. Noticing that she was becoming aroused again, she stopped. After cleaning up, Donna went into her bedroom with a feeling that she was becoming a slave to her sexual desires. While this was not true, it was hard for her to feel any other way given that today she had had the most intense orgasm of her life, followed by another, and yet another, all in the space of a few hours and all with the image of Matt held firmly in her mind. Donna drifted to sleep reliving every fantasy of Matt over and over in her exhausted mind.

The next morning Donna awoke at eight and quickly dressed for work. She was late again and she knew that Matt would not approve of her constant tardiness. How could she tell him that thoughts of making love to him led to her many restless nights? She rushed to the studio apartment which doubled as Matt's work place. He barely looked up as he tossed her a robe and told her to undress quickly. She watched as he set out the many colors of paint, her mind floating back to last night's dream.

Donna took off her shirt to reveal a small black lace bra that had little to do with providing support and much more to do with presenting a sexy image. Reaching behind herself, she unclasped it and dropped it on the bed. Provocatively, she turned towards Matt and undid the top button of her jeans, followed by the zipper. Matt admired her text-book shaped tits as they bounced very slightly. As Donna lowered her jeans, Matt saw an expanse of skin which would normally have been covered by her white cotton panties. Today; however, she was wearing a deeply cut black satin thong, having planned ahead that this would be the day she finally seduced him. Donna removed her jeans and stood there in her satin and lace undies with her thumbs hooked into the waistband, ready to pull them down. Although Matt was trying not to look, he was responding lustfully to both her provocative lingerie and her supple figure. Donna pulled down her panties to her knees and absently scratched her sweet pussy as though a sudden itch had interrupted her movements. Slowly, she wiggled up and down while scratching so that the panties fell to the floor, leaving her totally naked.

Matt had a perfect view of Donna's mound and could just see the top of her pussy lips through her thick pubic hair. He stared at the sight, and found his eyes roaming over her taught tummy, up past her ribs, and on to her near-perfect tits which looked like two scoops of vanilla ice cream capped by her erect cherry-like nipples. Matt seized the moment and, much to her surprise, knelt down by the bed to talk to Donna more closely. He put his right hand on Donna's leg, just above the knee. His hand slowly circled around her stomach, using her belly button as a center and then ventured down, brushing the top of her pubic hair. Donna murmured several sounds of pleasure as Matt worked down her slender legs, and then started to caress their soft insides on his way back up, causing Donna to part them very slightly.

Donna pulled herself up to sit crossed legged and guided Matt's hand with her own down to her hot, dripping pussy. Matt gasped as he felt the soft folds of her inner lips surround his fingers. Donna felt a quivering deep within her body as he took his middle finger and ran it down through her pubic hair and landed on her swollen clit.

She pushed Matt down on the bed and sat next to him. She undid his zipper and the top button on his jeans, allowing his cock to burst upward. He raised his bottom and let her pull his trousers down to his ankles. She had her left hand inside Matt's underpants, massaging his balls and occasionally touching his stiff cock. Donna's body had the same idea and she put Matt's hand over her sopping wet mound to show him her eagerness. He tugged at the curly hairs lightly and Donna smiled at him as he moved his fingers to glide up and down her legs. She took his T-Shirt, pulled it off over his head, and finally removed his underpants, leaving him in only his white crew socks.

Matt pulled her up, running his hands over her tits. His rough hands glided gently over her back and down to her waist. He found the little curve in her back and caressed it lovingly. He knew that the real prize was waiting for him below, and he was determined that if Donna was going to taste his cock, then he was going to have a taste of Donna. And so, parting Donna's legs, he ran his tongue over her stomach and along her inner thighs. Donna knew what he was going to do and was delighted.

Matt licked very slowly along Donna's thighs as he held her legs up and apart with his strong hands. Donna slid a down a little, exposing both her pussy and her anus. Matt was watching the performance, amazed at her sudden lack of inhibition. He silently brought his hand up and placed it on her neck, reassuring her. He ran his hand softly across her cheek, pulling her lips gently towards his own. He kissed her upper lip very romantically as he stroked her face, his hard cock now searching out, begging for entrance to her wet pussy.

Almost immediately, Donna felt something prodding between them, and realized that his erection was gaining strength. Matt's cock, for reasons unknown to Donna, grew fully erect, pushing into her leg. Donna took his rigid rod in hand and re-directed it towards her dripping vagina. Both Donna and Matt twitched, not sure who was doing what to whom. Donna gently let out a long breath as she moved her head slightly to return his scorching kiss. Matt knew that Donna was becoming aroused by the way she ground her hips against the bed, positioning herself very slightly to accept the rigid pole heading for her vagina. He was intrigued how she seemed to be so knowledgeable and free with her loving caresses. He had always shied away from women in case they found him lacking or wanted him to do something he couldn't, but this was proving to be so easy.

Donna pulled her legs up against her chest, but her right hand slipped down and started stroking her pussy very lightly. She let her legs stretch out as her hand moved in between them, the back of it brushing Matt's hot cock as it began to stroke in and out of her. For several minutes Donna squirmed while playing with her pussy. Then she took a deep breath. Her fingers were sticky from playing with herself, and she licked them, tasting her own juices. The smell and taste of her own excitement intoxicated her and as a result she began to push her hips up to meet his now-insistent thrusting.

The feeling of Donna's soft warm tunnel engulfing his raging hard-on drove Matt to furiously pound into her, beads of sweat running off his body and splashing onto hers below. He kept his eyes glued to her face, his sensitivity heightened by the image of rapture he saw there. Slowing his pace, he pushed his hard cock into her until it seemed that even his balls threatened to be swallowed by the tight hole of her dripping pussy. Matt held still, enjoying the sensation of being gripped, her sweet tunnel milking his cock as wave after wave of pure pleasure passed over her.

Donna moaned loudly and wrapped her legs around Matt's waist. She writhed and bucked as she forced him to start stroking in and out of her hot body again. Every long slow stroke gently rubbed her over-stimulated clit, prolonging the twitching and spasms of her orgasm until it seemed they would never stop. She slid her slender fingers over his back, her nails biting into his flesh lightly, just enough to tingle without hurting. Her hands moved round to firmly grasp the cheeks of his tight ass and with a strength that was remarkable in a woman of such small stature, she pulled him into her tightly, grinding her pussy against him.

The forceful way she took control sent Matt over the edge and he growled as his orgasm gave way. His cock jerked inside its warm prison, more in protest of having to leave than anything else. The muscles in his arms grew suddenly weak and Matt let his weight fall on the soft body beneath him. He could feel Donna's heart beating against his own in perfect synchronization. Their heavy, ragged breathing was the only sound to fill the room. Matt couldn't believe that it had taken him so long to see what a beauty Donna was, both inside and out. He rolled to his side and pulled her against him, their sweaty bodies basking in the afterglow of their lovemaking session.

When both could breath easily again, Donna stood up and put her clothes back on. She couldn't pose today. She couldn't go back to business as usual when she had just given her virginity to the handsome man on the bed. She needed to think, to mull things over, and to decide what action she should take next. She leaned down and gave Matt a gentle kiss as his eyes closed in peaceful sleep. Then she walked quietly to the door and let herself out.

That night, as Donna lay in bed and looked through her bedroom window at the moon shining, she tried to visualize how the next day might be. She ran through the conversation she would engage in after arriving for work on time, where they could go to have a quiet lunch together, and what activities they might do together during the afternoon. Her ideal afternoon would be alone with him, talking about his love of painting and finding out about his friends and family. Perhaps they would stroll hand in hand along the nearby beach.

As her dreams grew increasingly elaborate so they became more romantic. Her lips revealed a contented smile as she pulled the blanket up to her chin, turning onto her side to stare out at the glowing circle in the dark night sky. She thought back to the afternoon, and how they had made passionate love in the studio. She remembered the light blood she found on her thighs when she returned home, evidence that her body was now the body of a woman in every way.

In hindsight, she found it difficult to understand how she could have done it when she had only known him for a few months. They hadn't even bothered with mild petting or any of the other foreplay that was the staple of the romance novels she loved so much. She recalled his size and the feeling of it thrusting into her. She had felt a twinge at first but never any real pain and it hadn't taken long for the twinge to fade into pleasure.

Donna smiled, feeling the blanket brushing against her nipples. She brought her right hand out to rub them through the material, wondering what it would be like to spend a whole night with Matt, waking up in his arms and feeling his cock poking impatiently at her.

Her nipples hardened, causing tingling sensations to run through her tits as she rolled onto her back, her left hand exploring the elastic in the waistband of her silk panties. Using her left hand gave her the feeling that someone else was there, exploring, desperate to ravage her body and carry her off into the night, someone who might be Matt.

Her dreams flitted to him and their one and only love making session. She wondered what he was doing now. Perhaps he was also staring out of the window, playing with his hard cock, running his hand up and down the throbbing shaft as he thought of her. A surge of excitement ran through her stomach, reaching her pussy at the same time as her hand found her swollen clit. She needed satisfaction. She looked at the clock beside her bed and saw it was past eleven, too late to sneak back to Matt's studio under some pretense of work. Her middle finger explored the deep valley between her pussy lips, teasing her clit and then probing down toward her wet opening. A wonderful idea came to her.

She pushed back the blanket and shrugged off her negligee and panties, leaving her naked in the moonlight. She walked over to her dressing table and took her hair brush, checking its contours and imagining it inside her. She compared its width to Matt's hard cock and considered it to be quite thin. It was reminiscent of a vibrator she had seen in a magazine although not as long and she giggled to herself as she wondered if there was such a thing as a vibrating hairbrush. She tip-toed across to the window, and ran her hand across her pussy lips, pleased to feel that there was the familiar sticky feeling already. She brushed the little hairs as though introducing her pussy to a new friend and slowly pushed a finger inside herself, checking that the handle of the hairbrush was not going to be too wide. The thought of someone being able to see her naked body in the bedroom window excited her, giving her extra encouragement as she licked the handle liberally and offered it to her pussy.

Very slowly, she pushed it in, finding it somewhat difficult. Her thumb rested halfway along the handle, and when she felt it touch her pussy lips, she judged that she had entered as far as she safely dared. She let the brush squeeze out, it's handle slick from her saliva and natural juices.

Donna experimented with the angle of the brush as she bent slightly in the pale light. Moving in and out was difficult, until she realized that by placing one foot on her desk, she could have all the room she needed. Steadying herself against the wall, she increased the speed of her efforts, producing a whole new feeling inside which spidered upwards through her body, warming her and causing her stomach to flutter. She could feel her orgasm beginning deep inside her pussy, slowly but surely. She pulled the brush out, moved over to her dressing table again and dripped a little Baby Oil on the handle. She administered a little over her hands and rubbed the lotion over her clit in slow, lazy circles, ensuring that every inch of her pleasure center was oiled.

Donna realized that she would be unable to orgasm standing with one foot on her desk, so she lay back on the bed, spreading her legs, and parting the lips of her pink pussy with one hand. The hardness of the brush entered again. She moved her thumb further down towards the bristles, breathing heavily as the remaining few inches disappeared inside her. The oil combined with her efforts provided a pleasing mix, the brush gliding smoothly in and out as her breathing increased. She thought of Matt, his scorching sensual kisses, the exploratory tongue, and the gentle and loving way in which he had pushed his massive cock into her inexperienced pussy. His stroking had built up once she was used to his size, and he had whispered lovingly to her as she came.

Her hand dropped down to rub her clit, massaging the oil around the proud little bud, as her thoughts returned again to how he had first entered her. Her orgasm was approaching, her muscles contacting involuntarily as she raised her rear off the bed with her weight on her feet and put her free hand underneath her bottom to support herself. Her stomach muscles tightened as her thighs pushed her body up to meet the thrusting brush. Now past the point of no-return, she frantically pushed the brush between her legs, oblivious to pain, remembering how as she came with Matt, how he had gasped and moaned. The orgasm grabbed her consciousness as she collapsed back on the bed with wave after wave of pleasure. She pulled her legs tightly together against her chest, leaving the brush trapped, protruding behind her as she rolled onto her side and buried her face in the pillow. Donna held the brush loosely as she reveled in the intensity of her orgasm. She lay there for several minutes, toying with the brush, before rolling onto her back and slowly extracting it. The plastic handle felt slippery to her touch and she explored how the oil had coated it.

She was interested to feel the oil around her anus and rolled the handle of the brush over the little hole, noting the different feeling it created. She offered it gently to the entrance, pushing slightly to overcome any initial reluctance. It penetrated only half an inch before she decided that the handle was spreading her muscle uncomfortably and a dull pain protested against the invasion. She dropped the brush and put her middle finger against the hole, pushing until it was allowed access. A warm surge of pleasure met her finger, increasing as she pushed deeper. Donna felt satisfaction as she realized that she could push her finger no further. Her knuckles were against the cheeks of her rear.

She removed her finger and wiped it on her blanket as she pulled her negligee back on. Naked from the waist down, she pulled the covers over her, leaving her panties inside the bed by her feet. As she curled up on her side, the moon disappeared behind the clouds and she slept. She smiled in her sleep as she dreamed of what her next encounter with Matt would offer.

Her dreams were full of a strange mixture of work and pleasure. Matt was back to his usual painting with one exception. In her dream world, Donna had become the canvas. Every stroke of his brush caused ripples of pleasure to run throughout her body as the tiny wire-like bristles tickled her flesh. She watched as he splashed color after vibrant color over her naked tits, across her tummy, and down to cover her dripping cunt.

The next morning, Donna awoke with a new feeling of vitality and the erotic dream still fresh in her mind. She dressed in the outfit she had worn during her night time fantasy and carefully prepared for her adventure. Today, she had determined when she awoke last night in the middle of a crashing orgasm, was going to be the day that she made the recurring dream a reality. Today she would place herself between Matt and his beloved canvas, slowly and sensually remove all her clothes, and lean over to whisper seductively in his ear, "Paint me perfect, baby!" She could already see the smile on his face as he took his tool firmly in his hand and advanced toward his willing canvas.

Printed in the United States
140050LV00010B/91/A